Need Me

By Tessa Bailey

VINE MESS
Secretly Yours • *Unfortunately Yours*

BELLINGER SISTERS
It Happened One Summer • *Hook, Line, and Sinker*

HOT & HAMMERED
Fix Her Up • *Love Her or Lose Her* • *Tools of Engagement*

THE ACADEMY
Disorderly Conduct • *Indecent Exposure* • *Disturbing His Peace*

BROKE AND BEAUTIFUL
Chase Me • *Need Me* • *Make Me*

ROMANCING THE CLARKSONS
Too Hot to Handle • *Too Wild to Tame*
Too Hard to Forget • *Too Beautiful to Break*

MADE IN JERSEY
Crashed Out • *Rough Rhythm*
Thrown Down • *Worked Up* • *Wound Tight*

CROSSING THE LINE
Risking It All • *Up in Smoke* • *Boiling Point* • *Raw Redemption*

THE GIRL SERIES
Getaway Girl • *Runaway Girl*

LINE OF DUTY
Protecting What's His • *Protecting What's Theirs* (novella)
His Risk to Take • *Officer Off Limits*
Asking for Trouble • *Staking His Claim*

SERVE
Owned by Fate • *Exposed by Fate* • *Driven by Fate*

BEACH KINGDOM
Mouth to Mouth • *Heat Stroke* • *Sink or Swim*

STANDALONE BOOKS
Unfixable • *Baiting the Maid of Honor* • *Off Base*
Captivated • *My Killer Vacation* • *Happenstance*

Need Me

A Broke and Beautiful Novel

TESSA BAILEY

AVON

An Imprint of HarperCollinsPublishers

NEED ME. Copyright © 2015 by Tessa Bailey. Excerpt from WRECK THE HALLS © 2023 by Tessa Bailey. All rights reserved. Printed in the United States of America. No part of this book may be used or reproduced in any manner whatsoever without written permission except in the case of brief quotations embodied in critical articles and reviews. For information, address HarperCollins Publishers, 195 Broadway, New York, NY 10007.

HarperCollins books may be purchased for educational, business, or sales promotional use. For information, please email the Special Markets Department at SPsales@harpercollins.com.

FIRST AVON IMPULSE MASS MARKET PUBLISHED IN 2015.

Designed by Diahann Sturge

New York City illustration © wanspatsorn / Shutterstock
Butterfly illustrations © ainul muttaqin; sara saedi/the noun project

Library of Congress Cataloging-in-Publication Data has been applied for.

ISBN 978-0-06-332937-9

23 24 25 26 27 LBC 5 4 3 2 1

To my neighbor in 2C
Wish I'd said hello.

Acknowledgments

*A*s always, to my husband and daughter for believing in me. Thank you.

To my editor, Nicole Fischer, for being incredibly encouraging. This series is so fun to write because of the freedom I've been given to develop story and character without boundaries. Thank you.

To Jessie Edwards, a publicity dynamo, thank you for your support and enthusiasm. And everyone at Avon Impulse, including the copyeditors, proofreaders, formatters, and cover designers who make my books look good. Thank you.

To my agent, Laura Bradford, for having my best interests in mind and always being honest. Thank you.

To my parents for being proud and supportive of me. Thank you. I love you both!

To the readers who continue to pick up my books and trust me to deliver, thank you. Your confidence gets me in front of the laptop every morning.

Need
Me

Chapter 1

When choosing the perfect panties for a seduction, one couldn't be too selective. Careful consideration had to be given to the cut, the style, and, most importantly, the almighty color. Honey Perribow rifled through her underwear drawer from her position on the rug, picking up and discarding undies with the efficiency required of premed students the world over. Red silk was a little too on the nose. It didn't give the guy any credit. Blue? Hinted at mood swings. Yellow with a strawberry pattern . . . *what am I, five?*

There was no help for her. She had to call in the big guns. "Roxy!"

Her roommate of one month propped a hip on the inside of Honey's door a moment later, biting into a piece of toast. "Did you lose your indoor voice in that pile of underpants?"

"What color would you wear if you wanted to seduce your English teacher?"

The toast paused halfway to Roxy's mouth. "Aw, shit. Today is the day?"

Honey took a deep breath and nodded. "I've finally worked up the nerve. No more hiding under my hoodie in the back row. Professor Dawson is going down to Honey town."

"How long have you been waiting to say that?"

"A while. How was my delivery?"

"Not too shabby." Roxy shoved the remainder of the toast in her mouth and plopped down onto the floor, cross-legged, eyeballing the mountain of panties. In the month since they'd become roommates in one of the oddest interview processes of all time, they'd formed a friendship that sometimes seemed as if they were feeling their way in the dark. Honey could still sense some hesitancy on Roxy's part to open up completely, but Roxy's new boyfriend, Louis, seemed to be unlocking a new part of her. Considering Roxy had hidden out in her room at the outset, commiserating over panties was a vast improvement. "All right. So, we know he's studious. He teaches Intro to Literary Theory. How does he dress?"

Honey hid her swoon by turning and pressing her face into the rug. "He has this tweed jacket. It's like a greenish-brown, which should be ugly, but it looks so dang *amazing* on him. If I got up close, I bet it would smell like honest-to-goodness man mixed up with old book leather. He keeps candy in the pockets, too. I can't tell from the back of the room which kind of candy he always pops into his mouth, but if I had to guess, I'd say butterscotch. So the jacket might have a hint of butterscotch smell going on, too."

"Are you telling me *tweed* inspired all that?"

"It's crazy, right? I know it. I can hear myself." Honey rolled back over and stared up at the ceiling. In the few weeks since she'd started courses at Columbia University, Professor Dawson had wiggled his way under her skin like a splinter from a yellow poplar tree. No one back home in Bloomfield, Kentucky, would ever have accused her of being shy. In fact, they would have laughed over the very suggestion. She'd won first prize two years in a row for mud wrestling a pig at the county fair, after all. Shyness and pig wrestling simply didn't add up. But the day she'd walked into the lecture hall, a mixture of confidence and nerves, and seen Professor Dawson, quietly gorgeous, in his tweed jacket and black-rimmed glasses, she'd slunk into the back row like a scolded basset hound.

Then. *Then* he'd spoken. Good Lord, she still remembered the shift of energy in the room. Each and every female student had leaned forward and propped their chin on their hands. Spellbound. There was no other word for it. His voice filled the room like sexy fog, rich and nuanced. It held a subtle hint of New England, not an all-out Boston accent, but occasionally he would drop an *R* in a way that made her shiver. It wasn't just the sound of his voice, either. His passion about the subject material came across in every word, every endearing head scratch or thoughtful chin rub. She'd been more of a science girl in high school. Give her physics or chemistry any day of the week, but English had become her favorite subject with enough speed to inflict whiplash.

Since she'd been bitten by the shyness bug, talking to the object of her nightly fantasies *directly* hadn't been an option. Yet. Oh, and there was that *teensy* little issue of college professors not being allowed to fraternize with students. But she'd cross that rickety bridge when she came to it.

All her life, she'd lived in a small town where the most exciting thing to happen was a fistfight between two grannies at the Dairy Queen. She'd purposely applied for universities with strong premed programs in New York City because she wanted, *needed*, excitement. Needed to take life by the short and curlies and tell it who was boss. She loved her parents and her hometown dearly, but she wanted *more*. Starting small wasn't an option, either. She wanted to start with something so far outside her wheelhouse she needed binoculars to see it. This was her life, and it was time to live it.

Starting today, she would seduce Professor Dawson. Just the thought of it raised goose bumps all over her arms. From the back of the room, he looked like a movie star. Something she watched on a screen from a safe distance. What would he be like up close?

"If you rub your thighs together any harder," Roxy broke into her thoughts, "this pile of panties is going to turn into a bonfire."

"Sorry." Honey pushed some unbrushed blond hair out of her face. "Let's focus on the matter at hand."

Abby, their third roommate, breezed into the room. "What are we focusing on?"

"*I* was focusing. *She* was fantasizing about tweed."

"Tweed is still in style, but elbow patches are out," Abby stated offhandedly, taking a spot on the floor. Of the three of them, Abby was the one gainfully employed in a corporate gig downtown, which explained her tailored black pantsuit at eight in the morning while Honey and Roxy, an aspiring actress, were still in pajamas. "What's with the panty mountain?"

"I'm beginning the seduction process this morning."

Roxy rolled her eyes. "Try not to make it sound so sexy, Perribow."

Honey threw a pair of plaid panties at Roxy. "I'm not you. I can't just flash a little leg and leave a trail of man-drool in my path."

"Have you tried?" Roxy asked, looking smug when Honey stumbled over a reply. "Look, you're not going to flash him your panties in class. That's not your style. Worry about the top layer *first*, drag him back to your cave later. Worry about the panties then."

"I agree." Abby nodded. "This is premature panty picking."

"Of course I'm not going to flash him." Honey shrugged. "I was thinking it might boost my confidence a little if I had something sexy underneath my jeans. Might give me an extra boost so I won't chicken out."

Abby gave her a warm, encouraging look. She fished through the pile with one manicured hand and picked out a silky, mint-green thong with lace detail. Still with the tags on. "Wear these. They're unique and subtly brilliant, just like you. You won't chicken out."

"And you're *not* wearing jeans," Roxy added, standing and dragging Honey to her feet. "To my closet, Batgirl. Where you will behold the wonder of humankind's finest invention."

Honey shot a nervous look over her shoulder toward an amused Abby. The brunette practically skipped along behind them down the hallway. "What would that invention be?"

"The strapless maxi dress," Roxy breathed.

BEN DAWSON GATHERED up the papers he'd spent his lunch break grading and tucked them neatly into his leather satchel. A quick check of his wristwatch told him he had seven minutes until his next class started. Since it took exactly three minutes to walk to the lecture hall from the teacher's break room, he should probably get moving. As far as arriving at class went, there was a sweet spot three minutes before class began that allowed him enough time to gather his thoughts and arrange his lesson plan on the podium, but didn't leave enough time for the students to engage him in conversation.

It wasn't that he didn't like conversation. He just liked to keep his social life and his professional life completely separate. He called it his laundry theory. Talking to students about their weekend plans or the shitty coffee in the cafeteria was the equivalent of throwing a red sock in with a load of whites. It just wasn't done.

He snapped his bag closed with a definitive click and took a deep breath before leaving the break room. Yes. Separation of his social and professional life was key. The minimal age difference between him and the college sophomores he taught sometimes gave them the false impression that they were his peers. Being a professor at the age of twenty-five made him seem accessible, when, in fact, he wasn't. He came to class, he lectured, and he went home. If he wanted to grab a beer and talk baseball, he did it with his buddies, Louis and Russell. Not students. Never, *ever*, students.

Ben taught English because from the moment he'd cracked his first book, words had hummed in his blood. They were something he breathed and slept and lived for. If his students left with an impression of anything, he wanted it to be his lectures, the contents of the assigned reading. Their opinion of him as a person couldn't be allowed to enter the mix, or it took away from their experience. Conversely, he didn't form opinions of them. Ever.

Which is why he shouldn't have read Honey Perribow's latest essay seven times. *Seven.*

He didn't know which of his students happened to be the insightful Ms. Perribow. They were just a sea of faces, none of which he focused on for more than a few seconds now and again. He wouldn't find out, either. Didn't want to know what she looked like, because it didn't matter. It *couldn't* matter.

His reading assignment of *The Things They Carried* and subsequent essay had been met with the usual moans and gripes. Honestly. The book was a work of art. But his students' lack of enthusiasm for anything other than a rooftop kegger had carried over into their lackluster essays. Then he'd read Ms. Perribow's paper and he'd actually spilled his coffee in his haste to turn the pages. Instead of listing the items men carried into war, as was done in the book, she'd written a clever modern spin about what college students carry to class. What they'd chosen to bring from home. What they kept in their book bags and dorm rooms. It was obvious from her nods to the book that she'd not only read it but *enjoyed* it, too. She'd made him laugh. He couldn't remember the last time he'd heard the sound coming from his own mouth.

Ben banished that depressing thought as he entered the lecture hall, where students were flopping down into their seats, clicking pens, finishing up their oh-so-urgent text message conversations. He hooked a thumb into the strap of his bag and lifted it over his head, placing it carefully on the podium. *Don't look up. Don't try and figure out which one she is. It's irrelevant.*

The problem was, he kind of felt like he *knew* her after reading the essay. Her voice had drawn him in and locked him up inside of it. More, he felt like she'd been talking directly to *him*. That simply wouldn't do.

The big hand on his wristwatch landed on one o'clock. He made sure the edges of his lesson plan were perfectly lined up with the podium and looked up at the class to begin.

And stopped.

Front row. Who was that blonde in the front row? He might not pay any attention to what his students looked like, but Ben was certain he would have remembered her. Yes, he definitely would have remembered a petite little goddess with big golden eyes and shoulders made to be gripped. Oh fuck, where had that thought come from? *Stop looking. Stop looking.* But he couldn't, because her lips parted just slightly, as if she was surprised to find him staring at her. Who *wouldn't* stare at her? Okay, as long as he didn't look any lower than her face—

He looked. There was no stopping his gaze from dipping down to her cleavage. Not enough to be classified as provocative, but enough to be sexy in an *I-don't-even-have-to-try* kind of way. Thank God her legs were covered. He wished her legs weren't covered. What was happening here?

"Lolita."

When every head in the class came up, Ben realized he'd said the single, horrifying word out loud.

A male student wearing a Rangers hat spoke up. "Lolita?"

This wasn't happening. It couldn't be. His neck had grown so hot that he swore it was on fire. Kind of like the rest of him.

Thank God he was standing behind the podium, because his dick was hard enough to give someone in the front row a black eye. What was wrong with him? He was acting like he'd never seen a beautiful girl before. This city was packed full of them, just walking around looking like they'd stepped out of a glossy magazine, but this one. Oh, this one. Something about her made him ache everywhere. Innocent looking with a hint of excitement in her eyes, like maybe he was making her just as hot. But that couldn't be right, because he was wearing the ugliest thrift shop tweed jacket he'd been able to find just to make himself the opposite of hot. Unappealing. Unapproachable. *Just their professor.*

This—all of this, including his hard-on—had to be dealt with later, though, because his students were still looking at him like he'd sprouted a third eye. *Think fast, Ben.*

"I, uh . . ." He started to adjust his glasses, but he forced his hand to lay flat on the podium. "I've decided to give extra credit for a paper on *Lolita*. The book, not the movie. Although, if you ever want to watch the movie, I'd recommend the Kubrick version. Not the one with Jeremy Irons." *Oh my God. This is such a massive fail.* "Um. Okay, so. Three-thousand-word minimum. Due this time next week. Let's talk about *The Things They Carried.*"

"I'd rather talk about *Lolita*," Baseball Cap said, earning a few laughs.

This was what happened. One crack in his armor and suddenly they're making jokes in his joke-free environment. He tried not to look at the blonde in the front row and failed miserably. When he saw her frown over Baseball Cap's comment, he found himself frowning at *her.* He didn't like how good it felt to have her on his side. They weren't on the same side. Teacher. Student. That's it. That's how it would stay.

Ben spent the next hour reading passages from the book and giving several different interpretations of what the author wanted the reader to glean about each fictional character based on the items they carried into war. Every once in a while, his gaze would stray to the blonde, and he'd find her watching him steadily from underneath her long eyelashes. Like clockwork, every ten minutes, she would switch the leg she had crossed. Right, left, right, left. Her toes were unpainted. He liked that. *Stop looking. Stop.*

At two o'clock on the nose, he dismissed the class with the promise to return their graded papers next time. As the students filed out of the class, he briefly wondered which one was Honey, but the blond Lolita captured his attention. She wasn't leaving like the rest of them. Why wasn't she leaving? He needed her to leave. His mouth went dry when he realized they were the only two people left in the room. They stared at each other, him behind the podium, her still seated. His cock strained harder and more insistently behind his fly the longer he kept his attention on her, but he couldn't look away. He should say something, otherwise it would be weird. She'd know how much she affected him. But he didn't. He could only stare back as she rose to her feet and saun-tered toward him, her breasts swaying underneath the dress. *No bra. Red. Alert. She's not wearing a bra. I'm screwed.*

She shook her long hair back over her shoulders and he groaned. He fucking groaned, right out loud. Amusement lit her eyes. Sat-isfaction. None of the pretense employed by females her age. Only confidence that her girl-next-door looks were hooking him like a half-witted sea bass. And they had. There was more, however. She looked at him as if they already knew each other on some level and this face-to-face meeting was long overdue. Which is exactly how he felt. Jesus. He'd never wanted to fuck a girl so badly in his entire life, and it was wrong on so many levels. *So many.* It broke every rule. The school's rules. More importantly, his own rules. He knew too well what happened when a man gave in to temptation. Knew what the consequences could be. He'd seen it. He'd lived it.

Her tongue came out to wet her lips, and he watched it happen in slow motion. Felt the muscles in his abdomen tighten at the image of her mouth skating down, down, to deal with the turmoil in his pants. She stopped right at the front of the podium and traced a finger over his lesson plans. No one had ever touched his lesson plans before, and it felt intimate. Maybe more intimate than a kiss for someone like him. She opened her mouth to speak—

"*Ben.*"

The familiar voice broke through his red haze of lust. His colleague, Peter, stood at the entrance, eyeing him strangely. Why? Oh, probably because he was sweating and staring at a student like he wanted to eat her for lunch. Eat her . . . fuck. What color panties was she wearing? He'd give anything to know.

"Hey, Ben," Peter said with a little more oomph. "We've got that faculty meeting."

The blonde, looking more than a little disappointed with their audience, gave him a small smile and walked away. Just like that. She'd aroused him out of his mind, made him question his strict rules, then walked away so casually she might be headed to a beach party. When she passed Peter in the doorway, the fellow teacher looked at her speculatively, and something ugly reared its head inside of Ben. *Don't look at her. Don't you fucking look at her,* he wanted to shout.

Jesus, man. Reel it back. Repeating those words on a loop, he gathered his things quickly and joined Peter at the door. At least he had his body under control now. The icing on this cake of a day would be explaining his peter to Peter.

"What was that about?" his often nosy colleague asked him. "That looked . . . bad."

Ben scratched his chin. "No idea what you mean. It was nothing."

"It didn't look like nothing." Peter bumped him with his shoulder, and Ben gave him a dark look. He found Peter irritating on a regular basis, but something about him discussing the blonde in any capacity was making him twice as unbearable. They were both new to the faculty, though, and taught the same course. They were required to share notes and compare lesson plans, which put them in one another's company pretty frequently. "Listen, we have to be careful. We don't have tenure yet. One wrong move—"

"Stop. I don't know what you think you saw, but you need to drop it."

Peter held up his hands. "Just looking out for you."

Ben stayed silent the rest of the walk to the meeting. He thought of the blonde the entire way.

Chapter 2

*H*oney walked into the apartment that evening and froze. Was she in the right place? She leaned back slightly and checked the apartment number. Yup. She lived here.

Candles everywhere. Streamers. Balloons. Sugary pop music pumped from Abby's pink MacBook where it sat on the kitchen table. Bottles upon bottles of booze were lined up on the kitchen island in every flavor imaginable. Red plastic cups and an ice bucket were placed handily beside them. The lights were out in the entire apartment, but the candles flickered, lighting the walls with an orangey glow. This was what she got for staying late at the lab to finish her organic chemistry project, hoping to distract herself from thoughts of Professor Dawson. She came home to a whole new world.

No, not Professor Dawson. Ben. She knew his name now.

Abby almost bulldozed her as she ran into the living room with only one eye of makeup and two different shoes on her feet. "There you are!"

"Here I am." Honey gestured to the room. "Why does it look like Mardi Gras threw up in here?"

"Roxy landed a part today." Abby was practically vibrating. "A *big* one."

Honey's hands flew to her mouth. "No way. Oh my God. What is it?"

"I don't know yet. She wanted to tell everyone in person." Abby latched onto Honey's arms, and they both started jumping up and down. "Louis brought all this stuff over and went back out for more. We're going to surprise her."

"She's going to hate this."

"I know, right? She'll get over it."

The apartment door swung open and Louis backed in, holding a . . . fog machine? Honey might have had her reservations about Louis in the beginning. No way could this gorgeous lawyer with a trust fund that could purchase a small island be as nice as he seemed. But she'd warmed to him when it had become obvious he would do just about anything and everything to make Roxy happy. As in, saw his own arm off if it improved her day by even the tiniest degree. The fact that he always brought over butter pecan ice cream for them didn't exactly hurt his cause, either.

Louis set down the fog machine and started jumping up and down with them, sending them both into a laughing fit. Another thing about Louis? He'd grown up with two—certifiably insane—twin sisters, which had made it easy for him to fit in with their girl crew. Roxy had once called him the Pussy Whisperer, and it had kind of stuck. For the sake of brevity, though, they simply called him P-Dub.

"Rox just texted me that she's hopping on the train," Louis said, holding up his phone. "That gives us about twenty minutes."

"Where is every—"

Honey was cut off when the door opened and people began to stream into the apartment. She recognized Louis's sisters from a picture he'd once shown them, although she would have known anyway, since they shared his good looks. Walking in behind them was a huge group of people, including two girls with yoga mats and tattoo sleeves, three guys with scraggly beards carrying guitars, and a woman dressed like Madonna, circa 1989. Louis's coworkers and Roxy's actor friends continued to arrive until their voices drowned out the music, forcing Abby to turn up the volume.

Honey jogged to her room, threw her book bag into the corner, and quickly changed her clothes, opting for overalls that ended in a skirt instead of pant legs. She paired it with a white tank top and her beat-up Converse. Damn, she needed to think about a new pair of shoes soon. Maybe it was time to think about getting some waitressing shifts to ease the strain on her parents. Little things like shoes could shoot their whole budget to hell. She'd had an amazing stroke of luck finding this apartment and Abby, who only charged them two hundred dollars for rent, but she needed to remember how tight money was back home. Everything that had been sacrificed so she could be here. Living her dreams.

Her throat feeling a little tight, Honey ran a brush through her hair and left the room, locking it behind her. Didn't want anyone getting busy on her grandma's afghan.

As soon as she walked into the kitchen, Louis waved her over.

He was standing with another guy. A *tall* guy with a shaved head. He was attractive in a rugged, works-with-his-hands kind of way. Kind of . . . dangerous looking. The exact opposite of who she would expect lawyerly Louis to hang out with. Then Abby joined them, and Shaved Head's entire demeanor softened, Adam's apple bobbing in his throat as he shifted back and forth in his work boots. Honey almost laughed out loud. This giant man was clearly infatuated with Abby. And Abby clearly had zero clue. She had to meet this guy.

Louis put a friendly hand on Honey's shoulder. "Honey, this is my boy, Russell. We met because of beer." Russell shook her hand with a half smile and went back to watching Abby.

Honey nudged Abby. "You've already met Russell?"

"Yes," she confirmed with a precise nod. "When Russell and Ben came to yell at Roxy for making Louis sad. You weren't there to witness the fireworks."

"Oh." Honey felt a flutter in her throat just hearing the name *Ben*. Even if it wasn't attached to her Ben. *Her* Ben? When had she started thinking of him that way? Maybe when he looked at her like he wanted to devour her. "I wish I could have seen that."

"It wasn't pretty." Russell's voice sounded like thunder rumbling. "She would have gone back to him eventually. We just gave her a nudge."

Louis looked lost in his thoughts for a moment. "Yeah, well. I guess you're good for something. Speaking of Ben, where is he? He always shows up exactly on time."

"On his way. He got caught up at some meeting."

Louis checked his phone again, obviously restless for Roxy

to show up. He scanned the room, gaze landing on everything in one swoop. "We need more chairs. Would you mind running downstairs and grabbing some out of the super's closet, Russell? He told me we could borrow a few fold-up ones for the night."

"Sure thing," Russell said, looking around for a place to set down his beer. When Abby took it from him, he smiled like she'd just crowned him king of England.

"You know what? I'll go," Honey volunteered. It seemed like a shame to pull Russell away from Abby. Not to mention, she wanted to be useful, since Abby and Louis had set up the whole party without her help. Growing up on a farm had instilled an almost obsessive need to pull her own weight, whether it was cooking for her roommates or lugging shit up three flights of stairs. Russell and Louis started to protest, but she cut them off. "I might be small, but I'm tough. Be right back."

She skirted past a group of guys in various styles of plaid and dipped out of the apartment. After peeking down the hall to make sure Roxy wasn't coming, lest she ruin the surprise, she skipped down the stairs to the first floor, letting her mind drift back to her literary theory class that afternoon. Either she'd been breathing too many fumes in the lab and had become delusional, or she and Ben had shared a . . . moment. She hadn't expected that. Hadn't expected him to *react* to her. She'd expected him to maintain his careful detachment to anyone and everything apart from his lecture, the material. Just like always. Instead, he'd looked at her as if he'd recognized her. Then . . . oh *then*, he'd let his mask slip, and there'd just been heat. Heat everywhere, licking over her skin and dragging her toward him. The way he'd made her feel shouldn't be felt in a lecture hall, surrounded by a hundred students. It should only be felt in the bedroom or the shower . . . or in a field under the moon.

All right, now she just sounded ridiculous. She could no more picture the professor lying under a Kentucky moon than she could picture him in jeans and a T-shirt. No, if she succeeded in seducing him, he would probably keep on his tweed jacket and glasses the whole time they got it on. He'd probably quote Salinger when he came, instead of giving a good old-fashioned moan. Which was fine with her. Oh *mama*, was it fine with her.

Honey reached the super's supply closet and found that he'd left it propped open with a block of wood. "So helpful," she murmured, making a mental note to bake Rodrigo some brownies to say thank you. The kind with walnuts and frosting on top. Humming to herself, she reached over to flick the light switch. Nothing happened. "Looks like I'll be operating in the dark."

BEN WAS LATE by five minutes. It really shouldn't matter, five minutes. Three hundred seconds. It wasn't even enough time to boil an egg. But it did matter. It mattered because he'd been thrown off his game already today and it had now carried over into his evening. He hadn't finished grading papers on time because of his fascination with the faceless Ms. Perribow's work, which he'd read twice more on the subway ride to Chelsea, bringing the grand total to nine. *Nine times.* And yet if he was honest with himself, he'd read it again to distract himself from thoughts of the blonde. His Lolita. Granted, she was clearly past the age of consent, unlike the character he'd secretly named her after in his mind, but as a sophomore, she couldn't be more than nineteen. Twenty, tops. Young. *Way* too young.

As far back as his first date in high school with Janine Conway, he'd dated older women. He *liked* older women. They had more in common with him. Shared similar interests, such as The Moth podcast or Diane Lane movies. Not to mention, they were easier for him to communicate with. If they wanted something, miracle of miracles, they told him instead of playing head games and confusing the hell out of him. They didn't fiddle with their hair or drag him along on group dates with their always-laughing friends. He could hear himself *think* with older women.

But there was more to it. A lot more. His parents' situation had instilled a healthy fear in him from a young age. A clear picture of what could happen if you let sex overrule your common sense. You got trapped. And when it was all over, you were left with nothing but bitterness. So when he got the urge to be with a woman, he made sure he could keep his head. He maintained control over his emotions, and if for some reason he ever felt the control slipping, which he hadn't felt until *today,* he got out. Quickly.

How could he get out of this situation, though? He couldn't very well meet with the administration and ask them to remove Lolita from his class. On what grounds? That he wanted to drag her onto his desk and bury himself between her legs? That would go over like a dream.

What's more, he hadn't even spoken to the girl. Hadn't exchanged a single word with her. For someone like him, who placed more value on someone's thoughts than their attractiveness, it made him a little disappointed in himself. And rather absurdly, it made him feel unfaithful to Ms. Perribow. She'd been sitting in that lecture hall today with her brilliant, witty thoughts, and he'd only been able to think about jumping Lolita's bones. Shameful.

Ben rang the buzzer for 4D and was let inside immediately. Six minutes late now. An egg would be boiled at this point. Totally edible. He was halfway up the stairs when he heard a loud crash from below and a very distinctly Southern, feminine voice say, "Ouch." And, "*Shit.*"

He contemplated minding his own business in the interest of minimizing his lateness, but it was a girl. She could be hurt. He couldn't very well take out his current frustration with a certain golden-eyed blonde on this girl. It wouldn't be fair, and it kind of made him a dick for even considering it. Ben reversed his progress and covered the hallway in eight quick steps. He heard shuffling coming from inside what appeared to be a closet. After pulling open the door, he was unable to see a damn thing in the dim glow the hallway light provided, so he stepped inside, peering into the room.

I'm being tested. It's the only explanation. He only caught a brief flash of the most beautiful, bent-over ass in history, mint-green panties peeking out from beneath a jean skirt, before the door closed behind him and cast the closet into darkness.

A beat of silence passed. "Whoever you are, please tell me you didn't just shut that door."

Her husky voice affected him like fingertips coasting down his stomach, toward his belt buckle. It made him think of skinny-dipping, which made no sense. He'd never gone swimming naked in his life. "I, um." He reached behind himself and tested the doorknob. Jesus, it was locked. "Based on how you said that, I'm assuming you don't have a key."

A long moment stretched on without her responding, but he heard a slight hitch in her breathing and wondered at it. Then it hit him. Of course she would be worried. *Moron*. A strange man had just locked himself into a closet with her.

"Oh. Oh, hey." He held his hands out, dropping them when he remembered she couldn't see him. "Listen, I'm here for the party upstairs. I'm six minutes late, probably seven now." An egg timer went off in his brain. "I heard a crash and came to check on you. Please don't be nervous."

"Ben?" He heard her gulp. "*You* are *that* Ben?"

"I'm . . . *a* Ben." Confusion had him shaking his head. "Do we know each other?"

A long pause. "I'm . . . I'm Roxy's roommate. Louis told us *Ben* was on the way, but I didn't think or even consider . . ." An incredulous laugh. "Why would I?"

"Okay, maybe I'm the one that should be nervous."

"Nervous around me?" Her voice seemed strained. "I'm harmless as a June bug."

Since she couldn't even see him, he didn't bother to hide his amused expression. He'd heard about Roxy's roommates from Louis, but only briefly and in passing. His best friend had been a little tied up since meeting his girlfriend, and boy's night had been put on temporary hiatus. At least until Louis managed to convince himself she wouldn't disappear into a cloud of smoke. But Ben remembered hearing about the Southern roommate who'd given Louis a hard time, which had immediately earned his and Russell's unqualified approval. That kind of thing rarely, if ever, happened to their overachiever buddy, and it was cause to celebrate.

Ben opened his leather satchel and felt around for his cell phone. "I'll give Russell a call. He'll come down and let us out."

"Oh."

Did she sound disappointed? If that was the case, did that mean she *wanted* to be stuck in the closet with him? How could that be, when she hadn't even seen his face before the door closed? Up until now, he'd been trying to forget the glimpse he'd gotten of her tiny green panties. The ones that had been wedged in between two sweet little ass cheeks. God, after the day he'd had, a day that had put him in the eye of a sexual frustration cyclone, this was a test he wasn't prepared to pass. His hand closed around the hard case of his cell phone, and he hit speed dial for Russell. No answer. He tried Louis. Twice. Again, his friend didn't pick up.

"The music must be too loud," she whispered. Oh, shit. Had she moved closer? *Don't think of the panties, Ben. Don't.* Too late. Jesus, was it a full fucking moon? His dick had been hard for three different girls today, all for different reasons. Intellect, beauty . . . now a soft Southern twang that he wanted to hear say his name again, right up against his ear.

"Tell me about yourself," Ben said abruptly. If he just kept her talking, eventually someone would wonder where their elusive roommate had gone and come looking. He was determined to circumvent this attack on his self-discipline, if for no other reason than to prove he could. To himself. Why this victory seemed so important, he couldn't quite decide, except he resented how easily he'd been tempted today. Distracted. It never happened to him, and he needed to keep his house of cards standing. "You're from down south, right? What are you doing in New York?"

Her feet shuffled in the darkness. "I'm premed at Columbia. It's my first year."

"Really." He called himself ten kinds of asshole for being surprised that a girl with a gorgeous ass wanted to be a doctor. *Honestly, Ben.* The fact that she attended the same school he taught at barely registered. Columbia was massive. They would likely go her entire college career without crossing paths once. Still, he was curious about her. Annoyingly curious. "What made you want to be a doctor?"

Her breathy sigh washed over him, and he closed his eyes before forcing them back open. "Actually, I always wanted to be a veterinarian. My family owns a farm in Kentucky, you see, so it just seemed natural. I'd get to work with animals and help my daddy at the same time." Oh Lord, he loved the way she spoke. They weren't even done talking yet and he already missed the sound of it. He'd begun to crave lemonade and sunshine, things he knew little about, being from Concord, Massachusetts. "When I was thirteen, my little brother, Teddy, who really isn't little at all, got thrown from his horse and broke his leg. My parents weren't home. It was just me and my poor brother. And I couldn't do a thing. I had no idea what to do to make him better." Her shrug moved the air around him. "Something changed after that. I didn't like feeling helpless when someone I loved needed me."

Ben's heart started to knock against his ribs. There was something familiar about how her words made him feel, but he couldn't place it. Couldn't think through the sensual web her voice continued to spin around him. He only knew one thing. *Screwed. I'm screwed.*

Chapter 3

*H*oney couldn't believe it. If she closed her eyes and tried to come up with the ultimate fantasy scenario, it couldn't compare to this. She was locked in a closet with Professor Dawson in all his tweedy, leathery, butterscotch glory. The second he'd spoken, every nerve ending in her body had stood up and done the cha-cha, and they hadn't stopped for a rest yet. At some point in her short life, she must have done something right, because he was so close that she could feel his body heat, hear him breathe as she spoke. Was she rambling? Probably. Stop rambling and ask him about himself. Anything to prevent him from making another phone call. She didn't want to be pulled from this musky, dusty heaven anytime soon.

And yet her conscience, the conniving wench, was preventing her from enjoying this moment completely. As her professor, Ben had something to lose here. Even after a month at Columbia, she knew students engaged in relationships with professors, but it wasn't *allowed*. By not telling him he was sharing the darkness with his student, she was taking away his choice to do what he might consider right. After today, though, after what she'd seen in his expression and body language, would he really turn her down in the name of following the rules? She didn't know. How could she? She only knew Professor Dawson. She didn't know Ben. Just a little longer, a few more minutes to get to know him better without their roles as professor and student in play, then she'd tell him.

After her story about the day she replayed in her head early and often, Ben had gone silent. She swallowed the worry that she'd rambled him into a coma and spoke. "What about you? Why did you decide to become a—" She cut herself off. Maybe she should take this as a sign that deception wasn't really her thing. "What do you do?"

"I'm an English professor," he said after a minute, voice a little deeper than before. It sent a warm shiver down her spine that abruptly ended when she reminded herself she already knew that and wasn't telling him. "I wasn't supposed to be," he continued almost thoughtfully. "My father was a wide receiver for the Patriots, and everyone expected me to follow his lead."

Talk about unexpected. She hadn't thought much about how he'd been raised, but no one expects the answer to be "by a professional football player." He would have been the equivalent of a rock star in her hometown. "But you didn't want to play football?"

"No. Well, *yes*. I did. Every son is supposed to . . . make an attempt to follow in their father's footsteps, right?" He laughed under his breath, but it didn't sound like he meant it. "Unfortunately, I didn't hit a growth spurt until junior year of high school, and by then, I'd discovered books."

She thought of his broad shoulders and the way his thigh muscles flexed when he walked around the classroom. "That must have been some growth spurt."

"What?" Oh wow. Had he moved closer? The body heat he gave off felt like it came from a radiator. Was that his breath on her forehead? She wished she could see in the dark. Wished she could see what he looked like close up. He'd be breathtaking. "How can you say that—'that must have been some growth spurt'—when you didn't even see me before the door closed?"

Honey shook a little at the underlying harshness in the question. There was no irritation or suspicion. No, he sounded like she felt. Edgy and breathless. Hungry. "Well, your voice is coming from a good eight inches above my head, so I know you're tall." There was a reason this was supposed to be wrong, but she was fast losing the ability to reason. Professor Dawson, Ben, the man she'd been fantasizing about for weeks, was right in front of her. Wanting her. She couldn't be imagining it, right? Just a little longer. "Maybe I can figure out the rest a different way."

It sounded like he bit back a groan. "That sounds like a bad idea."

"Why? Because our friends are dating? Are you worried that—"

"No. It's because you couldn't be further from my type."

"Oh." Ouch. More than ouch. Honey rubbed the heel of her hand over her chest, trying and failing to ease the epic sting of rejection. Hadn't seen that one coming. Maybe she should have. He was all smooth Yankee perfection, and she was a country bumpkin in ratty sneakers. Heck, they probably still had mud stains on them from the farm. Ben never looked anything less than put together and polished. In a mere two seconds before the door had closed, he'd summed her up and found her lacking.

Screw. That.

Honey put a lid on her insecurities. They were always there, waiting to pop up like some kind of needy jack-in-the-box toy, but she'd come to this city to shed them. She knew what she'd seen in his eyes this afternoon in the classroom, and he was full of shit. *Not his type.* This was *her* seduction, and he had another think coming if he thought a well-delivered lie could knock her off course.

She took a deep breath and eased closer to him. The door rattled, telling her he'd backed up and hit it. Good. He couldn't go any further. She placed her palms on his chest and felt him shudder. Heard him curse in an almost desperate manner. Memorizing every inch of terrain encountered by her hands, she smoothed them higher, over his shoulders, before dragging her fingertips back down the way she'd come. When they reached his hard abdomen, Ben heaved an exhale and tunneled his hands into her hair. It was so sudden and so fierce that Honey's knees almost gave out.

"What are you doing?" he demanded.

"Touching you. Feeling what you look like." It was part lie, part truth. She knew what he looked like, but he kept himself hidden behind tweed and podiums and glasses. Her hands moved on their own, scrubbing over his unyielding stomach while his breath accelerated at the top of her head. Her pulse sounded like a storm in her ears that only increased in volume when he tilted her face up.

"You want to put your hands all over me?" He slipped his mouth over her open one, his breath gliding over her tongue without actually kissing her. "It's only fair if I do the same. So if that's what you want, by all means, keep going."

Honey was reeling from the touch of his mouth. Butterscotch. She'd known that was how he'd taste, yet she hadn't had a clue. When combined with his unique flavor, he was . . . drugging. *He wants to touch me. Wants me to keep going. Yes.* Without reservation, her palm dragged over his belt buckle and encountered his hardness. The evidence of how she'd turned him on, the feel of him after weeks of imagining it, had her moaning loudly against his parted mouth.

Ben's responding groan made the muscles in her belly contract. One of his hands left her hair to cover her grip, tightening until they both squeezed his length. "Fuck. I've been so hard all day, babe."

She felt dazed at hearing her straightlaced professor curse. Admit to a weakness. "Why?"

"So many reasons." His laughter sounded pained, turning into a hiss of breath as she began to stroke him through his pants. "But it feels like it was all for you. I don't know how to explain that."

The beating in her chest expanded, reaching her throat. Her limbs felt heavy but pliant at the same time. Coupled with the darkness, the anonymity, his words emboldened her. *I've been so hard all day, babe. It feels like it was all for you.* She went up on her toes and laid her mouth on his ear. "I've been soft for you all day, so I guess we're even."

Her back hit the cinder-block wall before she'd completed her sentence. The breath whooshed from her lungs, and Ben swallowed it with his mouth. Time stood suspended as he kissed her. *Finally* kissed her. And it was *nothing* like she'd imagined as she'd lain in her bed at night. At all. It wasn't proper or romantic or precise like everything else he did. No. Professor Dawson kissed like a certified bad boy. His mouth taunted her with gentle bites and teasing licks, before he swooped in and kissed her hard enough to bruise. It was glorious and . . . oh God, it was making her wet and achy. Excruciatingly so. She still held his impressive arousal in her hand, and the harder she gripped him, the more he growled and—

Ben tore his mouth away, and she almost dropped like a stone. Strong hands yanking her skirt up to her waist and settling firmly on her ass anchored her, though, made her fight to keep standing. To see what he would do. "Soft for me," he breathed against her throat. "Should we find out where?"

"Yes." She rubbed her thighs together, trying to dull the pulsing, but the movement made it worse. Strengthened it. "Please."

Slowly, so slowly, he sucked her bottom lip into his mouth. At the same time, his fingertips trailed down the back of her thong, dragging lightly down the center of her bottom until they were between her legs. Honey held her breath as he placed pressure over her clit with two fingers, testing, torturing. He let her bottom lip go with a *pop,* then moved to her top one, sucking it into his mouth with a savoring noise. His lips, his fingers were sparking so many sensations inside of her that she couldn't focus on any of them. She could only hang in some sensual balance and wait for what he chose to do next.

Ben released her top lip, and she could feel him staring at her in the dark, even though the air was ink black, impossible to see through. His breath was warm and ragged on her face as he hooked his two fingers into her panties and drew them to the side. Their lips slipped together, meshed, but didn't kiss. There was too much anticipation hanging in the air, and neither of them wanted to upset it. His knuckle nudged against her clit and Honey gasped.

"This is where you're soft, babe. Right here." He drew his knuckle through her folds, back and forth, in a devastating pattern. "Does this soft pussy need something hard?"

The closet door flew open.

BEN OPERATED ON instinct, crowding his girl—*his girl?*—against the wall and yanking down her skirt at the same time. As soon as light had flooded the closet, she'd ducked her head and tucked it under his chin. It was a gesture that had taken the crazy, protective feeling she'd instilled in him and ramped it up about eighty notches until he wanted to strangle whoever had interrupted them. Sweet. She was so sweet and hot, and *fuck*, why wasn't he still kissing her? She'd been so wet for him that he could barely think past the need to feel her again. Jesus, she still had her hand on his cock, like she'd forgotten it was there. He hadn't forgotten. And his cock definitely wasn't showing any signs of forgetting anytime soon, either.

He squinted into the hallway light to find Russell and—was that Abby?—staring back at them, mouths agape. Of course, Russell spoke first. What else was new? "Well, this explains why you were late."

"Do you mind shutting the goddamn door?" Ben growled. His girl shook her head, bumping his chin and reminding him of their predicament. The initial one, anyway. "Oh, right. Don't close it. We were locked in." *Let me out of here so I can get this girl somewhere private. I'll worry about my bullshit rules tomorrow. Need her now.*

"Honey?" Abby looked concerned. "You okay under there?"

Honey. Ben shook off the recognition at hearing the name of his student, Ms. Perribow. Abby had obviously meant the word as an endearment, not a name . . . right? But the longer his girl stayed tucked under his chin, refusing to raise her head, a sinking feeling took over his stomach. She was completely covered now, and thankfully—or *not* thankfully, depending on how you looked at it—had removed her hand from his dick. There was no reason for her to be hiding. Unless she was extremely shy, but he hadn't gotten that impression from her. Quite the opposite, in fact.

"Hey." He pushed her blond hair out of the way and leaned down to murmur in her ear. "You okay?"

She blew out a breath and looked him in the eye. And his world ground to a halt. *No* way. This was a dream. His alarm clock would go off in a minute and he'd be back in his studio apartment in Bushwick. Not looking down into the eyes of his student. No. Not just any student.

"Lolita," he whispered.

"Who?" Abby asked from the doorway. "Her name is Honey. And I'm not judging, but that seems like something you might have chatted about before kissing in a dark closet."

Ben grabbed her shoulders and eased her away, his throat dry as dust. Lolita, Ms. Honey Perribow, and closet seductress. All the same girl. One and the same. The holy trinity of hot, intelligent, endearing girl, and he couldn't have her. But she hadn't given him a choice, dammit. He hated, *hated*, the desire that flared even brighter at the sight of her face in the light. Beautiful. Way too young for him. But completely and utterly beautiful.

And a liar.

"You knew it was me," Ben grated, scenes from his past rushing through his mind like a sick slide show. "There's no way you couldn't have known after listening to me lecture for hours. You knew. And you pretended not to."

"Uh-oh," Russell said to his left. "She's one of his—"

"Students?" Abby finished, then gasped. "Oh my God, this is him? This is—"

"Abby, *stop*," Honey croaked, face bright red. He could tell it wasn't easy for her to look up at him, but he squashed any kind of sympathy. "I'm sorry. I didn't expect you to lock yourself into a dark closet with me, and I just . . . it wasn't supposed to go that far."

Ben laughed a little too loudly. His neck was on fire. He had to get out of there. When he looked at her, all he saw was her deception. The same deception his father had faced so many years ago. The one that had bankrupted him, his family. All for a pretty young girl. Ben had sworn it would never happen to him, that he would never allow his body to overrule his common sense, and she, this girl, had done it to him three times in one day. No, four. Four. If you count his insane urge to throw her up against the wall and give her a nice, hard fuck for doing this to him. Stranding him in lust with a liar.

"What did she mean? 'This is him.'" He pointed at Abby, but he kept his gaze trained on Honey. "What did she mean by that?"

Out of the corner of his eye, he saw Russell shoulder his way into the closet. "Hey man, let's go upstairs and have a beer. This just sounds like a misunderstanding."

Ben ignored his friend, batting away the hand he tried to lay on his shoulder. He couldn't look at anyone but her, and God, she looked miserable. Too bad. Not his problem. "Answer me, Ms. Perribow."

She flinched at the formal use of her name, those golden eyes imploring him to understand. "She didn't mean anything. *I* didn't mean to—"

"Was this your plan when you walked into my class this morning?" He could see immediately that it was. She ripped her gaze away so quickly that he almost stumbled forward at the loss of it, which made him twice as angry. *I have my father's weakness. It's in my blood. What if she's already there, too?* "Did you stop to think of the consequences for someone besides yourself? Or has pretending to be a grown-up in your big Chelsea apartment gotten boring? *So* boring that you thought, *I'll fuck with someone else's life today.*"

Abby stepped in between them and got right in his face. "That's *enough*. You made your point, Ben."

He didn't like having Honey distanced from him. *Not at all.* He should want to get as far away from her as possible, but as soon as Abby blocked her from his view, he tried to get Honey back in his sights. Needed to. *What the fuck was wrong with him?*

Russell shouldered up beside Abby. "Let's go, Ben. I'll walk you out."

He actually considered shoving his friend out of the way to get a final look at her. That was when he knew he had to go. Something told him that if he saw even an iota of hurt in her expression, hurt *he'd* caused, he would take back everything he'd said. He refused to do that. Refused to absolve her. If she chose, she could report him to the administration for misconduct with a student, and everything he'd worked for would vanish. Someone holding that type of power over him was unacceptable.

Not giving himself another minute to think, he left the closet and slammed out of the building.

Chapter 4

*H*oney set down *The History of Medicine* and picked up *Lolita*. Really, she was only torturing herself, but she figured she kind of deserved it. What a complete clusterfuck. She groaned at the memory of Ben storming out of the super's closet last night, his parting shot still hanging in the air so heavy she could have reached up and plucked out the vowels. Thank God she didn't have her Medical Sociology class until later this afternoon, because she needed a few hours to work up the nerve to leave the building. She'd come up to the roof in hopes of escaping Roxy and Abby, who were both a fun combination of hungover and annoyingly curious about what had gone down with Ben in the supply closet. Hell if she knew.

She rolled out the beach towel she'd brought from downstairs and lay back, sighing as the sun warmed her neck and shoulders. If she closed her eyes, she could be back in Bloomfield, sunbathing in the field behind their house. Dad would be blasting Tom Petty inside the barn, Mom would be exercising the horses, and they'd all be pretending not to smell the occasional marijuana smoke drifting from her brother's room. Just a typical day in the Perribow household.

No. She didn't want to be in Bloomfield. New York City was where she'd decided to make her mark, and one incident, albeit a mortifying one, wouldn't ruin the experience. Since she'd decided to become a doctor all those years ago, her parents had busted their butts and saved to make that hope a reality. Now she was here, and there would be no picturing herself riding in the back of her father's pickup truck with their dog, Lolly. Or having a spitting contest with Jasper Burns, the old man who never left his post outside the town liquor store.

Aw, shit. She was homesick. Maybe because back home, she hadn't gotten herself into situations like the one last night. She'd been the smart one. The one with ambition and a one-way ticket to big, bad New York after graduation. Sure, once in a blue moon she'd gotten up to no good, having had one too many helpings of spiked punch and gone streaking through the convenience store, but those antics had been harmless. What she'd done last night to Ben hadn't been harmless. This wasn't Kentucky, and she wasn't seventeen anymore. This was real life, and there was comeuppance for each and every decision she made.

If her pulse still skittered and danced when she thought of Ben, it couldn't be helped. She wouldn't be going there again. No ma'am, you couldn't drag her there by her hair. Even if the memory of Ben's mouth moving across hers, where his hands had gone and almost *done* made her feel miles closer to the sun. Good Lord, she'd never kissed a man before. She'd kissed boys. Been on the receiving end of sweet summer kisses after chowing down on slices of watermelon and sloppy kisses after a triumphant keg stand. Last night, in that closet, she'd been well and truly mouth fucked.

But just like all liars, she would now pay for what she'd done. Her punishment would be going to class every day, listening to Ben's smooth baritone voice fill up the room like a thousand plush cushions and never hear it in her ear again. Never taste his mouth or have the pleasure of his hands on her body. Atonement was a bitch, but she'd take it like a woman. That's what she was now, after all. Not some Lolita with a lollipop and pigtails who went around tempting men at their own peril. Although, hell. It had been kind of fun while it lasted.

Honey's cell phone buzzed on the tar roof beside her. She lifted her sunglasses and peered down at the screen. Elmer Boggs, calling again. Her ex-boyfriend, God bless his soul, had called her every single day since she'd left for New York. Now, Elmer might be a little on the lazy side, but he was a good guy who cared about her, so she didn't fancy stringing him along. She hadn't answered once for that very reason. But she could admit that today she felt a little vulnerable and a lot homesick. It wouldn't hurt to see how old Elmer was getting along, would it?

She answered on the third ring. "Hey hey, Elmer."

"Well, I'll be damned. Honey Perribow is alive." Elmer chuckled good-naturedly, and she couldn't help but smile back. "I thought you might be too good for me now. Landed in New York and forgot all about Elmer."

"Aw, I won't be forgetting you anytime soon. You're too damn big."

His laughter boomed down the line. "You never complained when we won first prize every year at the apple picking competition."

As always, when she spoke to someone from back home, her accent thickened. "You never complained when I baked them into pies, neither."

He made a pained sound. "Now that is just plain cruel reminding me of all the pies I'm not eating. When are you coming back, Honey?"

"I'm not, Elmer." She rolled onto her stomach with a sigh. "Tell me some gossip."

Elmer was silent a moment, and she pictured him as he always was. Backward hat, faded jeans, goofy smile. His class ring glinting in the sunshine. She'd wager he'd be buried with that ring someday. Strong, dependable Elmer. His image was comfortable and familiar, so she let it linger, but it didn't remain long. It was bulldozed by an intense, dark-haired professor with magical lips and sinful hands.

Finally, Elmer spoke, breaking into her wayward thoughts. "Katie and Jay got engaged last night at the homecoming game. Right there in the stands. Said he wanted to score a wife in the same place he used to score all his touchdowns."

Honey felt tears pool behind her eyelids. It didn't seem real. That the people she'd known since she'd been in diapers still had lives going on, so far from this place. She wasn't self-centered enough to think life in Bloomfield suspended itself when she left, but it hurt to know she'd missed moments like the one Elmer just described. Maybe that was real life and this New York City dream of hers was an illusion. "Wow. How long do you give them before they're having babies?"

"Now, I reckon there's already one on the way."

Honey giggled into her elbow, and it felt so good. Felt like she'd never left. "How's your mama?"

"She's keeping busy. Misses you." He huffed out a breath. "So do I. Come home, Honey. I've got a gig working with a road crew, fixing potholes and whatnot. It's steady. I can support us while you do the doctor thing here."

Her smile vanished. "Elmer, don't make me sorry I picked up the phone. I love talking to you, but I'm not coming back. I need to make my own way."

"You always were stubborn." He cleared his throat. She knew he was doing that nervous move with his hat, twisting it around his head. "I'll let you go. Answer next time I call, will ya?"

"Okay, Elmer. Bye."

Honey hung up the phone and stared at it a while, thinking of everything happening on the other end. Lives being lived. Babies being made. She thought of Elmer and his mama. Her own family. Ben. *Always* Ben. And she wondered if her course, the course she thought she'd always wanted, was the right one when it hurt this bad sometimes to follow it.

BEN KNEW HE should stop drinking. It wasn't that he was a lightweight. He couldn't *afford* to be a lightweight with friends like Louis and Russell, who drank beer like they might discontinue the shit. But he had a train ride back to Bushwick in front of him.

Falling asleep on the J train and ending up in Queens would only ice this shit cake of a day, so really, he should stop.

Fuck it, I'll get a cab.

Louis and Russell gave identical whistles as he reached for the pitcher of beer and missed. "Exactly how much beer do you need to consume before you tell us how *you*, Mr. Rule Follower, ended up with your hands up a student's skirt?"

He abandoned his quest to get a decent grip on the pitcher and slapped both hands over his face instead. "Please, for the love of God, don't say things like 'hands' and 'skirt' and 'student.' Not out loud."

Louis looked amused. "You want us to come up with some kind of code?"

"Yes." Ben pushed up his glasses, but they slipped down again almost immediately. "That should have been obvious."

Russell threw an arm over the back of his seat, shit-eating grin firmly in place. "All right, Professor. How did you end up with your jackhammer so close to an off-limits coconut?"

Now Ben *knew* he needed to stop drinking, because in his drunken state, that nonsense actually sounded vastly better. At least it created some comical imagery to replace the decidedly *not funny* memory of what his hands had felt like up Honey's skirt. No, not Honey. Ms. Perribow. Lolita. Jesus, how had he let things get so far? There was a *process* to getting your hands up a lady's skirt, and it involved dates, drinks, conversation that lasted longer than ten minutes. It certainly didn't involve your heart lodging in your throat, your hands clenching with the burning need to *touch her touch her touch her.* He couldn't even begin to reason with that Ben, storage closet Ben, to deduce what the fuck he'd been thinking.

He hadn't seen her face, obviously, but he'd known from her sweet voice and innocent rambling and *God,* her supple ass, that she'd been young. He stayed *away* from young girls. In order for her to be a student in his class, she had to be . . . young. She was young. There had been no decision involved, though, which wasn't just unusual for him, it had never happened. He always made decisions based on sound logic and possible consequences. It scared him that she'd taken that away with so little effort. *I've been soft for you all day.* Christ. He'd practically thrown her up against the wall with the need to discover the soft. Touch, taste, *take* the soft.

Worse, his lust hadn't exactly taken a hike since he'd found out Closet Girl was Honey and Honey was Lolita. No, it had revved higher. How was he supposed to stand in front of her tomorrow and lecture to a hundred students when her eyes would be on him? He didn't have many options unless she transferred out of his class, but they were too far into the semester for that to be a viable option. Plus, it would mean he wouldn't get to read any more of her work, and that upset him just as much as not being able to touch her. Okay, *almost* as much. He wouldn't lie.

"Ben, you over there thinking about coconuts?"

He flipped Russell the bird, but turned to Louis. "How did this happen? You've been dating Roxy for a month and we've never met her friends? This could have been avoided."

"Sorry, Ben. I've been kind of busy in my attempt to ruin her for other men." Louis sipped his beer. "The party on Friday night was supposed to be the meshing of two super groups. You kind of fucked that up by trying to jackhammer the coconut, man."

Ben felt an ugly flash of anger. "All right, stop talking about her like she's some kind of object. I don't like it." In fact, he really, *really* didn't like it. He knew his friends were just trying to lighten his mood, and hell, they'd had their fair share of beer as well, but someone talking about Honey in a less-than-respectful manner didn't work for him. *No, not Honey. Ms. Perribow.* He thought of the way he'd shouted at her, the things he'd said, and swallowed the lump in his throat with a swig of beer. *Hypocrite.* "She's not my type."

"That sounded convincing." Russell ran a hand over his shaved head. "Look, you want my advice?"

Ben and Louis both groaned, abandoning their beers on the table. Russell had developed a reputation in their group for giving out the worst advice. The fact that he retained his belief in its golden value, no matter how often it failed, made it even more unbearable to sit through. Still, in his present state of mind, Ben would take a distraction from thoughts of Ms. Perribow in any shape or form. *Don't think of her shape or form. Don't think—*

"Fire away," Ben croaked, ignoring Louis's look of disbelief.

"The way I see it, you only have one option." Russell shrugged, rather awkwardly. "We get the super groups back together and you guys learn to get along. Without any jackhammers or coconuts."

Louis dropped his head forward on a laugh. "You're too obvious, Russell."

"What?"

"This has nothing to do with Ben. You just want to see Abby again. Admit it."

Ben's mouth dropped open when his usually too-confident friend sputtered in response. "I don't know what you're talking about. Abby and I are just friends."

"You don't want to jackhammer her coconut?" Ben asked with a raised eyebrow.

Russell's jaw ticked. "Don't talk about her like that."

Ben and Louis high-fived Russell's showing his hand. The construction worker had it bad for the debutante. How would that play out? Damn, it felt good to have the focus momentarily off himself. "So if you like her, what's the problem? You've got all the best advice, now's the time to use it."

"I told you, we're just friends," Russell grated. "I'm *fine* with it."

"Did Abby friendzone you?" Louis held up a finger while he swallowed a sip of beer. "She did, didn't she?"

"I'm not talking about this anymore with you assholes." Russell took out his wallet and threw a couple of twenties onto the table. "Ben, here's my real advice. Stop acting like that gorgeous girl did you a huge disservice by making out with you. We should all be so lucky. Fuck the rules. They were made by old men who couldn't land a girl like Abby." He gave a quick head shake. "I mean, Honey."

"Oh my God. I think I agree with Russell." Louis's head whipped toward the window. "Was that a pig that just flew by?"

Russell sent Louis a look, then focused back on Ben. "But if you do pursue her, keep the upper hand. Take her somewhere nice for dinner, but not too nice." He tapped a finger to his temple. "Women get notions. You take them to places with white tablecloths, they start picturing their wedding receptions. Flower arrangements and shit. They can't help it. It's in their genetic makeup."

"*And* there it is," Ben said.

"Thought we'd lost you for a minute there, man."

"Take her to get Thai food," their ill-advising friend continued, completely ignoring them. "For the love of everything holy, *never* take her to an Italian restaurant."

Louis raised an eyebrow. "I took Rox to get Italian on our first official date."

"And just look at you now. Next you'll be getting a dog together."

Russell stood, giving Louis and his blissful grin a look of disgust. "I'm going to take myself somewhere my intellect is appreciated. Xbox Live. Goodnight, ladies."

Louis and Ben were silent for a while after Russell left. Ben hated the freedom Russell had so fleetingly thrown at his feet, as if it were that easy. Fuck the rules, huh? He'd seen firsthand what happened when people didn't give rules, *vows*, the respect they deserved. There was an undeniable part of him that wanted to let go of the restrictions he'd placed on himself and just *give in* to his painful attraction. Maybe it would only take one time and he'd be free of it.

Ben almost laughed at that hopeful thought. One time and she'd have him. He'd be fucked in every way imaginable. He didn't know where that certainty came from, but it was there. Strong and sure.

Louis cleared his throat beside him, drawing his attention. "I know you're smart, Ben, probably the smartest of all of us, so I probably don't need to tell you this. But not every relationship ends the way your parents' relationship did."

"There's only one way to guarantee that, though, isn't there?" Ben stared straight ahead, remembering things he didn't want to remember. Nights of screaming matches, his mother dragging him from their house in the middle of the night. Losing his father to another, newer family. Then another. Until their original family ceased to exist. "She wasn't honest with me. The situations are too similar. That's all I can see when I look at her."

"You sure about that?" Louis crossed his arms and leaned back in his chair. "If that was all you saw when you looked at her, you wouldn't be this fucked up, Ben."

He'd heard enough. He didn't want anyone making sense to him. It was clear what he needed to do, and it actually surprised him that Louis and Russell were too blind to see it. "Thanks for the advice, but I know what I have to do."

Stay the hell away from Lolita.

Chapter 5

*H*oney wasn't about to sit in the front row of literary theory class again. The forced proximity would only serve to antagonize Ben, and that would simply be pointless. She'd antagonized the man enough. But she'd be damned before she'd hang her head and sit in the back row, the way she'd done before he'd opened his eyes and noticed her. One of the middle rows would have to do. It said, *I'm contrite, but go to hell if you think I'm going to say it again out loud.*

She took a steadying breath and slipped into the lecture hall behind a group of sophomore guys discussing some bar downtown that didn't check IDs. One of them winked at her as she bypassed them, and she gave him an absent smile. It froze on her face when she saw Ben standing behind the podium, wearing his delicious tweed jacket. The one she wanted to crawl inside of and spend a week there. Every inch of her skin turned sensitive, buzzing and heating in his presence. The professor's gaze was flat as it gave her a cursory head-to-toe look, just before it landed on the Winker. As she took her seat smack in the middle of the class,

Honey decided she'd misinterpreted Ben's spark of irritation at seeing a boy give her a mere wink. Her fantasies were getting out of control. He couldn't have made it clearer that he wanted nothing to do with her.

"I have your graded papers." Ben tapped the pile of documents he held briskly. "As I call your name, please come and get them."

Oh boy. She hadn't anticipated this. In the past, he'd left them on his desk at the end of class and let the students sort through and find their own papers. Suddenly her white tank top felt too tight, too transparent. Her short, flowery skirt felt several inches too short. How could she get up and walk down the aisle, him watching her the whole way, and not combust? Honey tried not to let her nerves show, but when the Winker tapped his pen on her desk, she jumped in her seat.

He leaned toward her, running the pen along his bottom lip. She wondered if he realized it was leaving ink in its wake. His cocky smile said probably not. "Nervous about the grade?"

"Um." Ben had started calling names, so it was hard to focus. Should she be worried about her grade? He wouldn't fail her out of spite, would he? If he did, she would raise ever-loving hell. "No. I think I'll do just fine. What about you?"

"Didn't read it. Winged it."

He smirked at her, like she should be impressed by that. She wasn't. "Cool," she said politely.

"Ms. Perribow," Ben's smooth voice called from the front of the room. His eyes were no longer flat. They were on the Winker sitting next to her. Hard and analyzing. Honey suppressed a shiver and scooted out of her row, descending the seven steps toward

Ben. He held out her paper, keeping his attention firmly on some unseen spot over her head. She took it from him, careful not to let their fingers brush, and turned away. But not before his gaze dropped to hers, just in the nick of time for her to catch it.

Breathing ceased to be a possibility under the heat she encountered there. Only a split second's worth and not intended for her to see, she suspected, but there all the same. It singed her, that look. It made her aware of every curve of her body, how they shifted with each step on the way back to her seat. He couldn't still be looking, could he? He'd called another name, but she could feel his awareness smothering her like the August heat in Kentucky.

She sat back down feeling as though no time had passed since he'd kissed her in the storage closet. Her nipples had formed hard peaks beneath her shirt, so she crossed her arms to hide them. When she chanced a glance at Ben, she saw him take notice of the action from beneath heavy eyelids. It was as if they were the only two people in the hall, but that couldn't be right. After what he'd said to her, the *justified* things he'd said to her, this was supposed to stop. Maybe it *couldn't* stop?

Did she want it to stop?

No. *God*, no, she didn't. How could she have forgotten what it was like to merely be in the same room as him? Like every particle in the air around her was charged, electric. His voice, the passion he exhibited for teaching, had captured her. Initially. Then he'd focused it on her, and she'd seen that intensity was reserved for every area of his life. Possibly her. And now that she'd felt his touch, it almost felt like torture. She felt starved and miserable, while at the same time exultant that these kinds of feelings were even possible. When they were this close, she felt . . . like a woman.

Honey realized her thighs were clenched tight on the wooden seat to the point of shaking, and she forced them to relax. She had to get through the next hour without disgracing herself in a room full of her fellow students, and that meant *not* having a spontaneous orgasm in their midst. As Ben started his lecture, she wondered at her own mental state. She couldn't be the only woman in this room attracted to the professor. Could she? Had she created a fantasy Ben that didn't translate to real life? Nope. A chic brunette had taken her seat in the front row and looked seconds from creating a drool puddle. Honey had met the real Ben on Friday night, though, and proven he wasn't some mirage sent to make her horny. He was a person with ambitions, just like herself. Ambitions she could jeopardize. She needed to stop feeling this way, stop wanting him. But her mind couldn't come to a truce with her body.

Needing to look anywhere but at Ben, she turned over her graded paper. An A. He'd given her an A. She waited for the rush of relief, but it didn't come. She must have known instinctively that he wouldn't hurt her academically because of what had happened. She flipped to the final page and tried not to snatch up the document when she saw a note in his clear, crisp handwriting.

Flawless, Ms. Perribow. Except you didn't list the items you carry. Professor Dawson.

Her heart rate turned erratic, the organ throwing itself against her ribs like it wanted to sprint down the aisle and slide into an imaginary home plate at Ben's shiny wingtips. He was right. For the assignment, she'd written a comedic reflection of the book he'd assigned, an updated twist on the classic. While she'd listed the often absurd items her classmates carried in their backpacks and pockets, she hadn't included herself. Why did he care? Had he written the note before their little closet rendezvous?

Knowing she shouldn't but unable to help it, she reached into her purple JanSport backpack and withdrew her extra-credit assignment on *Lolita*. She turned to the last page and wrote:

The Things Honey Carries: A sealed letter my mother wrote for me the day I left home. My first-place blue ribbon for pig wrestling (2013 Kentucky State Fair). House keys (keys are a good thing . . . you never want to get locked in an enclosed space with a stranger, right? Heh . . .). Life Savers. Pepper spray. Index cards for jotting down recipes. A diagram of the human anatomy. Number two pencils. Clean socks. Thank you cards (when someone does something nice, you should send one right away or you'll forget). A mixed CD my brother made me when I had appendicitis. Laffy Taffy.

She shoved the assignment back into her backpack, already debating whether or not she should trash it and print out a new one. Without the note. It was early, anyway. He'd never know about the note. Yes, that was what she would do. If he'd written his note and forgotten, he'd only be confused and exasperated by her subsequent note. Yes, he'd forgotten. That had to be it. He hadn't been able to get away from her quick enough.

The lecture took years. At least, that's how it felt. Every time he paused to take a sip of water, she'd grow rapt at his bobbing Adam's apple. The way his brows would furrow as he swallowed, as if deciding which point to bring up next. He needed a haircut, the dark ends climbing down over the edges of his collar, so incongruous with the rest of him. When he started shoving his lesson plan into his leather bag and students around her began to disperse, it took her a moment to realize class was over.

Without looking, she stood and started to sidestep out of her row. Big mistake. Winker was still sitting there—*why?*—and her foot caught in the strap of his backpack, sending her flying down onto the hard floor, contents of her backpack scattering in every direction. For one long moment, she was in denial. *Nope, not happening to me. This is happening to someone in a romance novel or a Disney Channel movie.* Time sped up again when Winker hunkered down beside her and began handing her papers, notebooks, pens, and other embarrassingly private items, such as the ones she'd listed for Ben.

"Oh God, kill me now," she muttered, shoveling everything into her bag as fast as possible. "Thank you," she managed to utter in Winker's direction.

"Nah, it's my bad. I was waiting for you to come out of your trance so I could ask you out to, uh . . ." He snatched up a flyer that had come from her backpack, scanning it with a frown. "This poetry reading. You're going, right?" Once again, he consulted the paper. "It's at Barnard Hall on Wednesday night."

She *had* been planning on going. Never having been to a poetry reading before, it had sounded interesting. Plus, free lemonade and cookies if it stank to high heaven. But Winker, very obviously, had not been planning on attending. "Well, I—"

"Class is over." Honey started at Ben's voice striking out like a whip in between them where they still knelt down on the floor.

Both she and Winker looked up at their professor, but he only seemed to be addressing one of them. And it wasn't her. "You're free to go."

WITH AN UNCOMFORTABLE laugh, Johnny Jerk Off lumbered to his feet. "Right, uh . . ." He scratched the back of his neck with one hand, waving the flyer at Honey with the other. "I'll see you at the reading. Looking forward to it."

Ben checked the swelling urge to give the guy a dead leg as he strolled past, which would only make the situation *infinitely* better, wouldn't it? Not exactly. He shouldn't even be standing there. Should be halfway to the faculty lounge by now, but he'd been unable to watch the Neanderthal—who, *by the way*, hadn't even spelled Hemingway's *name* correctly in last week's writing exercise—ogle and flirt with Honey.

No, not Honey. Ms. Perribow.

The guy had done it for a full hour. Every time Ben's attention had been drawn toward her, which had happened with *startling* regularity, Johnny Jerk Off had been casting her an appreciative look. Nodding at her and smiling at his buddies—also abysmal spellers—as if passing on some sort of signal that he'd be making a move. And he had. He'd made a goddamn move on her. It appeared they were both going to the poetry reading organized by Ben's department. One he'd had no intention of attending. If he wanted to read poetry, he read it to himself. He certainly didn't need someone reading it *to* him. But Honey would be there, and so would Johnny Jerk Off. He should be indifferent. Or, at the very least, relieved that she'd set her sights elsewhere. Yet he felt only sharp denial. Undeniable denial. Was that a thing? *No no,* he thought. *She doesn't date. She sits in my class and looks beautiful and writes papers that drag me under some velvet surface and waits for me to kiss her again, which I won't.* How absurd to think that way. Maybe he was as much of a Neanderthal as Johnny Jerk Off.

He really needed to learn his students' names at some point.

Ben looked over his shoulder to watch Honey's admirer saunter from the lecture hall, probably on his way to chug a Monster Energy drink. There was a shift in the air the second Ben and Honey were alone. Their positions—her on her knees, him towering above her—seemed to take on a new, dangerous meaning. A meaning that called his gaze to her parted mouth. Made his cock shift and harden in his pants. Since she was basically eye level with his lap, that definitely wouldn't work.

He set his satchel down on the closest seat and stooped down to help her collect her things. Those golden eyes widened a little, as if she hadn't expected him to help. *Awesome. She thinks I'm a prick.*

No, it *was* great. It *helped* his cause for her to think that. Not currently helping his cause? Her pointed nipples, straining against the thin, white material of her tank top. The way her tits swayed and bounced as she bent forward to retrieve what looked like a pair of clean socks. A hint of a smile tried to curve his mouth, but it disappeared with a quickness when they both grabbed for a pencil at the same time, the move bringing their faces close together. Too close. Way too close.

Think of why you have to stay away. "How old are you?" he murmured.

She didn't seem surprised by the question. No, she seemed too focused on his mouth. *I can't kiss you, babe. I can't.* "I'll be twenty in ten days," she husked.

"Jesus." He ran a hand down his face. "You couldn't even order a drink in a restaurant."

"Not legally, no." She lifted her gaze to his, and he immediately wanted it back on his mouth. "I still do, though. Sometimes."

"You're a little rule breaker, aren't you?"

"It's been said."

When she shifted a little, he noticed her blood on the floor beneath her knee. Without thinking, Ben circled her waist with his hands and lifted her onto one of the seats, trying not to growl over the feel of her. The ease with which he could handle her. He operated on instinct, outrage that she'd been injured because some dickhead had left his backpack on the ground. As soon as he realized what he'd done—made contact with her when he absolutely shouldn't have—he retracted his touch like she'd burned his hands.

But she had to go and make this *noise*. The second her ass hit the seat, her mouth fell open, and she whimpered. It was the sexiest fucking thing he'd ever heard in his life, and her body matched it. She writhed on the seat, ever-so-slightly, as if his hands on her waist had set off a chain reaction. As if she felt even a fraction of what he experienced when they were this close. God, his cock ached. It pressed against the fly of his pants, begging him to do bad things. Bad things that would feel really damn good.

He took a deep breath and dragged his composure forward. A

glance at her knee told him she only needed the scrape cleaned off, maybe a Band-Aid. Of which he had none. He reached into his bag, took out a napkin from the school cafeteria, and pressed it over the bleeding. Which presented a problem, because now his hand was technically on her leg. And her skirt was technically a little too deliciously short. Short enough that he could see most of the way up her toned thighs. If he ducked his head, he'd be able to see beneath the hem. See her panties. *Fuck.* He needed to get up and walk away. Needed to leave.

"I brought you my extra credit," she said.

Ben's brain had no idea what she meant. All he saw was her pretty, beaded nipples and naked legs. His ears only heard "extra credit" said in that aroused, feminine tone. Oh sweet hell, it was the beginning of every naughty porno video he'd forbidden himself to watch. He watched porn. He was a man, and the Internet made it too easy. But he never clicked on the teacher-student category. Uh-uh. Completely off limits. As a teacher himself, it would be unethical. Still, he knew how they started, because he had ears and two horndog friends. The gorgeous student shows up in a flimsy, plaid skirt and demurely asks her teacher for extra credit. In exchange for a ten-minute blow job, followed by sex. The dirty kind.

Is that what this was? Something foreign glowed hot in his chest. She didn't need to do things like this. Maybe it was all for fun. He'd leveled accusations at her Friday night in the storage closet, all but calling her a bored princess. Had he been right on target? It pissed him off that she thought he was so easily seduced.

And dammit if there wasn't a challenge in her eyes. If she'd expected him to be outraged, she'd succeeded.

Yet there was another, rebellious part of him that wanted to call her bluff. Did she think the way she made him feel was funny? Very deliberately, he let his thumb brush the inside of her knee, the skin so smooth he had to swallow a groan. She jerked in reaction, her taunting nipples growing even more pronounced against the front of her shirt. *For fuck sake.*

"Why didn't you sit in the front row today?" He brought his other hand up and placed it on the opposite knee, began drawing slow circles on the insides of both knees with his thumbs. "You could have been one hell of a distraction for me. Seems like a missed opportunity."

Honey's breath shuddered out. "Did you want me there?"

No way was he answering that. He'd either have to lie and say no or tell the truth, which was *absolutely fucking yes, I want to look at you every chance I get.* Instead of saying those damning words, he damned himself another way. He'd let himself feel her skin now. It had taken away his inhibitions. Blocked the rules written in stone on his memory. She felt too perfect, and he *needed* to feel more.

He locked gazes with her and slowly, gently eased her thighs open.

And she made that sound again, only this time it sounded more like a sob. Her knees trembled in his hands, and it splintered something inside him. Should she be reacting like this, when her plan had been to seduce him? It seemed so inconsistent. None of those thoughts, however, registered past his initial flash of concern, because his hands were moving by themselves, inching her legs wider until he could see her panties. Lacy, white panties that made her pussy look delicate and innocent, while being the epitome of temptation at the same time. With her thighs spread, round tits rising and falling with choppy breaths, eyes half closed, *she* was the epitome of temptation.

"Did you think of me when you put those good girl panties on this morning?" He coasted his hands up the tops of her spread legs, letting his thumbs drag up the sensitive insides of her thighs, taking her skirt higher as he went. "Did you think they'd make my dick hard if I got a peek at them?"

"Yes." The answer burst out of her in a desperate whisper, as if she'd been holding it in. "I thought of you when I chose them."

Her honesty only served to make him hotter. *So goddamn hot.* A voice in his head screamed at him to stop, reminding him they were in his classroom. She was a student. Anyone could walk in at any time. Yet none of it mattered. All that mattered was reaching that sweet spot between her thighs, covered in white. Waiting for him. Just one touch to see if those panties were damp so he could go home and work his own cock to the memory.

"If we hadn't been interrupted Friday night, I would have stripped off that little green thong and fucked you, Lolita." His hands slipped higher and higher to the softest part of her legs, which were completely exposed now. "You were so warm and wet. Is that because you wanted to be fucked, babe?"

A hoarse cry greeted his ears. "Yes." Her answer told him where she wanted his hands, but when he brushed a thumb over her mound, she grabbed his wrist, bringing him slightly out of his lust-induced haze, but not completely. Her gaze implored him for something. What? He *thought* he was giving it to her. "Don't touch me there," she panted. "Last time you touched me there, you walked away and it . . . it hurt, Ben. I still hurt. You can't follow through here, not here, so please don't tease me."

Her words made total sense. They couldn't do this here. Of course not. Except biting at the heels of that realization was a surge of denial that he'd left her unsatisfied and hurting. He'd had no idea she'd been so affected by one single touch, didn't think it possible that she'd been left feeling as needy as he'd been from their encounter in the storage closet. When presented with the fact that this girl who drove him crazy with need hadn't gotten what she craved from him, he didn't give a shit about their surroundings. He only wanted to make it right. Satisfy her body. *Please let me. . .*

Ben rose up on his knees and leaned over her. She let her head fall back. Surrendering. Possessiveness heated his blood as he lowered his mouth to hers, let it hover. He felt himself being pulled under, her beautiful eyes luring him to somewhere unknown. It was that threat of the unknown that reminded him who she was and what she'd come here to do. Seduce him. Turning him inside out was part of her game. His plan had been to call her bluff. He needed to stick to the plan, or she'd drown him.

"You want me to stop?" He brushed their lips together. "What about your extra credit?"

Her body went rigid beneath him. Just like that moment in the closet when their eyes had met for the first time, everything went still around him. This time, though, instead of panic and regret in her eyes, he saw fury. It grabbed him in a choke hold and strangled the breath from his lungs. Dread crept in . . . then it *poured* in, sealing all the cracks inside him. Something was wrong. This wasn't the reaction he'd expected. Especially a moment later, when she reached between them with frantic hands and tugged her skirt back into place before shoving him off her.

He went immediately, the shame in her expression impaling him through his midsection. Every word he formulated in his head was wrong. He didn't even fully understand what he'd done until she reached into her still-open backpack and drew out a small, stapled stack of papers.

"I did the extra-credit assignment. On *Lolita.*"

Oh, Jesus. This wasn't happening. He'd forgotten all about the assignment. What had he just done? He'd lost his mind. With shaking hands he wanted to cover with his own, she zipped up her backpack and held it in front of her chest. Like a shield. It made him want to drop back to his knees and beg her not to need a shield from him, but the horror and mortification wouldn't allow him to move.

Honey moved around him in an exaggerated half circle and trudged down the lecture hall stairs, stopping before she reached the last one. She turned and pierced him with a look. "I have an A in this class. I have an A in *every* class because I work *hard.* I don't need to sleep with my teachers for good grades." She gave a bitter laugh. "I don't know what I saw in you, but I'm starting to wonder if I was wrong."

She turned and headed for the door. Ben went down the stairs after her, not knowing what he'd do when he got to her, but positive he couldn't just let her walk away. When he reached her, he placed a gentle hand on her shoulder, but she slapped it away.

"Honey—"

That was when Peter appeared in the doorway.

Chapter 6

The thigh bone's connected to the . . . hip bone.

Honey hummed the familiar tune as she studied her human anatomy text book, one leg jiggling beneath the library table. A cleared throat brought her head up in time to receive an irritated look from a guy wearing a faux turtleneck one table over.

Okay. Apparently not everyone enjoyed the classics.

She flipped the book closed and massaged her eyes. What time was it? Without English class to distract her today, she'd spent Tuesday afternoon studying but had continually found her eye drawn toward the literature section. Was it ridiculous that she wanted to pull *Lolita* from the shelf and see if Ben had checked it out recently? She knew from watching him unload his bag before class that he carried library books.

It was probably best if she headed home for the day before she acted on her wayward impulses. Her hormones had obviously overridden her good sense, because she *should* be indignant. She should *curse* the day she walked into Professor Ben Dawson's classroom. Lord, when she thought about the way he'd accused her of something so sordid, she started conjuring up parting shots she wished she'd delivered. Ones that included the phrase *in your dreams* and involved throwing a velvet cape over her shoulder as she swept from the classroom.

So, yeah. The situation with Ben had definitely taken an unfavorable turn, but he'd made the mistake of throwing down a gauntlet. Now that she'd had some time to think about what had happened in the classroom yesterday afternoon—oh, and she'd thought about it—it became more and more obvious he'd been calling her bluff. Or what he'd *thought* was a bluff. While she might have made up her mind to leave seduction to the big girls, she hadn't expected Ben to come on to her. The way he'd touched her . . . stared at the spot between her legs as if he were famished after three days in the desert . . . she couldn't shake how that made her feel. Hot, limber. Wanted.

So while she might have gone into class that day with the resolve to let this fascination with Ben go, he'd quite handily solidified it. He'd played a game with her, and to her way of thinking, that meant she could now seduce with impunity. Or *tempt*, as the case may be.

A yawn overtook her as she shoved her textbook into her backpack. Her grand seduction plans would have to be put on hiatus until tomorrow afternoon. Besides, in a hoodie, leggings, and her ancient, torn-up Converse, she wasn't even fit to tempt a blind man.

Honey threw her backpack over her shoulder and turned, her progress grinding to a halt when she saw Ben. Tweed jacket thrown over one arm, glasses outlining eyes that looked as weary as she felt, he nonetheless looked mouthwatering. How did he get his hair to look messy and controlled at the same time? Her first instinct was to drop back into her chair, hiding inside her hoodie until he disappeared into the literature section, but she knew she'd be disgusted with herself later if she ducked him.

"I was here first, dammit," Honey muttered, earning her a "shhh" from the table to her left. "Seriously?" she mouthed at Faux-Turtleneck. When she returned her attention to Ben, he'd just turned into a stack. Nineteenth-century literature. Why did his predictability turn her on? This was clearly a slow descent into madness, but she couldn't help wanting to take the ride. And hey, if she showed him yesterday hadn't hurt her, pride would be restored and equal footing regained. Right? Right. Honey turned in a quick circle meant to psyche herself up and headed in the direction Ben had gone, entering the aisle adjacent to his.

She ran her finger along the middle row of books, searching for him through the various gaps. When his face came into view, she encountered the urge to retreat. He looked so serious, head bent over a book, eyebrows knitted together as he flipped pages one way and then the other. When he landed on the page he obviously wanted, he rocked back on his heels with a satisfied nod.

And she giggle-snorted.

His head came up, an indignant frown blanketing his features, as if a reprimand for her outburst in the sacred library hovered right on his tongue. Instead, when he saw her, he went still. "Ms. Perribow."

"Professor Dawson." She sent a sidelong glance down the aisle to make sure they were alone. The fact that he did the same sent fizzy prickles down her arms. Maybe because it was an acknowledgment that their conversations weren't innocent enough to be overheard. "What are you reading?"

He seemed surprised by her casual question—but he slowly held up the book so she could see the cover. "*Heart of Darkness.*"

She pulled out a book halfway and nudged it back in. "Fitting. What's up next? *Moby* Dick?"

His right hand came up to scrub over his jawline. "I assume you're referring to my behavior yesterday. My accusation . . . *everything* that happened . . . was out of line. I apologize." He snapped the book shut. "It won't happen again."

Somehow, his stubborn obstinacy only made her want to push harder. Definitely a destructive idea, but she couldn't seem to help herself. This dim, deserted corner was a neutral setting, and they were alone. The silence of the library felt like a cloak around them, the books muffling everything that took place.

A distinctive throb had started at the elastic waistline of her leggings, making her want to squirm. Amazing, when a giant row of books separated their bodies. The opportunity to make him experience the same couldn't be passed up. "No. It won't happen again." She propped her chin on the shelf. "But you'll wish it would. Won't you, Professor Dawson?"

YES. YES, *I wish it right now. I've been wishing it all day.*

Unbelievable. He'd come to the library to escape the constant thoughts of her that seemed to inhabit his classroom. Now, here she was, surrounded by books, which were fast becoming his second favorite thing to look at. Replaced by this petite, fresh-faced blonde who refused to be scared off. Why was he so goddamn relieved by that? By the fact that he could drive a wedge between them, the way he'd done yesterday, only to have her kick it free? The last thing he'd expected was to have her approach him— speak to him—and *why* did she have to look so cute with her hood drawn up over her head?

After the shitty way he'd felt since yesterday, remembering her shamed expression when he'd put the equivalent of *two* feet in his mouth instead of one, he was forced to admit he wanted to know more about Honey. Not just how hard she could take it before screaming or if she'd pull his hair, although yeah, he wanted that knowledge in his head, badly.

Hell, though. He wanted to know the girl who wrote the papers. The one who made him feel as if his lectures were having an impact somewhere. The girl behind the intelligent eyes that could go from inquisitive to seductive in a heartbeat. She fascinated him on more than one level, and while he *wouldn't act on it,* he wasn't blind enough to deny the different levels of attraction toward her, either. He was too curious.

"Why is your hood up indoors?" *Great opener.*

She tugged on the drawstrings, tightening the opening until only her nose was visible. "It's like my own little invisibility cloak. I can hide from mean librarians, chatty classmates, and the shushers."

"The shushers?"

"Mmm hmm." She loosened the hood so he could see her eyes once more. The humor in them made the bookcase between them feel ten miles high. "The shushers who shush. I can't even get away with a shoe squeak in here. You think in the noisiest city on the planet, people would cut each other a little slack." Her lips tilted at the ends. "You're a shusher, aren't you?"

"Shush. Don't tell anyone."

Honey laughed into her hoodie sleeve. Ben's hand turned to a fist to prevent himself from reaching through the gap to tug it away so he could hear the sound. God, was he flirting with her? What an odd turn of events. An unacceptable one that he should cut off immediately, but damn, he wanted a few minutes more. No one was watching. No one would know.

"Are you in this section looking for a specific book? Or are you just hiding from Miss Woodmere?"

Her eyes widened at the mention of Columbia's notoriously mean librarian. "She's terrifying."

"She is," Ben agreed, taking a step closer to the shelf. *Cinnamon.* "And she's rumored to feast on the bones of freshmen, so I'd limit my shoe squeaks if I were you."

"I appreciate the advice, oh sagest of professors." Her voice was solemn, but her eyes twinkled. "So do you have a book suggestion? I was thinking I'd pick up something by Austen." She wet her lips, the twinkle turning heavy. Was she looking at his mouth? "*Persuasion,* maybe?"

Jesus. Russell was always accusing him of being an epic nerd, and he was beginning to see the truth behind that accusation. Because her clear innuendo was turning him on, but so was the fact that she obviously knew her nineteenth-century literature. If he didn't reel himself back, he'd be joining her on the other side of the bookcase, and that could not be allowed to happen. All sense of accountability for his actions went out the window when she was within reaching distance. "*Persuasion* has a happy ending. Not everything does, Ms. Perribow." *Good grief, I just said "happy ending."*

Thankfully, she let it slide, but she didn't let him off the hook. "I'm young, but I'm not naïve."

"Everyone says that when they're young." He regretted being harsh when she looked away, probably wishing she hadn't wasted her time talking to him. The loss of her attention dragged his stomach to the floor, and he had to get it back. How? His mind flipped like the pages of a novel. "One time, I got locked in the library after hours. I'd been grading exams and lost track of time." Hesitant, golden eyes met his once again through the gap, and he immediately felt better. "I went to the front desk, hoping to find someone who could let me out." He lowered his voice to a whisper. "I *might* have seen Miss Woodmere and Dean Mahoney. And she might have been dripping candle wax onto his bald head. While George Michael might have been playing from her computer speakers."

"No. No way." Honey shook her head. "You're a dirty liar."

He held up both hands, palms out. "His head is pretty shiny. That's all I'm saying."

"It's *reflective*." She laughed into her sleeve again. "Why did you tell me that?"

The truth just fell out, tumbling into their dim, secluded corner of the world. "I thought it would be nice if, just once, we didn't walk away from each other angry or upset."

He heard her swallow. "I guess I should walk away now before you blow it, huh?"

Ben really didn't want her to leave. Could have stood there talking to her all damn night. But he'd had his time with her, and he couldn't be greedy. Not when every moment he spent with her left him wanting more. More. "That's probably a good idea."

She stepped back from the shelf. "Goodnight, Ben."

"Goodnight, Honey."

He didn't move again until she'd been gone long minutes.

Chapter 7

A quarter mile from where Honey had grown up in Bloomfield, there was a ramshackle baseball diamond. At least, it had been ramshackle. Every day of her childhood, she rode past it, watching weeds take it over a little more each time, no local kids making use of it as they should. When her parents asked her what she wanted for her seventh birthday, she told them she wanted to fix up the baseball diamond. It took six weeks of hard work. Her friends filtered in and out, helping one day, disappearing the next, but Honey and her parents kept on weeding, laying sod, cleaning up ancient garbage.

When they were finished, it outshined the school baseball diamond. Her father spent hours pitching her the ball while her mother fielded, and she got pretty damn good by the time she turned nine. So good that she signed up for the town Little League. Only to find out it was for boys only.

After her parents asked around and Honey talked to the kids in her class, it became obvious that she wasn't the only one who hadn't made the cut. Not just girls, but boys who weren't friends with the coach's son or couldn't afford the uniform fee. So she started her own little league, running it on Saturdays in the diamond near her house. She didn't charge or turn a single person away, and they had fun. Local vendors started donating items, such as uniform shirts and postgame snacks. It became so popular that kids from the first Little League began dropping out and joining Honey's. In the end, the original league acquiesced and combined the two, with the promise to run the league in the spirit that should have been intended. They actually called a meeting with Honey at the town diner, two grown men sitting across from a ten-year-old Honey as she sipped a chocolate milk shake and listened to their terms.

Bottom line: Honey didn't slink off into a corner when things didn't go her way. And she could be stubborn as hell. Never in her life had she gone after a member of the opposite sex, mostly because she'd always been with Elmer. And after yesterday, when Ben had implied she was naïve, she shouldn't give him another thought. Unfortunately, their conversation in the library had elevated the too-sexy professor from infatuation to . . . guy she wanted to spend time with. Talk to. Learn more about. In addition to messing up the sheets with him. Sheet messing was definitely still on the agenda.

Honey didn't know what made her so certain Ben would attend the poetry reading tonight, but she somehow knew he'd be there. Monday after class, he'd obviously been irritated when Winker had said he'd see her at the reading. Even shoving the flyer into his pocket rather than returning it to her. Before they'd parted ways yesterday in the library, she'd been so tempted to ask if he'd be there tonight, but she'd known that if she vocalized the hope, he'd stay away. Which would throw a serious wrench into her seduction plans.

Honey stepped back and looked at herself in the mirror. She'd once again raided Roxy's closet, and she'd come out with a vintage halter dress in a dusky rose color. It was modest on top, showing no cleavage, but it more than made up for that lack of boob action once you traveled downstairs. The hem brushed the middle of her thighs like a tease, making her legs tingle all the way down to her heeled sandals. She'd opted to pile her hair on top of her head because it kept getting tangled in the dress's tie at the back of her neck, which kind of made it look like she was dressed for a Homecoming dance, but hey, this was her first seduction, so she would give herself a pass.

Half an hour later, she'd taken the train uptown and walked to the English building on campus. She'd made sure to show up twenty minutes late so she could slide into an empty seat in the back row and not stand around pretending to be fascinated with the snack table. Since starting at Columbia, she'd tried to attend as many of these events as possible. In the back of her mind, it justified her being here, all the money her parents were spending and loans she'd be paying off for years to come. This experience wouldn't be wasted because she wasn't adept at small talk.

When Honey walked into the event hall located on the second floor, she was disappointed to see the poetry reading hadn't started yet. She didn't recognize anyone right away, so she paced around the perimeter of the room, resisting the urge to grab her phone and text Abby something meaningless, just to have something to do with her hands. As she always did when attending these events, she wondered how the attendees formed groups so quickly. Did they arrive together, or did they just walk up and mingle with each other? Maybe someday she'd arrive early enough to find out.

"Hey, you."

Honey turned to find Winker sauntering toward her from the men's bathroom. "Oh, hey. Before you say anything else, can you tell me your name?"

When he looked at her curiously, she started to ramble. "If we say too much, it won't be appropriate for me to ask your name. Really, I should know it already, since we've been in class together for a month. But I don't. And there's a brief window where it won't be embarrassing for me to ask. Your name."

"Todd?"

He'd said it like a question. "Are you asking me if that's your name?"

"Do you want some lemonade?"

"Sure."

Honey wanted to knock her head against the wall as Todd headed for the snack table. She'd never thought talking to new people would be this hard. Growing up in a small town as she had, everyone she'd spoken to on a daily basis had known her since she was in diapers. Every new person she met here was a fresh start. A blank slate that would start to fill as soon as she opened her mouth. No one else seemed concerned about that, and she wished that were the case for herself. This is why she'd chosen medicine as an eventual career.

Todd retuned a moment later with two plastic cups of lemonade, three cookies cradled in his arm. He handed her a glass of lemonade. She waited for him to offer her a cookie. He didn't. "You look hot."

Mental eye roll. "Thanks. This is my roommate's dress."

"Is she hot?"

"Her boyfriend thinks so." This was going well. "So are you from out of state?"

"Oh man, I can't believe that asshole is here." Todd turned slightly so both of their backs were toward the exit, his shoulder pressing against hers. Honey's pulse jumped, but not because of Todd's proximity. No, she had a good idea which "asshole" her quasi-date was referring to, and yes, their last encounter had been decidedly shitty, but she still didn't like him being called an asshole. Unless she was the one doing it. Three cheers for making sense.

"Which asshole are you talking about?" She sipped her lemonade. Store-bought. *Blech.* "There's a lot of them in this city. The overcrowding makes it kind of inevitable."

"I don't know what you're saying half the time, but the accent makes it cute." He popped a cookie into his mouth. "Professor Dawson. The man in tweed. Do you know he gave me a D on my last paper?"

The back of Honey's neck started to heat. Was Ben looking at her? The warmth in her neck traced a downward path to her legs, and she suddenly felt overexposed. It didn't make her want to cover up, though. It made her feel feverish. Sexy. As if they were back in the classroom, Ben's hands creeping up her thighs, those thumbs massaging devastating circles into her sensitive flesh. God, she hadn't even set eyes on him yet and already her body was reacting to him. Knowing her nipples had gone hard, she crossed her arms and tried to focus on Todd. What had he said? Oh right, he'd gotten a D. "Did you do the extra credit?"

"Hell no. I can barely manage the regular credit." Todd brushed a stray piece of hair off her shoulder, and she barely restrained a flinch. "Maybe you can help me study."

As inconspicuously as possible, Honey put a few inches of distance between her and Todd. There was no more help for it, her gaze immediately bounced around the room, looking for Ben.

She sucked in a breath when they finally locked eyes. Just like in the library yesterday, seeing him outside the classroom gave her belly an extra kick. He'd taken off the tweed jacket and draped it over his arm, black dress shirt rolled up to his elbows. His hair looked a little more haphazard than usual, as if he'd been tugging on it with his fingers all day. *She* desperately wanted to be the one to mess it up. When Ben raised an eyebrow, she realized her thoughts were showing on her face and quickly reminded herself she was mad as hell at him. With a raised eyebrow of her own, she turned back to Todd and smiled. "Should we find a seat?"

Honey and Todd took a seat toward the back, joining a few of her friends in the premed program, who had just started to arrive. Having gone a full five minutes without looking at Ben, Honey was feeling pretty smug until the professor took a seat two rows ahead of her. With another older woman who wasted no time resting her hand on his arm and whispering in his ear.

Honey didn't hear a single damn word of the poetry reading.

BEN LET OUT the breath he'd been holding since the reading started, grateful it was over. He liked Viv, one of his fellow English teachers. In fact, she was the type of woman he usually dated. Midthirties, divorced, and not looking for anything serious. Straightforward. Unlike a certain blonde in a short pink dress whose presence he'd felt for the last hour as if she'd been sitting on his lap, kissing his neck, talking in his ear.

Who is she, Ben? Imaginary Honey had asked him, her voice all soft and twangy, making him glad he'd draped his coat over his lap. *Why is she sitting so close to you? I know all you want to do is drag me away from Johnny Jerk Off in the back row and fuck me in the stairwell.*

But Honey wasn't sitting on his lap, nor was she talking to him. He'd once again proven himself a purveyor of douchebagery in the library, talking to her like a wayward student who didn't know her own mind, when he *knew* from her work that the opposite was true. Had she moved on already? Found someone who'd appreciate her equal parts of maturity and youthfulness? God, he'd enjoyed talking to her yesterday and hated that someone else was enjoying that privilege now. She was wearing that sexy forties pinup outfit for another guy, and since he'd decided to show up to the reading anyway, despite his better judgment, he was sitting with Viv, who apparently had no qualms about stroking his arm like a cat in front of their colleagues.

Ben stood from his seat, a little surprised when Viv linked their arms together and tugged him toward a group of English department faculty members. She'd expressed her interest in going out with him on one or two occasions and he'd considered asking her out, but he'd never expected her to make a move like this. Honestly, he should have been more than happy to go with it, perfectly content to let Honey see how different she was from his usual conquests. He shouldn't even be *thinking* about Honey. Unfortunately, she'd turned in another brilliant essay. So when he combined the heartfelt words she'd given him and her soft voice reaching him across the shelf in the library, then threw in the memory of silky thighs leading to touchable, lily-white panties, he more than thought about her. In fact, he was wondering if he'd maybe gone swerving past the boundaries of attraction and veered straight into the fixation lane.

Viv and his colleagues immediately launched into a discussion about the poetry reading, but Ben found himself glancing toward Honey. She wasn't looking at him this time. Jesus, he hated that. Hated not being able to command her attention the way he did in class, when she had no *choice* but to look at him. He'd gotten spoiled by those full hours of having her look nowhere else. Instead, those big golden eyes were trained on Johnny Jerk Off, as if his backward Texas Longhorns hat held the meaning of life. It was possible he'd completely cured her of the attraction she felt for Ben. Again, that should be good news. *Great* news. So why did it feel like acid was bubbling in his gut every time she laughed at another man's joke? Why did he feel like both of them were doing something wrong by spending time with other people and not each other? Because it felt wrong. It just did.

Peter wedged himself in between Ben and Viv, earning himself an annoyed female stare. Ben barely stifled the urge to slap the usually irritating Peter on his back in welcome. The urge died when he saw the concern on Peter's face. He should have known a conversation about last night's Yankees game wasn't in the cards. Not after Peter had seen the beginnings of an obviously personal argument between Ben and Honey.

"Hey, Ben." Peter tossed a look over his shoulder and lowered his voice. "Did you see who's here?"

Ben tossed back the rest of his lemonade, wishing it were a cold beer. "You'll have to be more specific."

"The blonde," Peter murmured. "In the pink dress." When Ben didn't respond, mainly because he was focusing on *not* getting in Peter's face and asking why he was paying such close attention to what Honey was wearing, his colleague continued with a sigh. "Look, she's obviously got some kind of crush on you."

Ben's stomach muscles flexed involuntarily to counteract the sudden hot ache. Honestly, all that over the idea of her having a crush on him? His mental status was beginning to appear questionable. "Say what you want to say, Peter."

"Look, I think you need to give some more thought to what I said before." Peter shook his head. "She stays after class to get you alone. She shows up here. All it would take is that sting of rejection to file a complaint and your job would be in jeopardy. Head it off at the pass. Be up-front and write a formal letter to Dean Mahoney, letting him know a student has shown interest in you. That way, if blondie ever claims you harassed her, you've already been honest. It will count in your favor."

Ben had to admit there was some truth to what Peter was saying. If he wanted to make sure his job stayed secure, this would be a way to ensure that. The problem being, anything he put in that letter would mostly be horseshit. No one had held a gun to his head when he'd lifted up Honey's skirt to get a look at her panties. Her thighs. Her pussy. No one had done that but him. She might have deceived him at the outset, but the blame for what happened after didn't lay squarely on her shoulders.

"Thanks. I'll think about it," Ben mumbled, mostly to end the conversation with Peter. He rejoined the conversation with the rest of his colleagues for a few minutes, resisting his impulse to glance over at Honey. Not with Peter standing there, seemingly watching his every move. But when Peter excused himself to use the restroom, Ben found himself unable to hold off any longer. He angled his body away from Viv and turned, just in time to see her leave the hall with Johnny Jerk Off.

He stood very still for a moment, trying and failing to ignore the rush of denial. Where were they going? Back to some smelly dorm room to hang a sock on the doorknob while they . . . No. Not her. Please not her. Why did that guy actually make an effort to show up here? Didn't guys like that blow shit off for nickelwing night at the bar down the street? It was possible the guy was genuinely nice, despite being a garbage speller. *Maybe* I'm *the jerk-off*. Yes, clearly that was the case, because he was standing there staring at any empty doorway while the girl who'd written a paper from Lolita's POV as the literary heroine traversed the politics in an old folk's home was leaving with another guy. He hadn't even said hi to her. His arm was once again being tucked into Viv's side, and he wanted to yank it away.

No, he just had. He'd yanked it away, and now the circle of professors was staring at him. Not Peter, though. Peter was still in the bathroom. Which only gave Ben a few seconds to get out of here.

"I . . . uh." He made a vague gesture toward his throat. "Need something to drink besides lemonade. Going to make a trip to the vending machine."

He thought he heard Viv offering to walk with him, but he was already halfway to the door. What the fuck was he doing? When he found Honey and Johnny, was he going to give them detention? Jesus, he didn't know. He only knew he needed to stop Honey from having bad dorm-room sex. He just needed to stop her, *period*, and make her *look* at him. With that convoluted goal in mind, he rode the elevator to the first floor and strode down the deserted hallway to push open the exit door, thinking he'd see them hopping into a cab or walking hand in hand toward the subway. The thought of it made him sick to his stomach.

Nowhere. He saw them nowhere. Honey, Lolita, his closet girl. She'd been spirited away by a teenager doused in Axe body spray. His head started to pound, drowning out the traffic on Broadway. He felt like he'd just stepped off one of those carnival rides whose sole purpose was to spin until it stole your equilibrium. He hated those rides, but they were nothing compared to this. Without a destination or plan in place, Ben pushed back through the doors leading into the building.

Honey stood at the end of the dim hallway. Alone.

Relief almost doubled him over, but he didn't have time for that, because he needed to get to her. She hadn't left with another guy. Halle-fuckin-lujah. As soon as he started walking toward her—because really, he didn't have a choice in the matter—she stepped into the classroom to her right. Ben knew exactly what would happen if the two of them got inside that classroom together with the door shut. He also knew it was fucking inevitable. He'd never wanted anything more in his life, and he wasn't capable of giving a damn at the moment that a faculty-heavy party was in full swing a few floors up. His girl hadn't left with another guy and he'd made her pussy hurt by touching it twice and not making her come. That was all he fucking knew.

Last time you touched me there, you walked away and it . . . it hurt, Ben. I still hurt . . . please don't tease me.

Ben walked faster, faster until he was almost jogging.

Chapter 8

*H*oney backed away from the doorway slowly, waiting for Ben to appear inside it. This Ben, the one she'd seen at the end of the hallway, was not the Ben who lectured about Hemingway to a hall full of students. This wasn't even the Ben who'd gotten mad at her in the storage closet. Not even close. The Ben she'd just watched launch himself after her had looked miserable and a little lost. Then. Then he'd looked a whole lot ready for something else. Like, hard, angry screwing. With her.

Good. She wanted it, too. She'd wanted *him* for a month, and he'd gone after her. Whatever had happened upstairs, he'd gone after her. So she would worry about the rest of it tomorrow. When tomorrow came and went and he realized she didn't do it for a grade, *that* niggling issue would take care of itself. They couldn't be together because he was her professor? Fine. *Fine.* But she'd watched that woman paw him for the last hour while he'd refused to even make more than the barest eye contact with Honey, calling territorial instincts she didn't even know she possessed to the surface.

Did going after him after he'd insulted her character make her weak? No, it didn't. Weak would be hiding in the back of the classroom for the rest of the semester, pretending she didn't want him. Denying the attraction until it went away. That wasn't what she was about. What *this* was about. She needed him, and if he followed her in here, he needed her right back. In her estimation, acknowledging what she wanted and taking it made her strong.

Ben sounded out of breath when he rounded the doorway into the classroom. He stood outlined by the frame for a moment, looking her over from head to toe. Burning her. God, he looked amazing. If possible, his stubble had grown more pronounced during the reading, hair standing out at every direction. Honey trapped a gasp in her throat when he slammed the door behind him and came toward her, moving so fast her heart shot to her throat. His long legs ate up the distance. The weight of his determined gaze had her gripping the large metal desk behind her for balance.

Just before Ben reached her, she shot forward and met him, their mouths preying on one another's, hot and hungry. He hauled her body up against his, bending her backward over his forearm and yanking her back up, as if he couldn't decide how he wanted her. How to get close enough. His fingertips traced the hem of her dress before slipping beneath to skim up the inside of her thigh. When his warm hand molded to the flesh between her legs and squeezed, Honey broke away with a moan.

"Does it still hurt?" He grated the question at her lips. "Tell me it still hurts so I can lick it better."

A sharp exhale burst from her mouth. "It still hurts."

Her ass hit the metal desk before she'd even registered him picking her up. It was the first time she'd ever seen him without glasses. At some point during their kiss he'd taken them off and stowed them somewhere unseen. She'd always wondered if he'd be even more handsome without them on and decided then that he was incredible both ways. With or without. Without, however, he didn't remotely resemble her English professor anymore. No. With his black dress shirt shoved up to his elbows and hair falling across his forehead, he looked masculine, sexual. Like a man. She'd never been with a man. Only boys. Excitement, anticipation, of what was to come whipped through her midsection before moving lower. *Lower.*

Ben gripped her knees tightly in his hands. "Is this going to get you out of my system?"

"I don't know." Honey took a deep breath and slid her dress up to her waist, revealing the tiny triangle of blue silk between her legs. "Is it going to get you out of mine?"

He groaned, hands kneading her thighs. "I shouldn't want the answer to be no, right?" As if irritated at himself for saying those words out loud, he twisted his fingers in the sides of her panties and yanked them down her legs. Honey said a quick prayer to the waxing gods that she'd let Roxy drag her to get her first Brazilian one week prior, because the fierce, blanketing lust that fell over Ben's face made it worth the pain. A gruff sound escaped his lips, and he shook his head. "You've been sitting in my lectures hiding this sweetness beneath your skirt, babe?"

My sweet Lord. "Yes."

"Not anymore. I can see all of your bare little pussy now. Can't I?"

"*Yes.*"

The hardening of his jaw was the only warning she had before he circled her knees with his hands and jerked her to the edge of the desk. In one movement, he got to his knees and shoved her legs open further. After that, Honey's thoughts were only of Ben's mouth. Ben's tongue. She wished she could un-bow her back long enough to watch him, but the wicked sensations he created kept her head thrown back, staring blindly at the classroom ceiling. His mouth moved like a wave, smooth and determined, devouring her with wide, openmouthed kisses that left her gasping. The first time his upper lip brushed against her clit, Honey jerked on the desk, hands darting involuntarily to weave through his hair and hold him closer. A vibration emanated from his mouth, buzzing over her sensitive nub like the greatest vibrator known to man as he brushed his lips back and forth over the sensitive spot.

"Please, Ben. *Please.*"

Another brush of lips. "Pull my hair. Harder. Show me how bad you want me to take away the hurt."

Honey tugged hard on the strands wrapped around her fingers, savoring Ben's growl. He took her ankles in his hands and threw them both over his shoulders, burying his mouth at her core. His lips closed around her aching bud, drawing hard. And she flew. She flew backward on the desk, body shaking as the climax gripped her, but her mind flew, too. Out of the classroom to a green meadow where bunny rabbits frolicked and someone strummed an acoustic guitar while lounging in a hammock.

She was brought back to reality by her own voice chanting, "*Oh God, Ben. Oh God, Ben,*" on a constant loop, but she was abruptly cut off when he pulled her off the desk. Her stomach encountered the straining erection in his pants as she slipped off the metal desk, a reminder that they weren't finished yet. Ben was breathing heavily, sweat dotting his forehead. As soon as her feet hit the floor, his hands disappeared underneath her dress and gripped her ass with strong fingers. He looked to almost be in pain as he walked her backward, around the desk, to push her up against the wall, his hands hard and punishing on her backside the entire way.

Ben snagged her bottom lip between his teeth and tugged. "*Fuck,* the way you come is so goddamn hot."

"You're not supposed to talk that way." He ground his erection against her belly, eliciting a whimper from her lips. "You're an English professor."

"Yeah?" He spun her toward the wall, pressing her cheek against the cool surface. Cool air on her backside told her he'd lifted up her dress. "Well, your English professor isn't supposed to fuck you, either, but that's exactly what's going to happen here." A heavy pause. "Unless you tell me no. You should *really* tell me no, Honey. In a minute, babe . . . I don't know if I'll be able to hear anything but the sound of me slipping in and out of you."

The visual nearly made her go limp. She could tell by the stilted way he spoke, by the hardness pressing insistently against her naked bottom, that he didn't want her to say no. Nor did she *want* to. Her belly was already tightening with the thrilling thought of taking him inside her. Feeling all that desire for her in one place. Listening to his harsh pants as he drove deeper.

Honey reached behind her back and worked his belt buckle with frantic fingers. "I want you so bad, Ben. Don't stop. Please."

He pushed his hardness into her hands, rubbing himself there. "Oh, thank Christ."

She heard the crinkle of a condom wrapper seconds before she freed the leather from his belt and undid the button of his pants. He took over then, drawing down his zipper and rolling the condom onto his erection. Honey braced her hands against the wall and angled her hips for him, biting her lip so she wouldn't beg out loud for him to hurry.

His lips moved on her shoulder, hot and wet. At the same time, the thick head of his arousal nudged between her legs, stealing an uneven moan from both of them. "You're slippery as hell, but I can eat you again, Honey. Just say the word."

"Inside me. Just get *inside* me."

BEN RAMMED HIMSELF home.

And then he pushed *further* and *harder* because he couldn't get close enough. Couldn't get *inside* this girl enough. She was up on her toes, possibly had already left the ground, and all he could think was *more, more, give me more.* Had anyone ever felt this fucking good? Honey squirmed around on his cock, whimpering and clawing at the wall, no idea that every movement she made was driving him toward some unknown brink he'd never been aware existed.

He needed to touch all of her. Every inch. His hands moved on their own, untying the string at the back of her neck and peeling her dress down to expose her breasts. God, he wished he hadn't turned her around, because he couldn't see them, but he could touch. At least he could touch. Still unable to move inside her without the fear of ending this perfect feeling too soon, he smoothed his hands up her sides and cupped her sweet, pointed tits in his hands. He had all of her in his arms now, surrounding his body, and the possessive instinct she'd been culling inside him went off like a cannon shot.

His body took over, but so did his mouth. His mind. Lust tunneled through his veins, lighting fires as it went that only burned brighter when her body moved with his in devastating precision. Like they'd been designed for one another and no one else.

No one else. "You wanted me to think you'd left with him, didn't you?"

Her palm squeaked on the wall. "M-maybe," she gasped.

"It worked," he growled into the crook of her neck. "It worked, didn't it, you brat?"

"What about you?" There was cutting anger in her tone, but it was ruined by the way she worked her hips in tight, tempting circles. "Who was that woman?"

Ben almost laughed out loud, but pleasure blocked anything else from the forefront of his mind. How could she question him when he was breaking every single one of his rules? Taking her like a crazed animal in his place of work? "Do you know what I thought about during the reading, Honey?"

"What?"

Her head fell to the side, giving him room to suck and lick

at her neck. "I thought that if we were sitting in the back row, I would have made you sit on my lap. With my dick inside you." He drove into her tightness, again and again. So wet. So damn wet. *Fuck yes.* The rhythm was perfect. Steady enough to give her time to come, fast enough to satisfy this urgency she made him feel. "No one would know except us. Unless you moved, even just once. Because then you'd have to keep moving. We'd need it. And we'd have to fuck right there in front of everyone."

"Faster." Her pussy tightened up and shook a little in a way that made his hands turn to fists. "Oh, God. I need more. I need fast."

Ben wrapped an arm around her hips to angle her away from the wall, edging her ass higher in his lap. She liked that. No, she fucking loved it. Her breath shuddered out like hot little gusts of air. She clenched around his cock as if in warning that she'd go off soon. *Go on, babe. Go on.* There was no slowing down now. He could only thrust into her rough and fast, demanding she keep up. His balls were drawn up so tight they hurt, the product of his denying himself, pretending he didn't need this girl, when it was becoming obvious with each passing second that he *required* her. He reached between her legs, groaning at the friction of them joining, the feel of her *taking* him. His middle finger found her clit, flicking it once, twice, just to tease, before rubbing it nice and hard. Like he knew she needed.

"Come on, babe. I'm right behind you."

"*Ben.*"

Sweet fucking hell.

No one came like Honey. She bent forward with her hands braced on the wall, practically giving him a vertical lap dance as her body trembled. Legs spread, hips grinding on his hard dick while she moaned his name. As if she needed to feel every damn part of what their bodies had produced. He'd never get over seeing it. Especially not at that moment, when release clamored in his stomach, successfully finding an outlet right between her gorgeous thighs. Thighs he couldn't help but stroke and grip as he came. And *God*, he came hard. It stormed through him like a Category 5 hurricane, wrecking everything in its path. He opened his eyes to see that he'd hauled Honey back against him, crushing her to his chest as he'd borne the brunt of what she'd done to him. What they'd done to each other.

It was embarrassing to admit even to himself that his legs felt a little weak. Honey might weigh next to nothing, but his chest was full, and the air felt so close that he knew he had to sit down. He just wasn't willing to let her go in order to accomplish it. Forcing his brain to work with marginal success, he took the two steps to the chair behind them. A chair in which a professional educator, some faceless colleague of his, sat every day. Ben sunk into it, stunned to realize it felt almost as amazing to have her boneless on his lap as it did to be buried inside of her. Her head lolled against his shoulder as she continued to take in huge gulps of breath. Which didn't suck. Knowing he'd winded this beautiful, intelligent girl to the point of exhaustion. This beautiful, intelligent girl whose tits were still on full display, light glancing off her still-pointed nipples. And *shit*, he was hard as steel again. This behavior was really out of line for an English professor. He should resign.

"Again? Already?" She tipped her head back and laughed a

laugh that reminded him of marshmallows and moonbeams. Not that he'd ever seen a moonbeam in his life. "Give me a few minutes to touch down on terra firma before you get firma again."

A laugh boomed out of him, so unexpected he had the urge to look over his shoulder and see if someone else had delivered it. Nope, it was him. He was sitting in a classroom with a student in his lap. A student he'd just given it to the dirty way. Somehow, at the moment, though, he honestly couldn't find the will within himself to care. Not when it was just them, no harsh fluorescent lighting or lesson plans burning a hole in his bag. This girl who'd dug herself into his gut was smiling up at him like they were two rascally high school students who'd just made out beneath the bleachers, and he wanted to go there. He wanted to let her take him there for a while.

"Whose idea was it to name you Honey?"

She sighed. Not in an irritated way, but in the way someone sighs when they've just taken a sip of hot chocolate or seen a picture of a newborn deer. "My mom. She's a whimsical sort." She picked up one of his hands and threaded their fingers together. "She and my daddy tried for five years to have a baby, but it wasn't happening. She even went to see a fancy doctor up in Lexington, but nothing worked. One night, she went to the diner for dinner and put some honey in her tea." Her slender shoulder shook with laughter. "There's a censored version to what happens afterward, the one I grew up with. But when I turned eighteen, we split a bottle of cheap red wine and she told me the real dirt. My mother swears up, down, and sideways that as soon as that honey hit her belly, she went home to my father and made a baby. Me."

Ben let his hand hover over her hair a moment, then gave in to the urge to stroke it. Felt like silk. No. *Way* better than silk. He just had no name for what that better thing might be. "So she named you that, even knowing you'd probably have to tell the story behind your name constantly."

Her lips curved into an even wider smile. "Where I come from, a good story is a gift."

"You must be buried in gifts, then."

She looked up at him. "What do you mean?"

Feeling a little uncomfortable, he tried to sit up straighter, but she shook her head and he stilled. "Your papers." He cleared his throat, and it echoed in the empty classroom. "I've read the classics ten times over, I've studied and written enough words to drown us both, but I bet I've never held anyone's attention the way your papers hold mine."

"You're lying." She shook her head at him, sobering when she saw his expression. "Really?"

"I think you've figured out by now I'm not the joking type."

"True." She fused her lips with the hollow of his throat, as if it were the most natural thing in the world. Just then, it felt like it was. "Why did you become a professor, Ben?"

Oh fuck, he liked hearing her say his name. In the heat of the moment, it had been potent, but now it made his limbs feel heavy. Like he could finally relax. "I love words. On the page. Knowing someone felt them and immortalized them." He swallowed a knot in his throat. "And sometimes it's easiest to do the thing least expected. Instead of trying to get close as possible to what *is* expected." God, he sounded like a jackass. This was definitely twenty-first-century pillow talk at its finest. "Never mind."

"No. Not never mind." She slid her hand into his hair and tugged comfortingly. "*Mind.*"

Ben's lips tugged. "Forget what I said about your talent with words."

She yanked his hair and his cock swelled underneath her ass. He'd never been turned on by such a thing before, but it appeared tonight was a night for firsts. Had he actually begged her to pull his hair a few minutes ago? Honey looked up at him in a way he recognized from having her sit in the front row of his classroom. It unwittingly spoke volumes. *See anything you like, Professor?*

"Yes."

"Yes, what?"

His body responded to her husky question appropriately. No. *Severely.* Get a handle on yourself, man. "Yes, we should go. We don't want to be sitting here when a janitor walks in."

"Or worse," she added before sneaking a look up at him from under her eyelids. "Would you . . . I mean, do you want to come over to my place? We don't have to go inside. Even though Louis is probably there watching reruns of *Arrested Development*. There's a roof . . ."

Immediately, his mind began forming excuses. Reasons why he couldn't go home with her. There were too many to count, really. Except he wanted, very badly, to go sit on a rooftop with Honey and listen to her talk. Watch her smile. And yes, fuck her as many times as possible before the sun came up. She was most definitely still in his system, more than before. So much more. He could go to the roof and no one would ever know. Nobody could stop him.

Honey trailed her lips over his jaw to kiss his ear. "Stop thinking so hard about it."

Holy shit, he was going to do it. "All right, I'll—"

His cell phone went off in his pocket, loud and mood-ruining. *Son of a bitch.* Honey sighed and hopped off his lap to fix her clothes, covering her breasts by tying the halter back behind her neck. It was quite possibly the most depressing thing he'd ever seen.

Until he looked at his phone and saw the name Tracy. His mother. When he let it ring too long, it rolled over to voice mail, but a text message popped up instead. *At your place. Need to crash.*

His neck started to burn, nausea rolling in his stomach. He could feel Honey looking at him curiously, and suddenly he wanted nothing more than to kneel in front of her and wrap his arms around her waist. Feel her fingers in his hair again. Get a nice, long pull of her cinnamon-and-sugar scent. But he couldn't. He had to go. Based on the resignation in her big eyes, she already knew. She just didn't know why, and he could see every possibility ping-ponging in her head. Another girl. The guys wanting to drag him out for a beer. Why wouldn't he go? He'd already gotten what he wanted. That was what she thought. He could see it clearly on her beautiful face.

She smiled tightly and started to move around him. "Maybe next time."

He should let her go. Had no business spending time on her roof in the first place. But his hand shot out and gripped her elbow before he gave the command. "It's my mother. She's at my place . . . visiting . . . and I have to go let her in." Remembering what he had stuffed in his jacket, he bent down to retrieve the discarded garment and slipped her *Lolita* assignment out of his inside pocket. "I graded your extra-credit assignment." When she quirked a brow but didn't take the paper he offered, Ben felt a flash of self-loathing. "I just realized this is an awkward time to bring up extra credit, considering the inexcusable thing I said to you last time and the fact that we just . . . *you know*. It's just that I enjoyed your work so much, and I—"

Honey's light, sparkling laugh shut him up. With a shake of her head, she clasped the sides of his face. "How can you throw me against a wall and say all manner of filthy things to me one minute and turn back into the befuddled professor the next?"

A smile tugged at the corner of his mouth. "Were they really filthy, these things?"

"All manner of filthy." She slipped the paper out of his hand and replaced it with her silky blue panties. He had to remind himself to breathe. "Go let your mama in, Ben. But think about me later on."

He yanked her close on a groan, taking her mouth in a hard kiss. *God*, he wanted her again. The desk was right behind her. He could just—

Honey broke away with a chuckle. "Good night . . ." Halfway to the door, she turned around and winked at him. " . . . Professor."

Chapter 9

*H*oney stopped just outside the door to her apartment, keys pausing in midair before they reached the lock. Her plan had been to escape to her bedroom to unfold the *Lolita* assignment before her roommates got hold of her. She'd never been accomplished at keeping her feelings from her face. She could hear Abby and Roxy on the other side of the door, shouting at whatever reality TV program they were watching, and she knew they would take one look at her and *know* something was up. So she would take a minute for herself first. One minute more where tonight was *hers*. Her secret.

Smiling to herself, she took the folded assignment out of her purse and savored the anticipation of unfolding it, flattening it against the apartment door to smooth the creases. Another A grade. Approval from the man she was seeing shouldn't, *should not*, make her hot, but it did. She could hear him whispering it in her ear. *Amazing job, babe. You get an A.* A tiny moan sailed past her lips, thighs clenching together. Oh God, the feminist in her was stomping her foot and shaking her head—totally justified—

but hey, this was *her* minute to savor the secret. She consoled herself with the fact that she deserved the A. Had worked hard on the paper. Anyone would have given her an A . . . but it seemed to mean more coming from Ben.

She flipped to the final page and did a little dance. Just below the note she'd written to him detailing the contents of her backpack, Ben had left one of his own.

The things I carry (it's only fair). . .

A guitar pick I caught at a Springsteen concert. A gym lock I've forgotten the combination for, but I'm determined to remember. My father's rookie card. An eyeglass repair kit. Numerous red pens. Numerous. Wrapped together in a blue rubber band. Postcards from my mother. A book of New York Times *crossword puzzles for my morning train ride. A backup wristwatch in case mine stops ticking. Lesson plans. House keys. Butterscotches. Band-Aids (an important recent addition, in case of falling students).*

Aren't you curious what the letter from your mother says? Professor Dawson.

Honey smashed the assignment to her chest, as if she were the lead in a romantic comedy and the director had just yelled, *Emote, emote, emote.* It couldn't be helped. Her knees wanted to give way so she could fall to the floor and roll around with Ben's note in her arms. The brief times they had spent together thus far had been stolen snippets, but through this note, she wondered if maybe he wanted her to know him better. Even if she had even more questions as a result. Where was his father now? Why did his mother travel so much? And, heck. He'd bought Band-Aids for her.

Wiping the cheeseball expression off her face, Honey tucked

the assignment back into her purse and unlocked the apartment door. Abby sat on the arm of the couch, a bowl of popcorn balanced on her knees. She waved a fist full of popcorn at Honey, greeting her around a mouthful. Roxy sat on the opposite end with her legs in Louis's lap, both of them nursing bottles of Sam Adams. Clearly Roxy being cast as "Tina, the wacky next-door neighbor" in a new television pilot starring Neil Patrick Harris didn't mean she was changing her habits anytime soon. Honey kind of loved that.

"Hey, you," Roxy called. "Where've you been?"

Okay, normally she would just tell Abby and Roxy everything, but she couldn't with Louis sitting there listening to her every word. "School thing."

Abby finally swallowed her epic mouthful of popcorn. "What kind of school thing?"

"A, uh . . . poetry reading thing."

Louis's bottle stopped halfway to his mouth. "Oh."

Roxy noticed her boyfriend's hesitation. "What was that?"

"Nothing, just . . ." Louis sent her an apologetic look. "Ben went to a poetry reading thing tonight."

"*Oh*," Roxy and Abby said at the same time, drawing the word out until Honey scowled at them.

Honey threw her purse on the kitchen counter and snagged a beer from the fridge, rolling the cool glass bottle against her cheeks to reduce her stupid flush. Bake something. Yes, she would bake something. It would give her something to do with her hands and give her an excuse to avoid her roommates.

No dice.

Roxy hopped up on the marble island, grinning like the Cheshire Cat. Abby tried to execute the same move, failed, and took a stool instead. "Hey, I'll eat whatever you make," Roxy said. "That has been proven. But you're going to talk while you cook."

"Good thinking." Abby crossed her legs, smoothing a hand over her striped pajama pants. "People are more inclined to let details slip when they're distracted."

"Yes." Roxy nodded. "What she said."

Louis came up behind his girlfriend, tossing his keys up in the air and catching them. "I think that's my cue to bail." He gave Roxy a quick kiss that immediately turned into an all-out tongue war Louis clearly wanted to win. When he pulled away, he looked satisfied to see Roxy's bemused expression. "Call me before you turn your light off, 'kay?"

"'Kay," she breathed, keeping her gaze plastered to him until he disappeared through the apartment door. "I'm keeping him."

Honey tossed a baking pan onto the counter, satisfied when Roxy and Abby jumped. "Corn bread or dark chocolate bark?"

Roxy snorted. "What kind of a question is that?"

"Dark chocolate bark, obviously." Abby toed off her slippers. "Dark chocolate will replace the endorphins you released during sex with Ben." When they both gaped at her, she blinked. "What?"

"You could have let me break the news," Honey complained, removing a tub of shortening from the cabinet. She had a quick flashback to her mother completing the same movement a million times throughout her childhood and felt another unexpected pang of homesickness. Boy, that had been happening way too frequently lately. "Anyway," she started, determined to shake off the odd feeling. "A lady doesn't give details."

They booed her. Which immediately made her feel better.

Honey poured a bag of dark chocolate pieces into a giant glass bowl and stuck it in the microwave to melt it. What could she tell them? Ben had basically taken any prior knowledge she'd had about sex and crushed it up against the wall, right along with her. He'd known what to do to make her climax, which didn't sound like an uber-amazing feat unless you'd been with members of the opposite sex who couldn't find a clitoris with a flashlight and magnifying glass. He'd played her body so effortlessly, so confidently. Part of her wondered if she'd just picked the wrong partners in the past—sorry, Elmer—or if it was just Ben. Yeah. She had a feeling it was just Ben. Or Ben and her, specifically.

"Forget the microwave, you're going to melt that chocolate all on your own," Abby observed, earning her a high five from Roxy. "Was it that good?"

"You guys, it was . . ."

"Next-level shit?" Abby breathed.

Honey gave a solemn nod. "Next-level shit. And Roxy is starting to rub off on you."

"Lucky her." Roxy pulled her knees up to her chest. "So, Professor Ben, huh? Please tell me he slapped your ass with a yardstick."

"Well it wasn't a full *yard* . . ." Honey coughed into her fist. "But it was impressive. It reminded me of that scene in *A Few Good Men* where Jack Nicholson yells, 'You can't handle the truth'" at Tom Cruise. Except Ben was Jack Nicholson and my vagina was Tom Cruise."

Roxy whooped a laugh. "What is it with this crew of dudes? They're all hung?"

"We only need confirmation on Russell." Honey took the bowl of melted dark chocolate out of the microwave. "Batter up, Abby."

She split a frown between them. "Well, that would certainly be a weird thing to ask Russell."

Honey and Roxy traded a glance. "No one said you should *ask* him."

A long pause ensued. "How else would I find out?"

Oh boy, it appeared they had their work cut out for them with those two. Honey took pity on Abby and took the focus off her for now, but she resolved to have a chat with her later. Abby obviously had no clue Russell would probably walk on nails barefoot to get to her. Nor did she have a clue what a guy like Russell would likely do once he made it across that bed of nails. "I invited Ben over here, actually, but his mother is in town or something."

"Really." It was Roxy's turn to look confused. "His mother? You're sure?"

"Yeah." Honey experienced an unwanted sinking feeling. "Why?"

Roxy swiped a finger through the melted chocolate and licked it off. "Not sure, exactly. I nosed around about Ben to Louis on your behalf. He wouldn't give up too much, in the spirit of the bro code and all, but he made it sound like mom and dad were out of the picture."

Abby tucked a strand of long brown hair behind her ear.

"That's too bad." Honey watched as Abby surveyed the massive apartment, looking thoughtful. She knew her friend was insecure about having so much fortune foisted on her, when Honey and Roxy were more or less dirt poor. Probably didn't quite understand what it meant to *have* parents out of the picture. At least not in the way Roxy, or possibly even Ben, did. Honey's heart gave a hard squeeze, even as she began to doubt his story for leaving that night. Had it really been his mother, or something else? Maybe he'd just latched on to the first excuse he could think of to get away from her?

When Honey felt Roxy watching her steadily, she turned and withdrew a plastic baggie of dried cherries from the cabinet, adding them to the chocolate. As the television droned on in the background and Abby rummaged in the fridge behind her for a beer, Honey poured the mixture into a baking pan and placed it carefully in the oven. She thought about the note he'd written her, the way he'd kissed her before she'd left. Could she trust this gut feeling that there was something happening between them? Something out of the ordinary? She wanted to. Didn't want to believe it could just be sex. If it was, would that be enough for her with this particular guy?

No. It wouldn't. But she'd done quite enough pursuing for now. She'd purposely flirted with another guy in front of Ben and lured him into a classroom, for heaven's sake. Not that she hadn't been shoved into it by a massive case of jealousy. Still. What happened from this point would be up to him. If he'd gotten her out of his system so easily, it was for the best. She had options, right? She might have blown off Todd, all but stuffing him into a cab and racing back into the building while he sputtered like a broken-down pickup truck behind her, but there'd be more Todds. Legions of Todds.

Resolved to leave the ball in Ben's court for now, Honey turned and snagged a beer for herself out of the fridge. She popped the top and tossed it into the garbage cab, saluting Roxy and Abby with her bottle. "Let's watch a movie that doesn't have a heart-throb in it. Something where women kick ass and don't need men to be happy."

Roxy headed for the living room. *"A League of Their Own?"*

"Load it."

Chapter 10

Ben's footsteps echoed in the dim staircase as he climbed the four flights to his apartment. He took his time, more than a little reluctant to greet what waited him outside his door. Located above a hookah lounge and across the street from an overgrown, abandoned lot, this building had never been a joy to return to in the first place. But he paid for the apartment on his own. No help. Same way he'd been doing since his second year of college. He wouldn't be here forever. In fact, his student loans were close to being paid off, and now that he worked as a full-time professor, he should start looking at places. Maybe even somewhere with a window in the bedroom and heat in the winter. Somewhere he wouldn't be embarrassed to bring his friends. Or a girl. Honey.

If he'd gone home with his Lolita, what would they be doing right now? Lying on their backs on her roof, talking? Or would he already have gotten her into bed, both of their bodies slick with sweat, hands wrapped around the headboard as they tried not to make any noise?

All right, probably best not to think of that right now. Not when he couldn't see her again tonight. Or maybe even tomorrow, since they didn't have class. Wait. Did such a thing even matter anymore? He could easily get her phone number, having a direct connection through Louis and Roxy. Come to think of it, he was an asshat for not getting it tonight. He could have called her to make sure she'd gotten home all right, at the very least.

He knew why he hadn't gotten it, however, and she was one more flight up. The call had thrown him, especially after what had just happened with Honey. It had to be tonight. His mother's timing had always been shitty, but was there ever a good time to blow through town and pass out on your son's couch? She hadn't shown her face for the better part of a year, sending him postcards from Miami, Cabo San Lucas . . . Brazil. Never the same place twice. Never with the same people, either.

Ben rounded the corner onto the fourth floor and saw his mother, perched on her Louis Vuitton suitcase, nails tapping away as she texted on her cell. When her head popped up and she smiled at his approach, he saw that she'd had more work done. The chin this time. What had been wrong with it in the first place?

"Ben!" She swung her tastefully highlighted hair over her shoulder and stood, tanned arms outstretched for a hug. He stepped into them because as much as she frustrated him or became more unrecognizable each time he saw her, she was his mother. Once upon a time, they'd gone through the same debacle. They'd been on the same team, even though at eight and twenty-seven years old, neither of them had been old enough to know how to play the game. A thousand years could pass and he'd always let his mother hug him. It hurt to realize, though, that each time he felt it a little less. Had to try that much harder to find familiarity.

"Hey, Mom." He stepped back, digging his keys out of his satchel. "Sorry you had to wait so long. The trains don't come as often this time of night."

"I would have paid for a cab." She tilted her head, watching him as he unlocked the door. "I was half hoping you wouldn't live here anymore. That maybe you'd found somewhere better. I could help with that, you know. Just—"

"I'm fine here." He pushed into the apartment, flipping on lights as he went. The studio was small, but he'd made it work. A bookcase he'd found at a consignment shop in Williamsburg separated his sleeping area from the rest of the space. His brown suede couch had been a gift from his mother, one he'd been unable to turn down when she'd sworn it was going to the garbage dump otherwise. Books. There were books everywhere. Stacked in windowsills and overflowing from his kitchen cabinets in between boxes of cereal. He bent down and swiped a stack off the couch, where he'd be sleeping tonight. His mother would insist on taking it, and he'd insist she take his bed. They repeated the same routine every time.

"Are you hungry?" he asked her. "I can order pizza or Indian. There's a really good Indian—"

"I'm fine. I had sushi at the airport." She rubbed her arms as she turned in a circle, looking at his apartment like it was a museum exhibit. *Living Habits of the Prodigal Son.* At the refrigerator, she stopped, peering down at the official letter attached to his fridge. Damn. He should have taken the job offer from NYU down weeks ago, but he could admit he enjoyed seeing it there every time he opened the fridge. "NYU offered you a job?"

"Yes, but I'm not taking it. I'm comfortable where I am." He'd applied to Columbia and NYU at the same time, but Columbia had gotten back to him first. At the time, he'd been hoping for NYU because it was more convenient to his living situation, but staying unemployed for any length of time after school hadn't been an option. NYU had finally found an opening and contacted him right away. He'd been prepared to decline this week, but for some reason—a reason he refused to consider—he'd asked for time to consider the offer.

"Ben, I hate to see you living like this. It's so unnecessary."

"We have the same discussion every time you're here." He pulled his bag over his head and set it on top of the bookcase, careful to keep his tone patient. She'd never understood his un-willingness to touch the money set aside for him by his father, and he didn't expect her to now. "Why don't we talk about what you've been up to? You came from Miami, right?"

"The Hamptons, actually." She finished her perusal to look at him. "I spent a couple weeks there with some friends, but it's starting to get colder, so . . ." Her smile looked brittle. "We all started going our separate ways. You know how it goes."

He didn't. Well, he knew a lot about going separate ways. But spending two weeks in the Hamptons and saying good-bye to people because the weather changed? No, he knew nothing about that. It had taken him a while after coming to New York to make friends for the very reason that he knew what it felt like when people vanished from your life. There one day. Gone the next.

Louis and Russell had been watching a basketball game beside him in the Longshoreman one night, and they'd started talking over beers. They'd all three kept coming back, until he'd kind of fallen into friendship with them. It hadn't been a conscious thing, or it might never have happened.

"What about you?" his mother asked. "How is the job going? I still can't believe you're a professor." She laughed a little uncomfortably. "It makes me feel so old."

"It's going well. Really well." Honey's face swam in his mind, along with a heavy, carved-out feeling in his chest. He hadn't experienced it since they'd been together earlier, and he'd been waiting for it to make an appearance. The reminder that he'd done something irrevocable. Something against his rules and the ones that had been laid out for him by his employer. He suspected his mother showing up had buoyed the feeling, bringing it past the surface sooner than it might have.

"What's wrong?" His mother propped a hip against the counter in his tiny kitchen. "I can tell something is bothering you, because you keep pushing up your glasses even though they're not slipping down. You've done it since you were a kid."

"Did I?" He cleared his throat. "It's nothing." Except that was a lie. He felt the need to get it out in the open. Relieve some of the pressure surrounding his rib cage. Yet there was something else, too, bolstering the desire to spill his guts. He knew the details would horrify his mother, and he hoped maybe that would give him the reality check he needed. "There's a girl, actually. She's—"

"A girl?" Her arched eyebrow didn't move, but he suspected it might have lifted if it hadn't been for the Botox she got injected regularly. "That's so exciting. Have you been dating long?" She pulled her phone out of her pocket and checked the screen. "If I delay my flight to Ibiza one more day, could I meet her?"

Ben contained the laughter that wanted to escape. He'd barely spent any time with Honey himself. Not to mention, this wasn't exactly the kind of relationship that warranted a *meet the parents* night. Was it? He'd just barely wrapped his mind around the fact that they'd had sex.

Jesus. They'd had sex. In an unlocked classroom. With his colleagues a couple floors away.

He sunk down onto the couch. "She's a student of mine."

His mother went very still. Ben thought she might have fossilized, but she turned and reached up into the cabinet over the sink, pulling out the bottle of whiskey she'd brought with her the last time. "Ben, you can't be serious." Her Massachusetts accent had come back in a big way. "After everything. Everything that happened with your father. How could you do something so stupid?"

"I don't know." His voice sounded dull, far away. "It just—"

"*Don't.*" She shook the bottle at him, mouth twisting in a grimace. "Don't say those words. *It just happened.* You know where I've heard them before?"

"Yes. I do know. I was there."

"And still you continue the pattern?" She uncapped the bottle and took a healthy swig. "I know I was one of the women, Ben. I know that. When I met your father, he was married, and I was the shiny, new model. I hate myself for that. But I didn't deserve to watch him trade me in so many times. They got younger and younger. He stopped hiding them, and one day it all caught up, didn't it?"

Yes. It had. He could still remember the day he saw his father's picture on the news. Although this time it hadn't accompanied news of a trade or some highlight from last night's football game. It had been him being brought up on statutory rape charges. The parents of the girl had pressed charges. Right after the news had broken, his father had assured him in his cocky, offhanded way that their family would be fine. That the girl had lied about her age and it would all come out in the wash. Then endorsement deals had started to fall through. Cars had started disappearing from their driveway. The Patriots had elected not to offer his father a new contract. Ben had been young, but as an adult he could look back and know what it had all meant.

His mother had seen the writing on the wall early and hired a lawyer, making sure she got her share of the money before it all went away. She'd been married one other time since then, to another wealthy man Ben had only met on a handful of occasions before they'd divorced. Her funds were seemingly unlimited, her social calendar full, but Ben knew she was lonely.

His father had thrown away everything in a moment of weakness. Hurt his wife. Lost everything he'd ever worked for. Years later, the girl admitted in the press that she *had* in fact lied about her age, going so far as to show his father a fake ID that had conveniently disappeared before charges had been filed. Nothing excused his father's actions. Nothing. Not even the girl's deception.

Deception. Deception. Just like Honey pretending she didn't know him that night in the closet. Openly seducing him even though she knew what it could cost him.

Ben had no idea how long he sat there, taking the bottle his mother passed him and drinking deeply. Eventually, she closed her eyes and passed out on the couch, her eye makeup smeared by her tears. He threw a blanket over her and grabbed his satchel off the bookcase, taking it to the kitchen, where light from an outside streetlamp shined in through the window. Peter's advice from earlier filtered in through his whiskey-drunk state, making more and more sense as it lapped around his head.

Head it off at the pass. Be up-front and write a formal letter to Dean Mahoney, letting him know a student has shown interest in you. That way, if blondie ever claims you harassed her, you've already been honest. It will count in your favor.

Could he do something like that? Did he have a fucking choice? He'd vowed to himself as a child and again as a man that he would never end up like his father. That he would never let his judgment be clouded by a woman. But he'd done it. Barely one year into his career as a professor, and he'd already broken his word. How could he respect himself if he left himself wide open for the same result? No. No, he had to avoid the same fate at all costs. He'd be damned before he ended up like his father, living in a halfway house somewhere in California. No contact with his family. Not a dime to his name because he'd let it be taken away. That wouldn't be Ben.

Ben pulled the notebook out of his bag that was usually reserved for lesson plans. He flipped it open with one hand while nabbing a pen with the other. And he started to write.

Dean Mahoney,

I'm writing to you about a matter of great importance.

Ben dropped his head forward. He sounded like a Victorian novel. *Just keep going. Change it later.*

One of my students, Ms. Honey Perribow, has taken an apparent romantic interest in me. Normally, I find it relatively easy to ignore these inconvenient situations until they run their due course, but she has actively pursued me. Aggressively, in some cases. To the point where I no longer feel she is capable of processing my polite and repeated rejections. I have no interest in any of my students, especially the student in question, beyond teaching them and giving appropriate grades.

He dropped the pen to remove his glasses. His head was suddenly pounding, as if he'd fast-forwarded to the hangover portion of this drinking process. Writing this letter felt infinitely wrong. They were lies. When had he become a liar on top of being a rule breaker? His stomach burned, the whiskey turning to lava and spreading to his limbs. *Almost done.* He picked up the pen again.

I no longer feel capable of handling this situation on my own. The longer it goes on, I worry that Ms. Perribow may grow even more insistent that there is a romantic connection between us when that is simply not the case. While I'm not requesting you take any active steps against the student, I would ask that you put it on record as a preemptive explanation on my behalf. Thank you.

Prof. Ben Dawson

After taking one final pull from the whiskey bottle, Ben shoved the notebook back into his bag and walked unevenly to his bed, Honey's tinkling laugh echoing in his skull.

Chapter 11

*I*t was Friday night. Honey should have been out raising hell. Letting the slightly older Roxy and Abby buy her drinks in a bar that didn't card at the door. She should have put on something sexy, like a . . . a sequined romper and paired it with lipstick several shades too dark for her complexion. That's what she should have been doing. Instead, she was sitting on the roof, staring out over the Manhattan skyline, dumping Pixy Stix into her mouth. A bona fide party animal.

Two days had passed since her classroom conga with Ben, and she'd heard nothing from him. On a personal level, at least. She hadn't known what to expect from him in class this morning, but it had fallen firmly on the less desirable end of the spectrum, to put it mildly. He hadn't looked at her once. Not once. She'd sat in the middle row, same as last time, careful to put some distance between herself and Todd, but her Monster Energy drink chugging classmate had lumbered over and plopped down beside her anyway. She thought she'd seen Ben flinch at that point, but when his gaze didn't find her once for the remainder of the hour, she decided she must have imagined it.

That told her everything she needed to know. It had been a onetime thing, and he regretted it. So . . . fine. Okay. Her affair with Professor Ben had ended with a bang. A seriously hot, unforgettable, drove-her-crazy-just-to-think-about-it bang. She shouldn't feel betrayed. Or like her insides were being prodded at with a hot poker. She shouldn't feel like she'd been picked up by a hurricane and set down somewhere else. But she did. Ever since class this morning, everything she'd done had felt like a considerable effort. Sitting down, standing up, eating, talking, comprehending words. She'd gone past her subway stop without realizing it and ended up halfway to Chinatown.

She was starting to think she'd imagined the whole thing. Ben had never been anything but her professor. There hadn't been a connection between them in the closet or that day after class when he'd noticed her for the first time. He'd never thrown her onto a desk and given her pleasure with his brilliant, insightful mouth. Never. She'd made it all up. While she knew that simply couldn't be true, the idea of it hurt more than anything. Knowing it could all be a memory so easily. No closure or even a formal rejection from either of them. When she'd walked out of the classroom that night, he'd been staring after her like he couldn't wait to touch her again. What had changed?

The roof door slamming made her jump a foot in the air. "Jesus!"

"Sorry!" Abby put her hands out. "I've never been up here. I assumed it would coast to a close."

"Well, it didn't." Honey pressed a palm over her pound-ing heart, seeing for the first time how Abby was dressed. In a short, black eyelet skirt and pink halter top, she looked incredible. "Where are you going?"

"Where are *we* going, you mean?" Abby clicked to the edge of the roof in her high-heeled Mary Janes and propped an arm on the brick wall. She kicked off one of the shoes and massaged her right foot. "Out. Louis has decreed that our two super groups are merging into one giant, unstoppable super group. He and Roxy are working on a secret handshake as we speak."

"He's downstairs?" Honey came to her feet slowly, irritated by the way her pulse started beating in Morse code. "Who else is there?"

"Russell is in my room killing a spider." She switched feet, massaging the left with relish. "It went under my bed, and unless he finds and kills it, we're moving."

"Obviously."

Honey swallowed heavily, resisting the urge to shake Abby and ask about Ben's presence, but her friend beat her to it with a knowing smile. "Ben is meeting us at the Longshoreman later. He had a late meeting."

"Oh." Honey tried to hide her cheeseball smile by ducking her head, pretending to survey her own boring outfit. If he was meet-ing up with everyone knowing she would be there, he couldn't have blown her off completely, right? Maybe he'd just been busy and she'd dramatized the whole thing. Either way, she was going to see Ben in a few short hours, and there was no denying the ex-citement fizzing in her bloodstream. "I guess I'd better go change."

"Roxy already picked out a dress for you. It's on your bed." Abby replaced both shoes and did a little dance. "How come you never want to wear my clothes?"

Honey pointed to Abby's outfit. "I'd wear *that*."

"It's Roxy's."

"There you go."

Half an hour later, Honey had changed into the most incredible little black dress she'd ever worn. It had white leather cutouts for pockets and showed just enough cleavage to be friendly. In the interest of making sure Abby didn't feel left out, she'd pilfered a pair of red Jimmy Choos from an unopened box in her closet, surprised when they fit her feet, considering Abby was so much taller. All four of her friends whistled when she walked into the living room, so she put on a fierce model expression and cat walked over to retrieve her purse.

They spoke over one another on their way down the sidewalk to the Longshoreman, telling stories and making good-natured fun of one another, the energy that comes from the start of a night out singing in the air around them. This was when Honey loved New York the most. When possibilities are laid out before you like bright, shining swimming pools and you just have to decide which one to dive into. She didn't have to wake up tomorrow on time or be in a lab until Monday. Free. She felt free. The homesickness she'd been experiencing was the furthest thing from her mind as cabs whipped past in streaks of yellow and stars winked between the skyscrapers. At the root of it all, she knew this exhilarated feeling came from the knowledge she would see Ben. Just seeing him was enough to make her float down the street on their way downtown.

When they reached the Longshoreman, they practically fell into the last available table. Louis pulled Roxy down onto his lap and propped his head on her shoulder. Russell yanked out two chairs for Honey and Abby, propping himself against the wall when there were no more seats available. He didn't seem to mind, though. As if being on guard duty came natural to him.

"So, Honey. How are those premed courses coming?" Louis spoke up over the loud music. "Cut anybody open yet?"

"No. Are you volunteering?"

Laughing, he grabbed the pitcher of beer the waitress set down in front of them, pouring the foamy, gold liquid into plastic cups. "This marks the second time you've threatened me with a knife. Is that some kind of Southern custom?"

"Nope." She sent him an exaggerated wink. "Just mine."

Roxy held up her beer for a toast. "To threats of castration and slightly terrifying Southernisms."

"*Cheers.*"

They all drank. Abby tilted her head back and looked up at Russell. Who was already looking down at her with a frown. "You work construction all day while I'm in an air-conditioned office. Why don't you take my seat and I'll stand a while?"

He nodded toward something beneath the table. "Because your feet hurt."

"How do you know?"

"I know because your shoes are at least two sizes too small. You could barely walk on the way here." He actually looked irritated at her, tugging the collar of his Hart Brothers Construction shirt. "Why would you wear uncomfortable shoes?"

"Because they match."

"Oh, they *match*." He shifted against the wall. "You're taking a cab home." Abby grinned up into Russell's frown until he shook his head, an answering smile forming around the hard edges of his mouth. "Women like you were sent here to drive us all crazy."

"Thank you."

Honey turned her amusement on Roxy, hoping to gauge her friend's reaction to the chemistry buzzing between Russell and Abby, but Roxy looked . . . ill. Beside her, Louis didn't appear much better. Both of them were staring at the bar entrance. With a pit of dread in her stomach, Honey turned in her seat.

Ben had just walked in, looking as he always did. Just out of work. A little stressed. His navy button-down was tucked into gray slacks, sleeves rolled up to the elbows. He wasn't alone, though. Walking in beside him with a megawatt smile on her face was the older woman he'd sat with at the poetry reading. They were holding hands.

OH SHIT. THIS *feels like a colossal, goddamn mistake.* But that had to be natural, right? Because hurting someone's feelings wasn't supposed to feel good. In this case, though, it was necessary. The entire subway ride there, Ben had been debating with himself over how to let Honey down easy. If he'd be able to let her down *at all*, once he got within the vicinity of her and could smell, hear, *see* her. So when he'd run into Viv coming out of the bookstore two blocks away, he'd thought he'd seen his solution. She'd beaten him to the punch by asking him out for a drink, and he'd said yes.

Or he'd heard himself say yes. Or maybe he hadn't said anything at all. She'd latched onto his hand, and here they were.

And now that he was standing in Honey's vicinity, now that they were standing in the same room, he knew with dead certainty that he wouldn't have been able to accomplish letting her down any other way. She was painfully beautiful staring at him from across the bar, her face flushed from laughing. She'd parted her hair differently so that it was all pushed over onto one side, and he had the odd, sudden urge to ask her why she'd decided to do that. His friends were glaring at him, but he only knew that because he could feel it. He couldn't take his eyes off Honey long enough to confirm.

The pink flush in her cheeks was changing, turning red, the sparkle in her golden eyes dulling and dimming. Viv was asking him something, probably what he wanted to drink, but he couldn't focus on the words. He forced himself to remember why he'd done this. Honey had lied to him, let him walk into a trap. She was everything that had ruined his father, his family. She'd willingly put his career in jeopardy. It was too familiar, and he needed to distance himself from it.

So when she jumped out of her chair and sped off toward the back of the bar, why did he drop Viv's hand like a live grenade and take off after her? Because he had no choice. His body moved before his mind registered the action, as if one end of an invisible rope was attached to him and Honey held the other side. He dipped in and out of noisy groups of people, feeling like he'd left his stomach behind him at the bar.

Oh God. Her face.

At that moment, even with the voice in his head telling him breaking things off was right, nothing seemed worth the betrayal and hurt he'd seen on her face. What the hell was he going to do if he caught up with her? Explain that he *had* to hurt her like this? Explain that if he left even a sliver of a chance for this relationship to continue, he'd be toast? He so would. Nothing could keep him away from Honey unless she wanted nothing to do with him.

Now that he'd handily accomplished that goal and couldn't take back what he'd done, he had the horrible suspicion that he hadn't thought it all the way through. That he'd missed something important and it would come back to haunt him. Or maybe it already was.

Ben ground to a halt outside the women's bathroom. A brunette walked out drying her hands on her shirt, giving him a funny look when he tried to look over her shoulder before the door closed. "Yeah?"

"Is there a blonde in there? She would have just walked in."

"Nope. Empty."

He cursed under his breath while turning in a circle. Where else could she have gone? Two swinging, wooden doors caught his eye, located opposite the bathroom. Several men bustled behind them, yelling over the loud music. The kitchen. Not stopping to think, Ben pushed through the doors, ignoring the strange looks he received as he jogged to the other side, toward the back exit he'd suspected was there. He saw a flash of blond hair and increased his pace, throwing open the door as soon as he reached it.

His heart started to slam when he saw her. Although it was

possible it hadn't beaten since she'd seen him walk in with someone else. But it kick-started now in a gear high enough to make
breathing difficult. She hadn't seen him yet from where she stood
in the middle of the sidewalk, staring out into the side street. Her
fists were tightened into balls at her sides, body strung tight as
a bow.

"Honey."

She jolted, but didn't turn to face him. "Jesus. Go away, Ben."

His throat was impossibly tight. "I think I did this wrong."

"What were you trying to do?"

"Let you down easy." It sounded so insanely stupid now. Nothing about this girl or this situation or the way she made him feel
was easy. Everything she inspired in him was intense and concentrated.

She tossed her head back and laughed, the sound cutting right
through him. "Yeah, I'd say you did it wrong."

"I'm sorry it has to be this way."

"I'm not." Finally, blessedly, she turned those golden eyes on
him. And he was fucked. *Fucked.* They were hot-tempered and
magnificent. Just like the rest of her. They pinned him to where
he stood, daring him to move. He couldn't move, though, because
if he moved, it would be *toward* her, and he needed to move away.
How could he do that, when one look from her eviscerated his
resolve to end things? "I'm not sorry you did this, Ben, because
now I know what an unfeeling asshole you are. I know you're not
worth my time or thoughts. Now I know."

Her words scalded him in the worst way. Worst because that
part of him she'd woken up, the part that hated when other guys

looked at her, or ached to see her knee bleeding, demanded that he prove her wrong. It couldn't cope with her believing that about him. But he forced himself to remain where he was, not going to her even though it tore him open.

Honey narrowed her eyes at him, tilting her head as if she could see everything taking place inside his fucked-up brain. No, she could. When the corner of her mouth tilted up, he knew she could see it.

She turned on a heel and came toward him, hair streaming out behind her in the night wind. He swore his heart beat ten times in between each click of her shoes on the concrete, each swish of her dress against her thighs. The intention in her eyes was a warning he should be heeding, but it was doing nothing. All he could do was wait for her to reach him, because it felt vital. It was what she might have done in the bar if he hadn't walked in holding someone else's hand.

Her fingers dragging up his chest was all it took for him to grow hard as a fucking rock. He knew that if they hadn't been standing on a street with cars whizzing past, he would have grabbed her hand and put it on his cock, shamelessly begged her to jack him off. Anyone from the university could have walked past and seen them, but he could only hold his breath and see what she'd do next. When she flattened her palm on his belly and nudged him backward toward a recessed doorway, Ben went. He needed to. Needed her.

As soon as his back hit the door, she pushed up on her toes and attacked his mouth. The battle immediately went both ways. Her taste exploded through him, hot and delicious, but now it had a familiarity that battered him. He *knew* her mouth now. He *knew* the girl attached to it, and he'd fucked with her in the worst way, *goddammit*. The words zigzagging through his head commanded his mouth, using it as an outlet, and he kissed her, kissed her, kissed her like his life was at stake. He couldn't get close enough even though she was trying to climb him with that sweet, sexy body, so he flipped their positions and pressed her between him and the door. Hard.

Honey tore her mouth away on a moan. "You want me, Ben?"

He raked her neck with his teeth. "You can't feel me? I'm two seconds from fucking you in this doorway." Her hips rolled against his hardness, and he pumped his own in response. "Why did you have to be so tight and wet? I can't think of anything else. Want my mouth on it again. Want inside."

She brushed her lips over his gently. "Too bad."

Then she was gone. Slipped out from where he'd wedged her against the door, her body heat, mouth, touch, all stolen from him as he stood there panting into a void.

He turned to see her swipe a hand over her mouth, as if to rid herself of him. "Go ahead back inside, Ben. Go back to your sophisticated New York girlfriend and discuss Kafka over craft beers. Whatever makes you happy." She stepped back quickly when he reached for her. "I know you want me, even though you don't want to. Maybe you've never forgiven me for lying to you in the closet. I don't know. I *do* know I could wear you down and make you give in. But you know what? I'm not interested in *you* anymore. I'm not interested in *anything* you have to offer."

No. This isn't happening. He'd accomplished what he'd set out to do, but he hadn't taken into account what it would feel like to be on the receiving end. Is this how she'd felt? *Oh God.* "Honey—"

"Enjoy your night."

She put up a hand to hail a cab. No, he couldn't let her go like this. Ben tried to go after her, but two sets of hands held him back. His confusion over Russell and Louis's appearance behind him cost him precious seconds. She threw herself into the backseat of a cab and left. Left him.

Chapter 12

*H*oney peered down into the eyepiece of her microscope at the slide she'd placed on the stage. After observing for a few moments, she noted her findings in her notepad. The scratching of her pen sounded amplified in the surrounding quiet, alerting her that she was alone in the lab, half of the lights shut off. A glance at the clock told her it was after five o'clock. Shit. She rubbed at her sore eyes, knowing Roxy and Abby would be wondering where she was. The downside to being an awesome cook and preparing meals often was that people started to expect it. Not that she minded. Most of the time. Her roommates found other ways of making up for their constant need to be fed. Such as letting her stew all weekend without comment or setting a tub of ice cream down on the coffee table and handing her a ladle.

She shoved her notebook and pen into her backpack and cleaned her station before winding her way down the building's hallway toward the exit. Yesterday had gone by in kind of a haze, obviously brought on by Ben bringing a date to their super group mesh party. But also by the realization that she'd opened herself up to be hurt. Really, horrifyingly hurt. She'd had her share of dude disappointments in the past. Boys liking her friends instead of her. Elmer forgetting her birthday. It had always been the kind of pain she could get over with a good book or a sleeve of Oreos. But this? This was entirely different.

She might have made light of it to Roxy and Abby—because hello, the guy she just slept with walked in with someone else, and frankly, that was embarrassing as all get-out—but down in the root of her stomach, she felt torn to shreds. How had this man she'd known for such a short space of time taken such a huge chunk out of her? Her little stunt on Friday night just before she'd catapulted headfirst into a cab had only succeeded in getting a small portion of it back. But it had been a start. At the very least, she'd managed to walk away with her pride intact.

Tomorrow morning, she had English class, and she intended to walk in with her chin up. Look him right in the eye. She didn't run away from uncomfortable situations, and this would be no different. Honey shook her head when a traitorous spark of anticipation kicked up in her chest, telling her she still yearned to lay eyes on Ben after everything that had happened. God, when would that go away? Maybe when she stopped dreaming about his lips on her neck, thigh wedged between her legs, the way it had been on Friday night. Maybe she just needed to know why so she could get some closure. Was it her initial lie, the fact that she was his student, or something else? He'd looked so . . . tortured.

Honey jammed her headphones into her ear and blasted some old Dixie Chicks, thinking about the first concert her mother had brought her to up in Lexington when she was thirteen. They'd worn matching T-shirts and everything. The memory brought a much-needed smile to her face as she rode the train downtown to Chelsea, even though a half-empty Coca-Cola can rolled down the aisle and sloshed brown liquid over her shoes. When her phone rang twenty minutes later on her way into the apartment, she wondered if she'd somehow projected her thoughts to her mother all the way down in Kentucky.

"Hey, Mom."

"Hey, girly."

Instantly, Honey knew something was wrong. Her shoulders tensed as she hung up her backpack just inside the door. Her mother only called her by that nickname when something bad happened. Three times in her life, her mother had used it. When Granddaddy Perribow died. When the Little League phoned to inform them she couldn't try out because she had a vagina. And just now. "What's wrong?"

"Now, don't you go thinking you need to come home, Hon. I just want to get that out of the way up front. I mean what I say. I won't even pick you up at the airport."

"Yes you would, don't lie, and what happened?"

When her mother was upset, she strung her words together in one long breath. Honey did the same exact thing. Her father used to complain that the Perribow women had a secret, angry language that no one could decipher and he gave thanks for that fact every day.

Her mother's quick exhale echoed down the phone. "Your brother fell off the dang tractor, is what happened. Laid out in the field wailing for help and nobody was home. Broke both of his legs, the big idiot. I love him to pieces, but he is. He's a big ol' idiot."

Honey stomped her foot, mostly because she needed somewhere to put all the feelings. *Dammit.* Teddy was injured, and *again* she wasn't there. She was here in this giant city, a plane ride away from the people who loved and needed her. "Is he smoking while he works the fields again? I swear, he's going to turn green one of these days, and then what'll he have to say for himself?"

As far back as she could remember, her brother had liked to get stoned. He was as good-natured as they came, wouldn't harm a fly, and had never progressed to any harder drugs. So they'd all kind of learned to live with it, especially after he turned eighteen. He was a functioning pot smoker. Most of the time. Like when he wasn't getting so high he fell off the dang tractor.

She tuned back in to her mother's ramble. "Your father needs to get this crop planted by the end of the week, so he's gone into town looking for help. He's going to lose time either way, though, because—"

"No one knows how to work the tractor but us," Honey finished for her. It was true. Their rusted-ass tractor not only acted up with annoying frequency but it flat-out stopped working when it didn't like the way a newcomer treated it. Her father claimed it was haunted. Panic invaded her stomach at the thought of what her family could lose if they didn't plant a crop in time. All their extra resources went to pay for school. They couldn't afford such a setback. "I'm coming home."

"No, you're not. I told you, I won't pick you up at the airport."

"Yes, you will. Don't lie," Honey repeated.

"Well, if I've got an extra mouth to feed, I best get cooking."

"Bye, Mom."

"Bye."

Honey disconnected the call, a little stunned over what she'd just decided on the fly. She would miss an entire week of classes, but if she emailed each of her professors tonight and explained the family emergency, they would probably let her email her work from Kentucky. After all, she was carrying As in all her classes. The small amount of rent she paid left her with additional funds, so she could afford a flight. And damn, damn, she was just so homesick. Did it make her weak to want some time with her family? They needed her as much as she needed them right now.

She turned when someone cleared their throat behind her. Both roommates were standing in the living room, looking more than a little confused.

"Was that English?" Roxy asked.

Honey's laugh sounded unnatural to her own ears. "Not according to my father." She tapped her phone against her thigh. "I'm going home for the week. The tractor broke my brother's legs."

"Oh my God," Abby breathed. "Who is tractor?"

"It's not a person." Honey headed for her bedroom, knowing they would likely follow her. "It's an evil contraption that only my family knows how to work."

In the doorway to Honey's room, Roxy propped a hip on the doorframe. "So you're going home to plow the fields?" She frowned. "Are you sure this has nothing to do with Ben plowing your field, then acting like king asshole?"

"*Yes*, I'm sure," Honey answered quickly, having anticipated the question. "I'm not running because of a guy. I wouldn't."

Abby nodded, even if Roxy didn't. "Do you want us to come with you?"

Tears pricked behind Honey's eyelids, so she hid them by getting down on her knees to search for her suitcase under the bed. "I appreciate the offer, but it's just me. They just need me."

"Okay, but the offer stands." Abby clapped her hands together. "I can at least help by looking up flights. Aisle or window?"

"Aisle." Honey found her suitcase and yanked it into the center of her room, thinking both of her roommates had gone. But when she glanced toward the door, Roxy was still there, arms crossed. "I'm not running because of Ben," Honey said preemptively.

"Hmm." Roxy looked doubtful. "I'm kind of an expert at running from guys. Ask Louis." She sauntered into the room with a drawn-out sigh. "I won't pry, because I'm also an expert on hating people who pry. But promise me one thing?"

Honey gave up the pretense of rummaging through her drawers and looked at Roxy. "What's that?"

"Promise you'll come back."

Honey opened her mouth to make the promise, closing it with a snap when she realized she couldn't.

WHEN BEN SAW a message from Honey sitting in his email inbox early Monday morning, his first thought was, *Oh Jesus, she's dropping my class*. He'd done a *bang-up* job of keeping himself together over the weekend, drinking enough to drown two Yetis. But this was somehow the worst news he could have imagined receiving while still lying in bed with a motherfucker of a hangover. It meant no more heartbreakingly sincere papers that kept him up at night. No more certainty that he would at least *see* her. Nothing. She'd dropped him—for good reason—and now he wouldn't be her professor anymore, either. It made him want to pull the pillow over his head and block out the world.

He didn't, of course, because there was an urgency spinning around him madly, begging him to read the email. Any communication with her was beyond what he'd expected, be it good or bad. He had no right to be this desperate to read words she'd written, when he'd behaved like such an asshole, but no one was here to judge him, save the empty whiskey bottle lying at the foot of the bed.

Ben snatched his glasses off the bookcase, put them on, and sat up with a groan when his entire being rebelled. How much had he drunk exactly? Not enough to feel *this* horrible, but then again, he couldn't remember the last time he'd eaten. Russell had stopped by with a pizza at some point, which had basically been an excuse to tell Ben what a failure he was as a human being. Then they'd watched the Yankees game and polished off a six-pack without exchanging a single word. Ben had no idea which day of the weekend that had taken place, because he'd continued the party on his own as soon as the door had closed behind Russell. A pathetic, one-man party where the goal had been to drink until Honey's face blurred. It never did. It was still there, stronger and more beautiful with each passing minute. Sobriety was bullshit.

He tapped the email with his thumb and blinked to bring the bright electronic screen into focus.

Professor Dawson, it began. Ouch. No more *Ben* for him. Even through two simple words, he could hear her tone of voice. Detached. Formal.

A family emergency has come up and I won't be in class this week.

Ben sat up straighter. She wasn't dropping his class, but she wasn't going to be there, either. What kind of emergency sent you flying out of the state? It had to be bad, possibly a relative dying. Was she okay? God, he hated the idea of her dealing with bad news on top of what he'd done to her Friday night.

I have attached the assignment you gave out Friday morning to this email. Hopefully that is acceptable. If it isn't inconvenient, I would appreciate you responding with any assignments for the upcoming week, reading or otherwise, so I can email them to you on time. Thank you.

Honey Perribow

Ben tossed his phone onto the bed and grabbed his laptop off the floor, where he'd miraculously remembered to charge it. A minute later, he had Honey's email pulled up to open the attachment. He'd completely forgotten he'd even given an assignment on Friday, dropped it into the murkiness of the weekend. He remembered now, though. Remembered wanting to read something, anything, from Honey, so he'd asked for a creative writing piece on any topic, student's choice. It had been so unlike him, leaving anything up to chance. Not being specific. Even the students had shown their surprise. God, he'd crossed so many lines at this point to get close to her, to figure out how her mind worked, that he should really just resign. Honestly.

He read her abrupt message once again with the kind of voraciousness one reserves for a pie-eating contest. Perhaps when he was finished reading the assignment, he could figure out how to dull the sick feeling that had hit him at the realization that she was no longer in New York City. She was hours and miles and eons away from him at that very moment. If he wanted to see her, it wouldn't only be a bad idea; it would be impossible. Feeling helpless on top of miserable wasn't a great combination. Massaging his pounding forehead with one hand, he continued reading.

My family is like a baseball team. Dad is the third base coach, except he never tells you to stay on third. He'd say it was the coward's way out and God hates a coward. No matter how low your odds are of reaching home plate, he'll send you there every time, fully believing you'll make it. He lacks the ability to doubt, even when he should, and often to his detriment. Mom is the catcher, giving everyone subtle signals as to how they should proceed in every situation. A nose scratch means change your shoes. An ear tug means you're adding too much salt. Of course, if she ends up calling for the wrong pitch, it's not her fault. You should have known it was the wrong call. Maybe she was just testing you. My brother is the mascot. Loved by many, but forgotten by all unless he's standing right in front of you, big and colorful. High as a kite. He'll make you laugh in a way that has you forgetting why an hour later, but the content, happy feeling lingers. Making you want to be around him again.

I'm not sure who I am on the team yet. Sometimes I think I'm the team doctor, but the pull of running the bases is too strong. I want to drop my scalpel and sprint so fast my lungs hurt. So maybe I'm the pinch runner who steps in when someone can't carry their weight or is missing a step. But when I'm standing on first base, cheating toward second, I get lost staring into the outfield. The place where all your thoughts and secrets get swallowed up by a discreet blue sky. Blue sky never tells, it just listens. When I'm in the outfield and I hear the crack of bat meeting ball, when I see the ball sailing up, up, and know it will eventually come down, time elongates into something without boundaries. The ball hangs in the air so long, it could be plucked out of the sky with my daddy's barbequing tongs, flipped over like a sizzling burger. I want that ball more than anything. Anything. That's what I used to think. When I don't make the catch and the collective groans go up from the dugout, I used to think I was crushed. Used to wish for time to go in reverse so I'd get another chance.

Time does have boundaries, though. It puts you at the plate when you're not ready and it strikes you out. It strikes you out. It strikes you out. All the while, the things that used to be important, like a perfect pop fly, begin falling outside your reach. Or fade into memories. New things take their place. Jobs. Friends. A man.

If you look extra closely, you can see it happening. The smell of

a tweed jacket replaces the scent of freshly cut grass. Stolen kisses
replace . . . everything. A man becomes that perfect pop fly that
lands at your feet, not in your glove.

While I don't fear failure even though it hurts, I do fear the
answer to one question. Now that I know what real, consuming
want feels like, will I want to catch that ball as much next time
I'm in the outfield?

It was possible he didn't breathe until he'd finished the entire
three pages. Him. She'd written about him? The tone was the
same as her other work, but she'd never spoken about something
personal. Why now? Unless she'd written it Friday afternoon,
before the clusterfuck at the Longshoreman, she'd written those
candid thoughts *after* he'd destroyed what had been between
them. *Destroyed* it.

Ben shoved the laptop off his legs, not really caring where
or how it landed. Had she let him into her head as some devi-
ous brand of torture? His head ached twice as bad now, stomach
pitching as he gained his feet and headed for the bathroom. Halfway there, he stopped and paced back toward the bed. Then he
walked to the kitchen and turned in a half circle.

This was wrong. So wrong. He'd compared Honey to the
woman who'd burned his father. This country girl who assigned
her family members positions on a baseball field. Who wasn't
afraid to run for a pop fly or relay her feelings to the very person who'd shamefully abused them. Him. He'd landed outside
her glove, and he could have been inside of it. Could have been
caught by her, caught *her* in return. He hadn't even stopped to

consider that she might be everything she appeared to be. Not a liar or deceiver . . . but an amazing girl who'd gone after something she wanted. He'd been lucky enough to be that thing, and he'd punished her for trying, when maybe, just maybe, he should have been running toward her at top speed.

No, not maybe. He wouldn't feel this gutted over a maybe.

This couldn't be fixed. Could it? Could he . . . get her back? Convince her that despite his careless treatment of her thus far, he would make a stellar boyfriend? She had every right to laugh in his face. Furthermore, being Honey's boyfriend—and he *really* liked how that sounded—would still mean jeopardizing his job, but there had to be a way around it. Once she was no longer actively in one of his classes, which would only be another two months from now, she wouldn't technically be his student. They were both consenting adults. There had to be some sort of condition or allowance.

Unless . . .

Ben's gaze swung toward the refrigerator. To the offer letter from NYU. Taking the job would be the perfect solution, allowing them to be together without him losing his job as a professor. Or jeopardizing her education. Damn, though. It would be a huge leap of faith, when Honey could very well tell him to fuck right off.

Right now, all he could think of was her dealing with some crisis with her baseball team family. If she felt one-tenth as shitty as he felt, dealing with a crisis on her own was the last thing she needed. No way could he wait an entire week to fix this. So . . . what? He was going to Kentucky?

"Fucking right I'm going to Kentucky," he shouted into the silent apartment.

Peter could cover his classes for the week. He still owed Ben from the time he'd gotten pneumonia and Ben had subbed his literary theory class. He'd drop off his lesson plan to Peter on his way to the airport. And next time he landed back in New York, he'd have Honey with him.

It would appear he had a couple of phone calls to make.

Chapter 13

*H*oney's sore muscles protested as she hopped back up on the rickety wooden barstool. After arriving in the wee hours of Monday morning, two days had been spent plowing fields and planting corn, leaving her body feeling like one giant bruise. She'd been in New York less than two months, but it had made her soft, apparently. Her ass and thigh muscles were on fire. Shoulders stiff and aching. She'd had to get out of the house, because her father wouldn't stop teasing her for turning into a pansy-ass.

Lester, the bartender who'd worked at Calhoun's Junction since her mother had been in high school, placed a shot of tequila in front of her, hiding it behind a pint glass of Coca-Cola. "I know you're a college girl now, but we still can't serve you. Coke'll have to do."

She winked at Lester. "Thank you. Coke's just fine."

After making sure no one was looking, she tossed back the shot, welcoming the way it burned in her throat. Lester swiped the shot glass back off the bar and went to serve the next customer, innocence etched into his wrinkled face. To an outsider, the business practices at Calhoun's Junction might seem a little shady. Or illegal. Which they were. But Lester ruled over the bar like a mother hen, never letting anyone get so drunk they lost use of their faculties. Or got behind the wheel instead of calling home for a ride or carpooling with somebody sober. Senior year of high school was when Lester began sneaking her shots. All the kids knew his game, and no one ever squealed. It was just the way of things.

In fact, as she peered through the dimness toward the back of the bar, she could see several of those shot recipients playing pool, drinking Cokes, just like she'd left them. Elmer was there, bent low over the pool table, unable to take his shot for laughing too hard. A waitress in a black apron gestured wildly with a ketchup bottle as she spoke to Darlene Lennon, one of the first girls to join Honey's little league just over a decade ago. Katie and Jay were there, all sparkly in their new engagement and looking as if they'd never left high school. Jay still wore his letterman jacket. Katie still wore his class ring around her neck on a silver chain. None of them had seen her yet, so she took a moment to enjoy the picture they made. One that could have been taken straight out of her memory bank.

When she was part of the group gathered around the very same pool table not so long ago, she couldn't wait to get away. She didn't want to be standing there, collecting dust, when the college kids, such as she was now, came home to visit. She'd wanted to go places. Do things. Make a mark. *Damn it*, though. There was something to be said for a place that made you feel warm. Welcome. A place that could be predicted and didn't turn you upside down and shake you, seeing if you could stand it.

The worst part of this feeling? She didn't *know* if Ben was slightly responsible or not. She might have been feeling homesick before the shit pie was thrown at her face. Whatever the reason, a yearning for the familiar hit her now like a tsunami.

Elmer's head came up slowly from the pool table. "Well, I'd heard rumors, but I didn't believe them," he shouted across the bar. "Honey Perribow is in our midst."

She saluted her Coke, feeling like she'd slipped back into her old skin. "They let me back into the state against their better judgment."

Her friends abandoned their pool game, all talking at once as they made their way over. Just as she'd known he would, Elmer scooped her off the stool and crushed her in a bear hug. She squeezed her eyes shut, wishing for just a second she could feel a spark. Anything to prove Ben hadn't snuffed out any possibility of one. But all she felt was nostalgia over the familiar scent of Elmer's Cool Water cologne. Damn, the professor had done a number on her. She never cried. Never. With her friends' voices washing over her and Lester smiling from behind the bar, though, she was coming close. There was no denying it anymore. Something inside her had been damaged and needed to be knit back together. Would this visit home do it? Or would it take much longer, as she feared it would?

Elmer finally set her down, allowing Katie and Darlene to launch themselves at her. She ignored her screaming muscles and held on, coughing discreetly amid the abundance of hair spray as they hugged her. Darlene pulled back, smiling brightly. "What are you doing here?"

Honey accepted a one-armed hug from Jay, followed by a ruffling of her hair. "My brother fought the tractor and the tractor won."

"Again?" Jay asked, pulling back. "That tractor is a menace. My mom used to tell me if I didn't eat my greens, the Perribows' tractor would come and get me while I slept."

Honey gave a lopsided smile. "Well, Teddy definitely had some green, but not the kind you eat."

"Good old Teddy." Katie shook her head. "Ran into him in the supermarket last week. He was buying four boxes of Cocoa Crispies. Sweet as all get-out, but high as a motherfucker."

"That's my dear brother. I reckon that cereal didn't last him the ride home." Honey slid her Coke off the bar and took a sip through the straw. "I'm just here through the weekend helping out. My daddy has to get this crop into the ground before next week when the dirt gets hard and stops cooperating."

Elmer laid an arm across her shoulders. The most natural thing in the world, and yet it felt different. Too heavy. Too close. Like that arm was trying to suck her back in and she hadn't decided whether to be sucked yet. Damn. What was *in* that tequila? "Why didn't you call me when you got into town? I could have come by and lent a hand."

Honey felt a pang of guilt over the hurt in Elmer's voice. "Ah, you know that tractor. Only works for us Perribows." She tucked her hair behind her ear. "But I'm here now. What are y'all up to tonight?"

They all looked at each other. "This," Darlene laughed. "*This* is what we're up to."

"I—right." Honey's neck heated. Wednesday nights in Bloomfield were spent at Calhoun's. It was a constant this crew never deviated from. They were all staring at her now like they were seeing her for the first time, probably wondering if she'd changed. If she'd forgotten. Hoping to recover by taking the focus off herself, she smiled at Katie. "I haven't had a chance to say congratulations on your engagement. Have you set a date?"

Katie held out her hand so Honey could see the ring. It was simple and beautiful. Big enough to catch an eye, small enough not to get in the way. Something like Honey might pick for herself. "We're thinking next summer. Will you come on down and be a bridesmaid?"

Honey's throat felt tight. "Of course. Yes. I'd love to."

"It's not going to be fancy or anything." Katie and Darlene exchanged an excited look. "We drove to Lexington last weekend and picked out bridesmaids dresses. I wish we knew you were coming. Would have been one heck of a fun road trip."

Darlene rolled her eyes, but her smile was good-natured. "Maybe with two of us in the car, we could have convinced Katie to play something besides her worn-out Luke Bryan CD."

"You won't hear me apologizing." Katie nudged Jay with her elbow. "My future husband has given me a hall pass with Mr. Bryan's name on it. A woman can dream."

Honey was distracted from Katie and Darlene's friendly bickering when Elmer pulled her even closer. She could feel the group watching as he tipped her chin up with his fingers and smiled.

"Hey. It feels right having you here. You know?" He was so close. Too close. As much as Honey loved Elmer, she knew now what it felt like to feel breathless and desperate over a man. Settling for anything less wouldn't be fair to either her or Elmer. She needed to stop this before it got off the ground.

"Elmer—"

The bar's front door slammed—*loud*—and they all jumped. Honey's attention flew to the entrance, and everything stopped. Time. Her heart. Gravity.

Ben.

Here? No. No way. It had to be the lighting messing with her eyes. Or maybe something had really been in that tequila. Her brain could barely comprehend him in Calhoun's, in her tiny Kentucky town of Bloomfield, but he looked so out of place that she knew it had to be him. Because no one else on earth looked at her like that. Like he wanted to pounce on her. Read and decipher her thoughts. Then blow the very mind that held them together.

He wore a dress shirt as usual, white this time, and pushed up to reveal his strong forearms. His slacks were gray and travel-worn, wrinkled, but it didn't take anything away from the straight-up sexiness of him. She managed to drag her gaze from his and found his hand, white-knuckled around the handle of a suitcase. That sealed the deal. This had to be Ben. And if he was here . . . he had to be here for her. Why else would be come?

Too bad, though. Too bad, because all the pain rushed back in the longer they stood there, staring at each other. It gushed through her chest, knocking down dams and filling in cracks. She was suddenly so mad at him she wanted to throw her pint glass full of Coke at his head. For making her feel this way, for making her question herself. Her goals.

"What do you *want*, Ben?"

"For starters?" He actually had the nerve to look angry as he shoved his suitcase up against the wall, leaving it there as he came toward her. "I'd really like you *not* to have this guy's arm around you."

OKAY, THIS WAS starting off swell.

He'd shown up prepared to beg. In fact, he'd written it all down, neatly and concisely, in a notebook. Everything he wanted to say. He'd readied himself for the gamut of female emotions, according to Russell. Yes, Russell. Ben was *that* desperate. Tears, epithets, shouting. He'd come equipped for every possible scenario. And then he'd walked in and seen her cozied up to a guy who looked like he crushed Budweiser cans on his head for fun. The headache he'd managed to curb with the promise of seeing Honey had torn back through his skull like a rodeo bull. Someone was touching his fucking girl, and she looked so crazy pretty he couldn't stand it. So, yeah. Sayonara, notebook.

Ben stopped in front of the Beer Can Crusher. "Okay, look. I'm her least favorite person in the world right now. I've already got a mountain to dig myself out from under. We're talking Everest. But if I have to bury myself a little deeper in order to get your hands off of her, I'll do it."

The guy puffed out his chest. "How do you plan to do that, bro?"

Ben sent Honey a look. "Johnny Jerk Off and now this guy.

I'm starting to think you have a type, Honey, of which I don't fall within the boundaries."

"Who do you think you are, Ben?" Her eyes flashed, and *God*, he just needed to get right up in front of her and look into them until they calmed. Which wouldn't be any time soon. "You think you can just walk in here and start giving orders? Maybe you forgot how things ended."

"No." He stepped closer because he couldn't help it. She was *right there*. "No, I *didn't* forget. It's all I can think about. And I'm getting to that part. Honey?"

"What?"

"His hands are still on you."

Right before his eyes, her temper flared hotter, like a glowing coal from a campfire. Behind her, two girls stood staring at him with their jaws dropped down to their ankles. The beer crusher's head was swiveling back and forth, obviously confused by the scene playing out in front of him. "Who the hell *is* this guy, Honey?"

All right, he was done answering questions. Ben took off his glasses and shoved them in his back pocket. "I'm the guy who just flew to Lexington and took three buses to get her back. I'm the guy who would have flown or ridden *anywhere* to get her back. I'm hungover, missing this girl, and now I'm pissed off on top of it. So you want to go outside and be the person I take out my frustration on? Let's go."

Honey's jaw joined the other girls' on the floor, but it snapped shut when the other guy tried to go for him. Ben was ready for it, though. He'd always considered himself a pacifist, but at that moment, he wanted to hit something so bad his fists were already clenched and looking for a target. For too long, he'd kept everything contained inside him. Anger over the past had festered and ruined what Honey had tried to give him, and he was mad. Mad at himself. His preconceived notions. The blood in his veins heated with the need to release all the pent-up emotions.

"No." Honey stepped between him and Beer Can Crusher, finally succeeding in dislodging his arm from around her shoulders, but now her hands were on the guy's chest, holding him back. "Elmer, please. No fighting. I-I know him." She cast a look at Ben over her shoulder. "Go outside and wait for me. I'll be right out."

"Not moving an inch without you."

Elmer's laugh was incredulous. "I can't believe this guy."

"Yeah? Me either," Honey said. "But he won't hurt me. We're just going to talk."

That comment sent Ben spiraling back to reality. The here and now. For the first time, he noticed the entire bar had gone deathly silent, no one moving, all their attention centered on the drama unfolding. These people didn't know him from Adam, and his behavior since walking in the door hadn't exactly inspired confidence. Had he actually given them cause to be concerned for Honey's safety around him? Jesus Christ.

Ben held up his hands. "I'm sorry. Let me start over." He waited until Honey looked at him. "I'm guessing everyone here knows Honey pretty well, considering this town has one cab driver that

knew exactly where to take me from the bus station to find her.
So you know she's worth fighting for. I didn't come here to employ
the *literal* usage of that word, but—"

"Who talks like that?" Elmer muttered.

"An English professor," Honey mouthed silently, eyes still
shooting sparks at him.

"—but you can blame Honey for that. She makes me do crazy
things."

Okay, that might not have been the best thing to say. Even if,
in a roundabout way, it was true. Since meeting her, every single
thing he'd done had been out of character. He'd deep-sixed his
rule book and started acting on instincts he hadn't even been
aware of. Ones he didn't appear to have any control over, if his
entrance was any indication.

Honey really didn't seem sympathetic to his predicament,
however, as she rounded on him. At least she was finally facing
him, no part of her touching Elmer, accomplishing a short-term,
yet incredibly important, goal. "I don't give a rat's behind if you're
hungover or flew all this way to see me. No one *asked* you to come
here, and I don't owe you one minute of my time."

"I know," he said. "Give it to me anyway, please."

For one brief, terrifying moment, he thought she'd say no. He
really did. If she had, he would have come back and tried again
tomorrow. But going another whole night without repairing even
a fraction of the damage would have been unbearable. He needed
to be with her. Talk to her. Now.

"Did you really come here to fight for me?"

She'd whispered the question, so he answered in kind. "You're still in doubt after I called out every nightclub's dream bouncer?" When she didn't so much as smile, he figured serious was the way to go. "Yes. I'm here to fight. I'm bringing you back to New York with me."

For long moments, she just stared at him thoughtfully. Just when he was sure he couldn't take any more suspense, she skirted past him and headed for the exit. "I'll tell you one thing, Ben Dawson," she called over her shoulder. "You've got your work cut out for you."

Chapter 14

*H*ow had everything changed so drastically in five minutes?

She'd been standing there, conversation flowing freely between her friends, letting the ease of it suture her wounds for the night. Ben had been like a strike of lightning, knocking her emotional floodgates down like bowling pins. Fight for her. He was in Bloomfield to get her back. It wasn't an easy thing to believe, when she'd never been entirely convinced he was interested in her beyond sex. But guys, especially guys who looked like Ben, didn't fly seven hundred miles for sex. Even if the sex was mind-blowingly hot. Even if the mere suggestion of sex when Ben was walking beside her in the deserted parking lot of Calhoun's was enough to make her sweat. Sex. Ben. Sex. Ben.

Enough. She was still mad as hell, and he wasn't about to get off lightly. The things he'd said back in the bar—out loud in front of everyone, no less—might have made her pathetic heart squeeze, but that was neither here nor there. How could she maintain her self-respect if she gave in so easily? He'd been ruthless with her feelings, and despite how he made her feel, Honey wouldn't be able to trust him yet. No, he'd have to earn it from her.

"How much have you had to drink?"

She paused in the act of fishing her keys out of her purse. "One shot of tequila."

"I'll drive." He held out his hand. "Just to be safe."

Protesting would have made her seem childish, so she shrugged and tossed him the set. "Are you sure there's no alcohol still floating around in your system, Captain Hangover?"

He caught the set in midair. "It wouldn't surprise me. It takes a lot of whiskey to stop seeing your face when I walked into that bar Friday night."

Her footsteps faltered. "You're just going to bring it up like that without warning?"

"Yeah." He pulled her to a stop. His warm hand on her arm felt too good, especially after the fresh reminder of what he'd done, so she pulled it away. Ben looked as if he wanted to reach for her again, but he put his hand back down by his side. "Yeah. I'm bringing it up now. I want everything out in the open. If you need to scream and throw blunt objects at my head, do it now, so we can get back to the way you looked at me the day you sat in the front row of my lecture. I need you to look at me like that again, Honey. Like I haven't disappointed you yet or proven I'm just another bastard who isn't worthy of you. Okay? So, yes. I'm bringing it up."

"Oh. Okay, then." Her pulse went a little insane, making her feel light-headed. How the hell was she supposed to stay mad at him when he said things like that? *He's only been here ten minutes, Honey. Where's your pride?* She gestured to the rusted, sky-blue pickup truck behind him. "This is me."

He stared at her hard a minute before walking to the passenger side and opening the door for her. His hard body only left her a sliver of room to climb in, telling her Ben knew exactly what he was doing. It didn't matter if she was mad or hurt, their physical attraction had an obnoxious way of bypassing everything else. With a lift of her chin, Honey nudged him out of the way, put her foot on the truck's runner, and pushed herself up.

"Oh God. *Ouch.*" The words slipped out involuntarily, her abused thigh muscles nearly giving out on her as she heaved herself onto the seat. Ben's hands were on her immediately, assisting her.

"Honey?" His gaze raked her, obviously checking for injuries. "What's wrong?"

She blew a breath out toward the car's ceiling. So much for keeping her pride. Her legs were shaking like a newborn deer's. "Did anyone from the super group fill you in on why I came home?"

His lips quirked gorgeously, probably over her description of their friends. "Yes. Well, I got most of it out of Abby before Roxy hung up the phone on me. I'm not very popular with your roommates at the moment."

Honey felt a flash of gratitude for two dynamic girls having her back. "Did Abby keep switching from English to Italian? She does that when she's riled up."

"I've never been so impressed while being yelled at." Looking genuinely concerned, he cupped her knee, and every inch of her skin heated. Drastically. "I thought you were coming to help out with your brother, babe. I didn't know that meant physical labor. What have you been doing?"

"Nothing I didn't do every single day growing up." She let her head fall back against the seat, flexing her foot when she felt a cramp forming in her calf. "New York has ruined me. I'm a certified Yankee now, and you showed up before tequila could numb the pain."

He made a sympathetic noise. "I'm sorry. Will it help if I tell you I'm taking your place starting tomorrow?"

"What?" Her head popped up. "You can't."

"Why is that?"

"You won't be able to work the tractor." She gestured to his clothing. "I'm beginning to doubt you even own a pair of jeans. Or a T-shirt. You can't farm in a button-down and wingtips. No, it will never work."

His smile only got bigger the more she protested. "I guess we'll see, won't we?"

Honey could only stare as he closed the ancient, creaking passenger door and went around the front bumper to the driver's side. In a million years, she'd never expected to see Professor Dawson climbing into the bucket of bolts that served as her family's truck. But there he was. Starting it up just as naturally as he did everything else.

When he noticed her staring at him, he raised a dark eyebrow. "Yes?"

That familiar mannerism and tone reminded her of how Ben

spoke to students in his classroom, and a subsequent flare of lust ignited in her belly. Oh boy. This was bad. Very, very bad. "What am I supposed to tell my parents about you just showing up here?"

He gave her a serious look as he backed the truck out of its parking spot. "I can only tell you what I'd *like* you to say, Honey. That I'm your boyfriend who couldn't last a full week without you. The second half is already true. We're just working on the first half."

Don't throw yourself at him. Don't. "You have to stop saying things like that."

"Why? Is it getting to you?"

"Not ready to say yet." Ben pulled the truck to the edge of the parking lot, and she directed him to take a right. "What was your plan if I told you to go jump in a lake? Not that I haven't ruled it out," she rushed to add.

"For tonight, my plan would stay the same. Take you home and check into the motel in town. Tomorrow would be a little more challenging, since I'd have to convince you to change your mind."

"Motel?" She shot up in her seat, wincing at the flash of pain in her backside. "Are you trying to give me a permanent twitch?" When he only looked confused, she clarified. "This is the South, Ben. My mother would just as soon dance naked in our front yard than let a guest stay at a motel."

"Even if you're still angry with me?"

"*Especially* if I'm still angry with you. 'Keep your enemies close' might as well be the state motto."

He slid her a heated look. One that told her exactly what was on his mind. But not hers. *Definitely* not hers. "Well, this makes things considerably easier."

"'Easy' isn't the word I would use." She encompassed her body with a circular hand gesture. "This here is Fort Knox. Especially with my father around. Unless you want to go back to New York minus testicles."

"It's not on my top ten list." Honey tried not to be miffed that he didn't appear bothered by the lack of nookie on the table. It made her wonder if he had a plan cooking behind those scholarly looking glasses. "Who was Elmer to you, Honey? Please note that I'm speaking in the past tense."

"My high school sweetheart." She pursed her lips. "You jealous of ol' Elmer, Ben?"

"'Jealous' is too common a word. His existence is a threat to my sanity."

Lordy. If her heart kept fluttering to her throat, it was going to get good and stuck. "Well. It doesn't feel good, does it?"

His eyes closed briefly. "It wasn't my plan to arrive with Viv on Friday, Honey. I ran into her down the street and saw an opportunity to—"

"Let me down easy." Viv. She hated that he shortened the woman's name. Hated it. She shook her head while directing him to take a left turn onto the dirt road leading to her family's farm. "I don't understand. Nothing has changed since then."

Since there was only one residence on the dead-end road, Ben correctly pulled to a stop outside the old white clapboard house. Inside, she could see her mother's silhouette moving in the kitchen window. Shadows being cast on the walls of the living room, where her brother watched television from his permanent position laid up on the couch. Home. Only now she was seeing it through an outsider's eyes. She pictured him, with his education and a professional athlete for a father, in a brick town house with ivy crawling up the side. What would he think of her country family and their country ways?

When the silence stretched, she looked over at Ben, who was watching her closely. "You're wrong, Honey. Everything has changed."

BEN HAD NEVER met a girl's parents before. Ever. He'd dated a single mother once, which technically meant he had met *a* parent. Just not a parent of the person he was dating. *Don't get ahead of yourself, you're not dating her yet.* But somehow, by the grace of God, he was going to be sleeping under the same roof as Honey tonight, when he'd flown here fully expecting to sleep in some form of the Bates Motel. Those expectations, combined with his ferocious hangover, had led to some pretty disturbing dreams on the flight to Kentucky. More specifically, someone yanking aside his motel shower curtain and tossing live guinea pigs at him. Which was only slightly less daunting than meeting Honey's parents. Because he'd never met a girl's parents. He didn't get a test run, however, and this wasn't just any girl.

It certainly didn't help that as they climbed onto the porch Honey tensed up beside him and looked like she might be pondering a sprint in the opposite direction. As young as she was, she'd probably only brought home one lucky guy to meet her parents, and he couldn't think about that. It made him want to break things, and that probably wouldn't make the best first impression. *Nice to meet you, Mrs. Perribow. Smash vase.*

What had Russell said about meeting parents? Never bring chocolates for the mother because it implies you think she's unhealthy. Never discuss baseball with the father over dinner because it inevitably leads to indigestion and he'll associate you with a sour stomach for the rest of his life. Right. Not much help there, since he hadn't expected to meet Honey's mother tonight and was thus chocolateless. Dinner had long since passed. He was on his own.

"I don't know about this," she whispered, one hand on the screen door handle. "This isn't something I do. My family has long memories. They still bring up that time I dropped Baby Jesus at my fourth-grade Christmas pageant. Ten years from now, they'll say, 'Remember that man you brought home, Honey? Whatever happened to him?' I don't know if I can . . . subject myself to a lifetime of you being dropped into conversations."

Fuck. Her words socked him in the gut. She was already writing him out of the picture. He'd definitely done a number on her—maybe more than he'd originally thought. Even if he got her back to New York by his side, it wouldn't be over. He'd be making up for the hurt for a long time. He hoped he got the chance. They'd have a lot of time to talk, though. He'd make sure they did. Right now, he just needed her here with him. On the same side. Smiling. "Hey. Think of all the stories you could make up if I turn out to be an asshole. He joined a commune. He got eaten by a shark. That's years of entertainment."

The porch light illuminated her smile. "He runs a support group for ex–Elvis impersonators."

"Your mind is wasted on science."

Her laugh was interrupted when the front door flew open. A woman, Honey's mother if her eyes were any indication, paused in the act of drying a dish. "*Well.* What's this now?"

Honey held the screen door open with one hand. "Well, now, Mama. This is Ben. He's . . ." She stood up straighter. And proceeded to talk in what sounded like a new, undiscovered language. "The thing is, he's kind of my boyfriend and we're having a fight right now but he stuck his butt on a plane to come down and see me anyway. It was foolish and impulsive but here he is and I suspect he's probably hungry so can you make him a sandwich? Not one of your good ones, because like I said, we're fighting. But we can't just let him starve is all."

An older man in a trucker hat appeared at the door. "Who's that?"

"Her boyfriend," Honey's mother said without skipping a beat. "They're fighting, but it's not bad enough to let him starve on the porch."

Honey threw up her hands. "Can we come in?"

"Depends on what the fight was about," Honey's father drawled. "The devil is in the details, ain't it."

Don't bring up baseball. Don't bring up baseball. Ben could practically feel Honey wilting beside him. It was make or break time. *Man up, Dawson.* "Nice to meet you both. I'm Ben. Dawson. Ben Dawson. It's my fault we're fighting, sir. I brought another woman to our super group merger because I wanted Honey to realize I wasn't worth her time. But when she did actually realize it, I found out what it feels like to be without her." He chanced a look at Honey, but she only looked baffled. "It's awful. Without her. So I'm here to become worth her time again."

Honey's mother sank against the doorframe.

"You talk like a Kennedy." Honey's father ran a hand over his beard. "You a Democrat?"

"*Okay* and we're moving on." Honey grabbed Ben's hand and pulled him past her parents into the house. "Enough soul baring for the night. I'm putting him in Teddy's room, since he's sleeping on the couch."

Her father cocked an eyebrow. "That's right next to your room."

"My behavior will be above reproach, Mr. Perribow," Ben assured him with a firm nod.

Honey's parents exchanged a look. "Who talks like that?"

"An English professor," Honey muttered behind his back, low enough to reach his ears only. "Come on, Ben. Tomorrow will be soon enough to bring new meaning to the word *awkward*." She took his hand again and tugged him toward the stairs. "I'll be back down in five minutes. Feel free to set the oven timer, Mama, since I know that's what you're fixing to do."

"What about his sandwich?" Honey's mother complained. "You said I could make him one."

"I'm fine, Mrs. Perribow. I ate on the plane."

He was fucking starving, actually, but the need to be alone with Honey outweighed his hunger. He'd meant what he said to her father, too. Mostly. He would respect the man whose roof he was under and keep his pants zipped within those four walls.

Didn't mean he would pass up a chance to remind her what was between them. Early and often. He'd maximize every moment she'd let him have.

Knowing her parents were watching him as they ascended the stairs, he kept his eyes down, when he really wanted to get a good look at Honey's ass in that jean skirt. It felt like a year had passed since he'd had his hands on her, and the memory of her soft skin was wreaking havoc on his deprived senses. They turned right at the top of the staircase, and she led him into a tiny room, flipping on the light to reveal Bob Marley posters decorating the walls and a stuffed iguana mounted to the headboard.

"Don't ask," she said. "Teddy's a little eccentric."

"Okay." Ben propped his suitcase just inside the door and let himself finally get a decent look at her. Since he'd arrived, she'd had another man's arm around her, they'd been in the darkness of the truck, and meeting the parents wasn't exactly prime time for appreciating the new tan she was sporting. He started at the tip of her cowboy boots and let his gaze rake up her legs, her hips . . . God, those tits. Whoever had informed her she didn't need a bra was his first and last favorite person in the world. Didn't seem fair that other men got to enjoy the outline of her pointed nipples, but if she covered them up, angels would weep enough to flood the earth twice.

"Ben." Her tone held a warning. "You shouldn't be looking at me like that."

Damn. If she hadn't licked her bottom lip and shifted in her boots right after she said it, he might have listened. Might have. "What are we going to do with five minutes, babe?" Before she could answer, he closed the door as quietly as possible and flipped off the light. The only sound in the room was her little gasps of breath. He wanted to feel them against his stomach. Which couldn't happen. Not tonight. Not until she forgave him.

Ben hooked an arm around her waist and walked them backward toward the bed, seating her in his lap. "I don't like knowing you're sore," he murmured against her ear. He placed his thumb at the base of her spine, applying firm pressure all the way up to her shoulder. Honey gasped at the unexpected treatment of her tight muscles, but it quickly turned into a moan. "Ah, babe. You can't make noises like that or they'll think I'm fucking you in here."

"Okay. Okay, I'll be quiet," she panted. "Please keep doing that."

He wanted to laugh, but he didn't, for two reasons. One, that moan had made his dick hard enough to break through a block of ice. Two, they weren't in a place where he could laugh at her without damaging her pride again, and he wouldn't risk a setback. Instead, he dug his thumbs into her shoulders and neck, moving them in a circular motion, biting his lip when her head fell forward and she jerked it back upright. "If we were alone, I'd keep this up for an hour, Honey, but I want to get to the rest of you before my time is up."

"The rest of m—" He dropped his hands to her thighs and kneaded the flesh just beneath the hem of her skirt. "Oh . . . yes. There. Oh wow."

Hell, she was purring now, and he only had about another two minutes. He could feel the heat between her legs. It would only take him moving his hand two inches higher, and he'd be touching her pussy. *God. Damn.* In a move that seemed unconscious, she'd started rotating her hips in time with his fingers. "Keep that up and I'm going to give you more than a massage. I'm hard up for that pussy, Honey. Enough to forget where I am in order to get some."

Her hips didn't still. "Ben, I can't . . ."

She couldn't stop, either. He knew instinctively that was what she was trying to tell him. Which made the situation his to get a handle on. With a tortured curse, he clutched her around the waist and pushed her to her feet. But they were so close that the back of her skirt brushed over his mouth. Jesus. Nothing could stop him from sliding his hands up the backs of her thighs to glide over the flare of her bottom. No material existed between his palms and her firm flesh, telling him she wore a thong. "Tell me this is sore, too, babe, so I can rub it."

"Yeah." Her voice shook. "It is."

He molded her ass with his hands, once, twice, before pressing his thumbs into the very tops of her thighs. Then he stroked his thumbs over her cheeks, pushing her tight flesh up in the process. Her answering whimper made his cock throb all the more. "I remember what this ass feels like against my stomach. That's right where I had it when I fucked you. Huh, babe?" He gave in to the urge to lean in and plant a kiss on her right cheek. Then the left. "Next time, it'll be bouncing on the tops of my thighs. You know why?"

A sucked-in breath. "Why?"

Hating the time constraints they were under, Ben pushed to his feet behind her, giving himself the satisfaction of dragging his ruthless erection up the center of her backside. She stumbled forward a little on a moan, but he laid a hand on her stomach and kept her pressed to him. "Because next time, you're going to ride me. You're going to throw those thighs on either side of my hips and work me over." He circled his hips while humming into her hair. "I'm going to be so hard inside you, Honey. You'll be able to slide up and down me however you want. Take me deep or ride the tip. Whatever it takes to get you there."

Her stomach shuddered against his hand. "Ben, please . . ."

Must step back. Taking this too far. His intention at the outset had been to remind her of their unbelievable chemistry, how amazing it felt when they touched, but he hadn't taken into account how easily she stole his logic. Which was what had landed him here in the first place. He needed to get his hands off her before he did something stupid. He planted a kiss on her smooth shoulder and stepped back. "See you in the morning, Honey. Sleep well."

He tried not to be insulted when she lunged for the door like a prisoner during a jailbreak.

Chapter 15

*H*oney woke up feeling oddly well rested. Strange, considering she'd returned to her bedroom after the massage mindfuck with Ben, only to toss and turn for hours. Something felt different about the way she was waking up, but it took her a second to fight through the sleep-induced grogginess to put her finger on it. *Shit!* Daylight! She'd never woken up in the bedroom of her youth and encountered the sunlight currently filtering in through the gauzy white curtains. Enough to make her squint and hold up a hand to ward it off like a grumpy vampire.

Her family owned a farm. And when you owned a farm, waking at the crack of dawn was considered sleeping in. Especially now, when they were under a time crunch and her father needed all the help he could get. Honey snatched her Tweety Bird alarm clock off the bedside table and stared at the digital numbers. *Ten o'clock in the morning?* Why hadn't it gone off at five? She turned the device over and gaped. No way. Someone had turned off her alarm. Her parents sure as hell wouldn't have done it. Meaning . . . it had to have been Ben. Ben had been in her room while she'd slept.

Hot, delicious pressure settled in her belly. She stared down at the sheets twisted around her hips, baring her thin, white tank top and matching boy shorts. Had he seen her like this? Jesus, had she been snoring? A sound from outside broke into her thoughts. The tractor. Her father must be doing her job while she languished the morning away in bed. Not good.

She propelled herself from the bed, spending a mere minute beneath the shower spray in the bathroom across the hall, brushing her teeth at the same time, before yanking on jean shorts and cowboy boots. Brushing her hair would have to wait. It took her only five minutes to get down the stairs and burst through the screen door onto the porch. Where she almost ran smack into her mother's back.

Her mother said nothing, didn't even spare her a glance. She just handed Honey a glass of sweet tea and continued to stare out over the planting field. Honey took the offered glass and followed her mother's line of sight. The tea paused halfway to her mouth.

No, she was seeing things. Had to be. Her tweed-wearing English professor wasn't shirtless on top of the family tractor, handling it like a certified professional. First of all, no one without Perribow blood running through their veins had *ever* succeeded in handling the temperamental piece of farming equipment. Second of all? Second of . . . all. What had she been thinking about? Sunshine bounced off Ben's perspiring chest, arms flexing as he turned the tractor around and headed back in their direction. He was wearing jeans. Low-riding jeans. The kind that sat a good three inches below the navel and clung to strong thighs like a hungry lover. *Hungry. I'm so very hungry.*

She shot her mother an incredulous look. "What is happening—?"

"Shh." Her mother held up a finger. "Don't question it."

"You really are standing here shamelessly ogling a man half your age. Aren't you?"

"Just appreciating. Nothing wrong with that." Her mother tipped her head in Ben's general direction. "And don't look now, but I think he's found a way to end your fight."

Honey scowled at him, even though he was concentrating and not looking at her. "By being shirtless, useful, and . . . and way more muscular than I'd originally thought?"

"Effective, ain't it?"

They both took long pulls from their sweet tea. When Ben saw her standing on the porch, his mouth spread into a smile. Her mother mumbled something under her breath that sounded like *Lord help you* before heading back inside and leaving Honey alone. Ben cut off the tractor and hopped off in an irritating and sexy-as-all-get-out show of masculine grace. She stood there for a few seconds, watching him approach in slow motion, but decided she better meet him halfway so her mother couldn't eavesdrop on this conversation.

"Ben Dawson." She came to a stop, crossed her arms, and cocked a hip. "You can't just go around sneaking into people's rooms and turning off their alarm clocks."

"Honey Perribow." He ran a hand through his sweaty hair, leaving it slicked back. *Damn.* "You're lucky your mother is watching us from the kitchen window, or I'd kiss that sulk right off your face."

"You run a tractor for one morning and all of a sudden you're talking like a Southern boy." Her arms dropped to her sides. "How did you get it working, anyway? It only works for a Perribow."

"That's preposterous."

"There's the professor again," she murmured. "Which one are you?"

"Maybe I'm both." He eased into her personal space, smelling like salt and earth and man. "I read a guide to classic tractors this morning, that's how I figured out how to work it. Everything can be found in a book."

"The town library doesn't open this early."

He took off his glasses, wiping away a smudge with his thumb. "I'm not a caveman, Honey. I own a Kindle." The snobbery in his tone drew a laugh from her. Ben's head popped up at the sound, his gaze zeroing in on her mouth. "You were talking in your sleep this morning when I went in to turn off your alarm."

Oh God. "What was I saying?"

"You must have known I was there." His attention dropped to the hem of her shorts. "You told me I'd . . . made it hurt again. You also mentioned something about tweed. I didn't get the correlation."

"Well." She pressed her hands to her cheeks. "Never you mind."

"Oh, I mind. I fucking mind." He grazed her tummy with a knuckle, dipping it into her belly button and pressing. Such a simple move shouldn't have made her insides quake, but it did. All the way down to her boots. "I'd like to mind you on your hands and knees out in that field."

"Ben, stop."

His eyes were heated as they searched hers. "Why?"

She didn't know why. Only knew that every word out of his mouth confused her body. Her mind kept trying to reason with it, but her body kept giving her mind the one-finger salute. There was a reason she hadn't already jumped his bones, and she needed to remember that. He'd only gotten here last night, and she was already considering sleeping with him. The way she'd felt on the flight to Kentucky, or after the scene in the bar back in New York, hadn't faded in her mind, though. Even if the reasons for those painful feelings dimmed whenever she was around him. She felt certain about one thing, though. She didn't want to be confused by him the next time they were physical. This enigma that was Ben needed solving, and she wanted that to happen *before* he made her his shameless love slave again. So she threw up a barrier, a bluff, even though she really didn't want to. Maybe part of her wanted to see if he'd work harder. If he really wanted to know her, too. "If all you want is to have sex with me, you should have just said so." She stepped closer to toy with the button of his jeans. "There's a wildlife preserve not too far from here. We can take my truck and park somewhere private. Fog up the windows." She looked up at him from beneath her eyelashes. "We'd be back in time for lunch."

A groan rumbled in his throat. "Nice try, Lolita." He tipped her chin up. "If I gave you the impression I only want to get inside you, let me clear it up. I want to be your boyfriend. I want to take all those thoughts you put on paper for class assignments and hoard them, just for me. Make you say them while you're wrapped around me in bed. Fucking or not. I want to know your favorite movie, restaurant, and sexual position. All of it. I want it to be mine."

What was that thing you needed to go on living? Oh, right. Oxygen. With a concentrated effort, Honey reminded herself to breathe. Never in her nearly twenty years on this earth had she ever expected to be spoken to in such a way. A way that made her bones feel like microwaved Play-Doh. He'd meant every word, too. She could see the evidence of that in the hard lines of his shoulders, the way his expression dared her to contradict him.

"My favorite movie is *Bad News Bears* and I like Cracker Barrel. They don't have one in New York, and I miss the pancakes on Sunday mornings. I try to match the recipe, but it never comes out right."

She could see his mind working behind those glasses. Receiving information and cataloguing it like the hottest librarian that ever lived. "I'm waiting on your favorite sexual position."

"If you finish your chores by dinnertime, maybe I'll tell you."

He growled at her as she sauntered away, forcing her to duck her head to hide her smile.

THE DAY PASSED slowly for Ben. Not because he spent hours riding the sputtering tractor, dragging the three-furrow ridging plow through the fields, creating rows to plant potatoes and onions. Not because Honey's father dragged him to the edge of the property to repair a damaged fence, then laughed as he literally chased down the sheep that made it through the hole. And not because a chicken had tried to peck him to death while he'd collected her eggs.

No, it moved slowly because Honey was everywhere. All the time. Reaching up to unpin a bedsheet from the laundry line, giving him a glimpse of her flat belly. Exercising the two horses they owned, tanned thighs hugging the animal's flanks, hips moving in a hypnotic rhythm. Since this morning, he'd only been within a hundred yards of her once, when she'd brought him a glass of lemonade. She'd had her shirt twisted up and tied under her braless tits like some twenty-first-century version of Elly May, leading his thoughts into dangerous territory. Dangerous because her mother and father were watching him like a hawk, even though it had to be obvious at this point that he was patently obsessed with her. It wasn't something he could hide. Or put into words that might reassure her parents that he wasn't some creep with bad intentions. *Why yes, I'd like to bottle your daughter's cinnamon and sugar smell so I don't need to go a single second without it.* Probably wouldn't be well received.

Nor would it be well received if he told Honey his cock had been rock solid since this morning when he'd walked into her room with the most *honorable* of intentions, hoping to give her time to sleep and recover. But she'd thrown her arms up over her head, thighs falling open as she'd whispered his name in a sleepy, sex voice. The kind he wanted to give her from screaming too much. He'd been given no choice but to dive out of the room into the hallway before he did something unforgivable, like push her thighs wider and use his mouth to wake her up the best way possible.

On cue, Honey cut across the driveway, carrying a bucket in each hand. He could practically hear saxophone music accompany-

ing her seductive strut all the way to the barn. His instinct told him
to follow her, but he couldn't. After the day he'd spent fighting a
constant erection, if he followed her into the barn, his first course of
action would be pinning her to the nearest wall. But she'd thrown
down the gauntlet earlier by insinuating he only wanted sex. To be
honest, he wanted sex with Honey like a motherfucker. He wanted
to sink between her thighs and fuck an orgasm out of her. And he
wanted it bad. He'd meant what he said, though. All or nothing.
The problem with that being the fact that he was having a hell of a
time concentrating on the *all* when he'd been without her so long. It
blew his mind that they'd only had sex once. How had he survived
this long on once?

In an effort to keep from following her into the barn, Ben decided to take a break. He walked to the porch and fell onto the
top step. A minute later, the screen door opened behind him. Ben
turned at the sound of crutches touching down on the creaky
floorboards. One look at the young guy easing into the porch
swing behind him told Ben it was Honey's brother, Teddy. After
all, there was only one person in the house with two broken legs,
but they hadn't formally met yet, since he'd been sleeping when
Ben arrived the night before.

"Hey, man," Teddy greeted him affably. "Let me let you in on a
little secret. When you work too hard, they keep expecting you to
work up to that level. Like, every damn time."

Ben laughed under his breath. "You're probably right. Good
thing I'm only here for a week."

"That's what you think." Teddy dug in his pocket for something. "If you actually succeed in winning over my sister, you'll be back. She can't stay away for too long."

His comment made Ben's smile slip. "What do you mean?" When Teddy didn't answer right away, Ben turned toward him. Teddy gave him the international gesture for *wanna smoke?* Pinching his index finger and thumb together and holding it up to his lips, eyebrows raised. Ben waved him off, so Teddy shrugged and lit up a joint, right there on his family porch, before continuing the conversation as if illegal drugs weren't being smoked.

"I mean, she's only been gone two months, and she's already back." Teddy blew a stream of smoke toward the sky. "No need for it. My father could've hired some hands in town for cheap. She's here because she's got Kentucky in her blood."

Ben's stomach sunk to the bottom step of the porch. What if he wasn't just down there to convince her to come home with *him* but to come home *at all?* "You don't think she likes New York?"

"You haven't asked her that yourself?" The question must have been rhetorical, because Teddy coughed and kept going. "She's got all the expectations I could never live up to on her head. Carrying them for both of us, my sister. I'm not sure if she's there because she wants to be or thinks she has to be."

Ben stood without thinking. He needed to be proactive. Needed to do something. Say something. Maybe it was premature to worry about Honey not liking New York enough to stay, but he wanted to head it off at the pass. If she needed a reason to come back, a reason to love the city, he'd give it to her. Now. He'd already started toward the barn when Teddy's voice stopped him.

"Hey, I didn't even get to give the obligatory don't-hurt-my-sister-or-I'll-hurt-you speech." Teddy glanced down at his injured legs. "Although I guess it's a moot point, so I'll just say please."

Ben nodded. He wanted to laugh, but he was too distracted with the urgency to find Honey in the barn. This dancing around each other wasn't working for him. Especially not now, when he felt like a noose had been tied around his neck. God, if she wasn't happy in New York, had he made it that much worse? Pushed her a little closer into leaving?

She looked up as he entered the barn, the expression on her face reminding him of the evening in the deserted classroom when she'd been half excited, half deer in headlights. All perfect. When he got within ten feet of Honey, giving her no indication that he planned to slow down, she dropped the bucket she was holding, some type of feed spilling out onto the floor. Ben hooked an arm under her ass, dragging her up against him as he backed her into an empty horse stall. Her thighs wrapped around his waist like they'd been conditioned to do so. He planted his hard cock between those gorgeous limbs and ground against her in a rough twist of his hips, just managing to get a hand over her mouth, capturing a moan that would have easily reached the house.

He pressed their foreheads together and looked her in the eye. "Listen to me." He waited for her nod. "You're going to take me somewhere now where I can see you without your panties on. I'm going to get you off good and hard, maybe a few times. And then, Honey, we're going to talk." He bucked his hips into her twice. "But first, I'm going to fuck you so dirty, you won't be able to look anyone but me in the eye afterward. Have you heard everything I've said?"

He removed his hand so she could answer. "Yes. Okay, Ben."

"Good. I'll be at the truck." He stepped back, letting her slide down the wall. "Tell them whatever gets us out of here."

Chapter 16

*H*oney had driven this particular back road thousands of times in her life, but nothing looked familiar now. She drove straight into the potholes she'd been taught to avoid since age sixteen, when she'd gotten her license. In the early evening haze, the rooster mailbox signaling her nearest neighbor's driveway looked like a foreign object. The steering wheel didn't operate as she'd come to expect. It probably had something to do with Ben sitting in the passenger seat beside her, his warm hand resting high on her thigh, just beneath the hem of her shorts. His steady perusal of her body had turned her nipples into stiff, pointed peaks. She couldn't force enough air into her lungs to slow her breathing to a normal pace.

The place she was taking him was sacred. Was she taking a risk? Half of her best memories had taken place there. If she and Ben went their separate ways, would each and every one of them be shadowed by that failure? At that particular moment, she couldn't question her decision, though, because lust gnawed in her belly. Her sole purpose in life just then was to relieve this relentless, sweaty longing that wouldn't leave her alone. Would never leave her alone as long as Ben was in the vicinity. There was no denying that. Her body knew what his felt like, the heights it could bring her to, and she didn't have the kind of willpower it took to deny herself.

Ben moved closer on the bench seat and placed his mouth on her neck. "Calm down before you kill us both." His unexpected comment surprised a laugh out of her and he echoed it, although both of the sounds were strained. He pushed her hair away from her ear and breathed against it. "How much further?"

"I should know the answer to that, shouldn't I?"

His hand slid to her inner thigh. Higher. "Distracted?"

She exhaled hard. "Payback is a bitch, you know."

He began to knead her thigh. "Oh no. You've more than paid me back in the distraction department. Just by existing." His teeth teased her earlobe with a firm tug. "But I'm anxious to see what you think could be more distracting than this body."

Their destination was up ahead. She just had to get them there without combusting. "You'll find out soon enou—" She cut off her own words with a moan as Ben pressed his fingers to the seam of her jean shorts, right over her clit. "Oh God. I'm going to wreck the truck."

Ben made a sympathetic noise. "You soaked right through your panties to your shorts, babe?" He worked his fingers in a circle. "When did this happen?"

She didn't have the wherewithal to be anything but honest. "In the barn. I just wished we'd stayed in the barn and done it then and there instead of waiting. I don't know how you do this to me."

"Oh yes you do. You do it to me, too." He removed his hand from between her legs, untying the shirt beneath her breasts and unbuttoning it with impatient fingers. When her breasts bounced free, his hands moved over them possessively. "All day, walking around with no bra. Back and forth between the house and the barn. My dick has been so hard for you, I can't remember my own name."

"Well, it's Ben." She pulled off the road and onto the field, hitting the brakes and throwing the truck into park. "Professor. Ben. Dawson."

His jaw flexed. "Oh, now you've done it." He jerked open the passenger side door with such intention that all she could do was watch him round the front bumper, anticipation twirling like a ballerina in her stomach. She managed to take off her seat belt before he yanked the driver's side door open, took her by the waist, and pulled her out. A warning voice in Honey's head told her that if she let the inevitable kiss happen, he would have control of this entire encounter and *she* wanted the control. He'd been commanding her senses and brainpower all day, and she needed to call some shots before she drowned in him.

Letting her pent-up sexual frustration fuel her, she grabbed him by the front of his T-shirt, reversed their positions, and shoved him up against the car. Oh, he liked her being aggressive. He sunk his teeth into his bottom lip and watched her, waiting to see what she'd do with the reins she'd taken. She lifted the hem of his thin cotton T-shirt and scrubbed the heel of her hand over his abs, before going lower to snap open the fly of his jeans.

When her palm brushed over his erection, his head fell back

and hit the car on a groan. As she unzipped his pants, she leaned in and licked the column of his neck. "Whenever I fantasized about you during class, I pictured you wearing a tie when I did this."

"Did what?"

Honey gave him a sly smile in response. Having succeeded in undoing his pants, she slipped her hand into his boxer briefs and stroked his heavy arousal. "You asked me earlier about my favorite position."

"Tell me," he panted. "Say it."

She placed her mouth over his ear. "On my knees."

Ben twined his flexing fingers in her hair as she knelt. "Oh God, you know I want that mouth, babe. Just enough to let me feel it this time, though. I'm too hot and fucked up for you to last long."

The truth of his words was thick and swollen in her hand. She'd only done this with one other guy, so she didn't have the expertise to know when one was hurting. Maybe it was her undefinable connection to Ben or some instinct he'd awoken in her, but she knew in her core that his desperation not only matched but outshined hers. Ben was in serious need of relief. Having the power to give it to him went to her head like a shot-gunned bottle of champagne.

She ran her thumb up the smooth underside, following in its wake with her tongue. Ben's stomach hollowed on a sucked-in breath above her. "*Again.* Please, again."

Honey granted his wish twice more before taking the head into her mouth and inching her way down, wetting his length as she went, making him slippery, easier to take. Each time she took him deeper, she sucked her way back up, hand working in time with her mouth. Ben groaned and cursed above her, harsh, filthy words she'd never thought to associate with him, her by-the-book English professor.

"Thought about this in class, did you?" His hips began undulating, seeking the pleasure of her mouth. "I guess we both have the same favorite position, because I always fantasized about kneeling in front of your desk, spreading your legs and sucking your clit."

She moaned around his flesh, her clothes suddenly feeling way too confining. One hand continued to worship his erection along with her mouth, while the other dropped to unsnap her jean shorts in anticipation of getting them off. Ben must have heard the sound, because one of his fists released her hair to dig in his pocket, pulling a condom out between his index and middle finger. One second, she was on her knees with Ben in her mouth, the next she was on her back in the grass, the denim shorts being ripped down her body, along with her panties. Their hands were everywhere, groping, stroking. The silence of the falling twilight was broken by rough breaths, urgent requests. Honey took the condom from Ben's hand and tore the corner open with her teeth, but her wrists were pinned above her head before she could roll it down his hardness.

Her back bowed off the earth with a cry when Ben began sucking her nipples. Hard, hungry pulls that strengthened the pulsing between her legs. Keeping her wrists pinned with one hand, he rested the other on the apex of her thighs, not moving it, just teasing her with its proximity to where she needed him to touch.

"Ben," she gasped. "Please."

He ceased his torture of her breasts to lift his head. "You want me to finger bang you, Honey?"

"Yes. *Yes.*"

His eyes locked on hers as he drove two fingers inside her. *Oh God.* She was going to come. Going to come. But she *couldn't,* because his touch didn't move, granted her no friction. Her hips lifted and fell in a plea, but he didn't grant her request, choosing instead to study the movements of her body like one eyed a juicy steak. "If you move like that when I'm inside you, babe, I will fuck you all the harder."

Honey moaned, head tossing in the grass. Drowning. She was drowning. This was what she'd been afraid of, even if she'd secretly wanted to be overwhelmed by him. But she couldn't take another second of the agony. Reaching deep for the willpower, she extricated her wrists from Ben's strong grip and surged up, flipping him onto his back. His eyes flashed, jaw slackening. Encouraging her without words. Her limbs were shaking, pulse hammering. She couldn't think past having him inside her.

The truck's headlights were still on, partially illuminating his handsome features, the muscular chest he'd exposed by removing his T-shirt. His gaze was feverish as it devoured her body. An image flashed in her mind of what she must look like, naked and straddling him, just outside the glow of the headlights, but his commanding voice broke through her thoughts. "Don't keep me waiting, Honey. Not after the way you sucked me so good."

Fingers shaking, she reached between them and rolled the latex down his shaft. She wasted no time sinking down onto him, pausing halfway to breathe before sliding him home. The muscles in her stomach tightened to the point of pain, so intense she fell forward, catching herself with two hands on his shoulders. "Oh my God. Feels too good."

Ben lifted his hips, bouncing her a few times. "Does it fill you up nice and tight?"

"Yes," she whimpered, starbursts exploding behind her eyes. She had no choice but to move at that point or risk combustion. Her hips moved on their own, as if they were independent of the rest of her body. They snapped up until she was poised on the tip of Ben's erection, before scooping back down. His fingers had such a tight grip of her ass they had to be causing bruises, and she reveled in that realization. He was beneath her, head thrown back, chanting *fuck fuck fuck* in time with her bucking movements. She'd never felt more herself in her entire life, so damn alive it hurt to breathe. Twice she slowed down to stave off her inevitable climax, but the third time it loomed close, she let it take her, embracing it with her whole self. Her scream sounded distant, but it vibrated through her body, making itself known.

Then she was moving, shifting. Ben was still locked inside of her, rigid and thick, with her legs wrapped around his waist. He kept their bodies connected as he moved to his knees. Her body bowed backward over his hard forearm, hair tumbling into the grass. He thrust into her over and over, using his supporting arm to slam her body down to meet his driving hips.

"This is what we both needed, isn't it? A dirty fuck in the grass. Get up here." He jerked her upright so they were eye to eye, mouth to mouth. Being impaled once again on his lap, her hips automatically began to circle, eager and quick. Ben's hands on her ass urged her even faster. He pressed his mouth to her ear. "Your ex-boyfriend never fucked you this good."

"No." She threw her arms around his neck, hips pumping frantically. Oh Jesus, had he gotten bigger inside her? "No. Never."

Ben raked his teeth over her shoulder. "That sweet, wet pussy never came once for him, did it?"

"No," she sobbed, her actions growing jerky. Again. She was going to orgasm again. "*Ben*."

"I'm the only one who belongs inside you," he growled. "Show me why, babe."

She tightened her thighs around him and ground herself down as the climax shook through her. Her scream was swallowed by his hungry mouth as it claimed her, tongue pushing her lips wide to tangle with hers. His big body, plastered so tightly against her, began to shudder. He ripped his mouth away with a shouted expletive, eyes squeezed closed as his release took him.

Chapter 17

*O*ne of the most irritating parts of majoring in English had been the constant encouragement to express one's feelings. Picking English had been a no-brainer for Ben. He'd anticipated critical response papers, arguments in favor of popular theories. Perhaps the occasional assignment that would require him to pull from his own life experiences. Instead, he'd been constantly subjected to stream of consciousness writing exercises. Creative projects that had forced him to use examples of his own past experiences. Experiences he had no wish to revisit. More often than he'd been comfortable with, certain prompts had been given in his creative writing courses.

Write about a defining moment in your life. Write about what's important to you.

If he'd known then what he knew now, lying in a field with Honey Perribow tucked into his side, his answers would have been vastly different. Until meeting Honey, he'd never been afraid to lose anything. He'd lost everything as a child and he'd survived. Sure, his career was extremely important to him, but he'd only protected it because losing it would make him too similar to his father if the worst happened. But he'd never been afraid. He'd never been shaken by the idea of having to find a new job.

Nothing scared him as much as the idea of losing Honey did. This eight-foot-high electrified fence that had existed inside him as long as he could remember had been breached. She was inside his perimeter. Inside *him*. If he had to live indefinitely without this feeling, he'd be scared every morning. Scared to walk around without the fence at full strength, an open wound right in the middle of his chest.

Oh yes, he'd write those papers differently. A defining moment in his life? Realizing bigger things were at play than his useless insecurities and fear of the past repeating itself. When you found something that made you feel so much you could hardly stand it, that was the thing that counted. When the thought of being without someone well and truly scared the shit out of you, you decided not to be without that person, no matter what it took. So what was important to him? Keeping the person who made him feel. Keeping Honey. Making goddamn sure she had the same feelings for him. Working his ass off to make sure she never stopped having them.

Enough for tonight. If he kept up this line of thinking, he'd need to say the thoughts out loud. They might have just screwed each other's brains out in the sex session of his life, but he wouldn't take for granted that he was out of the woods. If he wanted to build a relationship with her, it needed to be on a foundation of more than sex. Un-fucking-believable, sweaty, tear-your-hair-out sex, yes. But still. He needed her to know him. Trust him. And he needed to achieve that without shaking her and demanding she let him keep her.

"Where are we?"

A breeze rolled over them, blowing a few strands of her hair across his face. "My baseball field."

"*Your* baseball field?"

Honey hummed in her throat. "Mmm hmm. I built it." She raised her head and looked around through one squinted eye. "Looks like we landed in the outfield."

"The place where all your thoughts and secrets get swallowed up by a discreet blue sky." He quoted her assignment without thinking. When Ben felt her staring—probably because he'd just let it slip how pathetic he'd become over her—he quickly changed the subject. "Tell me about this place. When did you build it?"

Her fingers drew circles on his stomach, making his eyelids feel heavy. "This place was just weeds and beer cans until my parents and I cleaned it up. Spent hours and hours out here." God, her voice was soothing. Soft and easy. "They wouldn't let me join the Little League because I was a girl, so I started my own. Right here." She paused for a while, and he sensed she was gathering her thoughts. "This place. It's the thing I'm most proud of in the world."

His throat tightened. "Thank you for bringing me here." She nodded against his shoulder but didn't say anything. As if she hadn't just crawled up inside his heart and put down permanent roots. After reading her latest paper, he knew baseball was important to her, but now he understood why. He felt humbled to be included in any way, and he wanted to return the favor. By opening up and talking about the past. Things he usually preferred to keep to himself but couldn't any longer. Not if he wanted her to see him and know him. "Honey, there's a reason I did what I did back in New York." When she stiffened a little, he pulled her closer. "A reason, not an excuse."

"Tell me," she said eventually.

Ben swallowed his nerves. "I told you my father played for the Patriots." She shifted so she could look up at him, but having her eyes on him was comforting rather than disconcerting. "We lived in a huge house with an indoor swimming pool. Gardeners, maids. Things nobody needs." He shrugged. "And then one day it was all gone. He'd slept with an underage girl, and it was just everywhere. Pictures of them together. Video."

"Oh, Ben . . ."

"He just kept repeating, '*She lied, she lied*,' but it didn't matter. He didn't seem to realize that. Our family was being torn apart. Who cared if she lied?" He took a deep breath. "Only, it must have stuck with me, Honey. It makes me sick that it did. Makes me sick that I let something that happened fifteen years ago have anything to do with us."

She was completely still against him. "I lied to you. That's why—"

"That was only part of it," he rushed to say. "I know what happens when a man loses his judgment. I've seen it. Before I met you, nothing could threaten what I had. Nothing made me feel strongly enough. You did. You *did*, and I thought if I pushed you away, I'd save myself. But I ended up doing the opposite. Watching you get into that cab . . . I didn't survive it. I was dead until I got here and saw you again."

Her breath hitched. She used his chest for leverage and sat up to stare out at the baseball field. Ben followed suit, ready to beg in order to find out what was going on in her head. Thankfully, she didn't keep him waiting too long. "I am a threat, though, Ben. It's all good and well to play house while we're in Bloomfield, but if—when—I go back to New York, I'm still your student. What happened to your father could happen to you, and it would be my fault."

"No." His heart pounded. "It won't happen."

"It *easily* could." She plowed her hands through her hair. "What are we doing here, Ben?"

He got in front of her and laid a hand over her mouth. "I can't lose my job. Or I *can*. But it wouldn't matter, because I've just accepted a new position at NYU. This morning, anyway." Her eyes shot wide over the top of his hand. What did that mean? "As soon as we get back, I'm going to hand in my notice at Columbia." Not an ounce of nerves accompanied that statement. "You might need to drop my class until the semester is over, babe. I wouldn't want to jeopardize you."

When Ben slowly removed his hand, her mouth fell open. "W-why didn't you say anything?"

He barked a laugh. "Why do you think? I don't even know if you're going to give me a second chance. I didn't want you to think I'd taken it for granted." Something hard stuck in his chest. "Jesus, I'm not even sure anymore if you want to come back to New York. With or without me. But I hate to tell you, Honey, I'm going to try and make staying here impossible for you. I'm going to make it as hard for you to watch me get on a plane as it was for me to watch you get into that cab."

Somewhere in the middle of his speech, her chest had started to rise and fall rapidly. Reminding him she was topless. Naked. While this had to be the only circumstance under which he'd ever forget Honey was naked, he was now being neatly reminded. So was his body. *Eyes up, Dawson. Don't look. Don't look. You just spilled everything out on the table, and what she says next is important.*

"Ben?"

"Yeah?"

She cupped and squeezed her breasts. "Fuck me again, please."

Christ. He dove for her, sending them both down onto the grass. Honey's mouth opened on a gasp, and he was all too happy to take that opening with his tongue, kissing her with everything he felt. Lust, frustration, possessiveness. Yeah, possessiveness. Big, bad, and encompassing. The hot little whimpering sounds she made every time his tongue stroked hers became an instantaneous addiction. So he did it over and over, fucking her mouth like he'd do with his body soon.

He tore away with a curse, inhaling the scent at her neck. "You know I'm going to give it to you, Honey. Probably two more times before we leave this field. But tell me what you're thinking first, though. About what I said. Okay? I'm going crazy here."

She was the most beautiful thing he'd ever seen. Blond hair spread out behind her on the grass, face flushed, eyes full of life. His life. It was all right there when she looked up at him. "I'm thinking I kind of want you to take me for granted in some ways.

I want you to know I'm coming back with you. That I'm going to be with you. Stay with you." Her voice fell to a whisper. "I'm sorry I let you wonder for so long. If you'd asked me to come home with you last night when you walked into Calhoun's, I would have said yes. Even though I wanted to scream at you."

Relief made him dizzy, so he dropped his head into the crook of her neck. She tilted to the side, and he grazed her skin with his teeth, making her suck in a breath. "Please don't get into any more cabs or airplanes for a while. Not unless I'm with you. Okay?"

"Deal," Honey whispered before wrapping her legs around his hips, arching beneath him so her sexy tits pointed straight up toward his mouth. God, she was going to have him walking around the streets of New York in a constant state of arousal. Already his cock felt full and heavy, as if he hadn't just come like nobody's business fifteen minutes ago. She bit her top lip while sliding her fingers into his hair. When she fisted it and pulled, Ben groaned. "You like when I pull your hair, don't you? When I did it that day in the classroom—"

"Yes, I fucking like it," he growled, nipping at her mouth. "I bet you think that's funny."

She shook her head. "No, I think it's hot. I think everything about you . . ." She tugged on the strands again, harder this time. *Fuck.* " . . . is hot. Every time you walked into class and lifted your bag over your head, a little bit of skin would show right above your belt. I wanted to lick it." Turned on even more by her confession, he slid his cock up through her wet pussy to rest on her belly, moaning when she started circling her tight, little body against it. "The way you push your glasses up with your middle finger. I used to imagine you pushing it inside me. All the way." Her heels dug into the small of his back. "One thing you do, though, is by far the hottest."

"Tell me. Tell me now. I'll never stop doing it."

Honey's lips twitched. "When you talk to me in that professor voice." Her eyelids fluttered, as if just saying it out loud was enough to get her going. *Sweet hell. This girl.* "You do it all the time, you know. Out of nowhere, your tone changes, and it . . ."

"What?"

"It makes me so wet," she murmured, hitting him with the full impact of those big eyes. "For you."

"Like maybe you want to please your professor? By being nice and ready?" His voice was strained. Everything about him was strained. With every word out of her mouth, his dick swelled thicker and became harder to ignore. Every instinct inside him demanded he thrust into all that snug heat and bang her into the ground, but she'd asked him for something in her own way. And he'd give her anything. *Everything.* Ben leaned down and placed his mouth over her ear. "Ms. Perribow, you've been squirming around in your seat for my entire lecture. In that ridiculous piece of fabric you refer to as a skirt. Is it your life's intention to distract me?"

Her energy snapped beneath him like a live wire. She threw her head back into the grass and moaned, thighs inching even higher around his waist. Fuck, he was going to give it to her so damn hard. She was going to feel it for days. But he wasn't finished yet.

"It seems there is something you'd like to share with the class, Ms. Perribow? Or is it just for your professor?" He leaned down and swiped his tongue over her hard nipples. "Come stand at the front of the class and lift up your little skirt. Let your professor see what's been warming your seat."

"Stop. Enough," she breathed, attempting to lean up and kiss him. "I need you now. Please."

Ben kept her pinned with his body, continuing to speak in the voice he usually reserved for lectures. "That's a good girl, Ms. Perribow." He rotated his hips, grinding the base of his cock against her clit. "Now take down your panties and bend over my desk. Stay that way until I've dismissed you. Not a moment sooner."

Honey cried out, her body going bow tight beneath him before it started to shake. Ben watched her with nothing short of awe. Unbelievable. He'd actually made her come just by talking to her. He liked the power of that. A lot. Maybe too much, because his body was now thrumming with the relentless need to be inside her. Now. Immediately. He had no idea where common sense got a foothold, reminding him to put on a condom, but he reached for his jeans, slipping one out of his pocket and covering himself within seconds. Honey still looked shell-shocked, lying on her back and sucking in gulping breaths. Her body looked gorgeous and satisfied in the moonlight. Too bad he wasn't quite done satisfying her. And after feeling the orgasm move through her body, he was pumped full of lust. *Need her. Need her now.*

Ben grabbed Honey by the waist and flipped her over, urging her onto her knees. He groaned at the sight of her ass in the air, just as he'd pictured it so many times. Perky and upturned. Asking for it. He led his cock between her legs and rubbed it through her wetness. "Just because I'm not going to be your professor anymore doesn't mean you shouldn't work hard for a good grade." He drove himself deep inside her, keeping her upright with an arm under her hips. "*Fuck*. You get extra credit for being tight, that's for goddamn sure."

Honey's back started to tremble, broken sobs falling from her mouth. "It feels so good this way."

"I haven't even moved yet, babe," Ben said through gritted teeth. He should probably get around to that, huh? But her warm pussy clenched around him so perfectly that he actually needed a moment to calm down before he gave in to his body's urges. "Tell me if I'm too rough, okay?"

She tossed her hair, looking back at him over her shoulder. "I'll only tell you if you're not rough enough."

Jesus. That fucking did it. Ben took hold of her hips, easing out of her on a groan before pounding back in. Honey whimpered his name, and that was the end of his control. He yanked her hips back to meet his as he started to thrust hard. It was insane how close he was already. She did this to him. Heightened his senses, made everything look, sound, feel better. More intense. He was fucking her *hard* and she only lifted her ass higher, arching her back for more. Her hot little cries were like the best song he'd ever heard, one he wanted to put on repeat, endlessly. When she tossed her head, that blond hair became too much of a temptation, so he fisted it and drove into her with even more force.

"Oh God, oh God, oh God. *Ben*."

Her hands slipped in the grass and she went down, landing on her belly. Ben went down with her, pushing her thighs open with his knees, not breaking his pace for a second. With her face turned to the side in the grass, he could see her eyes were squeezed shut, lips swollen from biting. Begging words fell from her mouth that only someone buried in her heat could understand. Ben wedged his hand between their bodies and stroked her clit, soft and easy, a complete contrast to his rhythmic thrusting. "Who's a teacher's pet?"

Her ass jerked up against his belly and she screamed. Ben went over the cliff right behind her, the unbearable pressure in his balls releasing, dragging his soul along for the ride. His mind went blank, void of everything but her and what she'd given him. *Good. So damn good.* No, better than good. There wasn't a word invented yet for what it felt like to shoot off inside of Honey while her body climaxed around him. He buried his face in her back as violent shudders took him over, absorbing hers at the same time. There were words in his head, so many words. His throat ached with the need to say them, to express this fucking tornado of emotion she whipped into a frenzy inside him. But he breathed her in instead, memorized the feel of her as he drew her up against his side in the grass. When he said the words, there wouldn't be any confusion as to why he'd said them.

They were silent for a few seconds before she spoke. "Welcome to the Bluegrass State."

Ben laughed long and loud. "I'd heard about Southern hospitality, but I had no idea. You really go above and beyond."

"We want to make sure our visitors come back."

The smile slipped from his face. He knew she was joking, but he didn't even like the possibility of them being separated by seven hundred miles.

Honey seemed to sense his inner turmoil, because she tucked her head under his chin, nudged his neck with her nose. "I told my parents we were going to a movie. That gives us another hour or so before we should head back."

Ben ran his fingers down her spine and back up. "What are the odds they bought that?"

"Pretty low." She yawned against his throat, and his smile fell back into place. He liked knowing what she sounded like when she yawned. "Wake me up in forty-five minutes."

"Okay, babe."

But the warmth of her, his lack of sleep and the relief of knowing she'd be coming back to New York, was too much. He fell asleep two minutes after her.

Chapter 18

*H*oney was having that dream. The one where she was late, but no idea how late. Or for what. Usually school was involved in some way, but those dreams of being late for class usually made her anxious. Tied her belly up in knots. That certainly wasn't the case here. She felt lethargic, warm. More comfortable than she'd ever felt in her life. As if she'd drunk just the right amount of wine before swan-diving into a pool full of goose feather pillows. Her body was molded around something hard, though. Very hard. And it was moving, albeit very slowly. A steady rise and fall. Something warm and firm—a hand?—traveled up the back of her thigh to cup her bottom, tug her closer.

"*Honey,*" a gruff, sleep-roughened voice husked at her ear. "Roll over and let me fuck, babe."

Ben. Oh God. Even as her body reacted swiftly to the command, she registered where they were. Baseball field. *Wake me up in forty-five minutes.* Honey's eyes flew open, but they slammed shut again when the overhead sun blinded her. Opening them again in a squint, she turned in Ben's strong arms and shook him. "Wake up. You have to wake up."

One eye eased open in his masculine face, made even more so by his morning stubble. Oh shit, he looked really good half asleep, hair all tousled and dewy. He appeared to have the same opinion about her, because his gaze dropped to her still-naked breasts and he groaned. She couldn't help taking a peek at his morning wood, which was growing by the instant. When he saw where her attention had been drawn, his lips quirked up into a lazy smile. "Climb on. It's been hours."

She considered it. She actually considered mounting her naked boyfriend in broad daylight and taking one for the road. Sanity prevailed, however, when she heard an approaching car rumbling in the distance. That was the exact moment Ben woke up fully, his face clearing of any hope of morning sex. His gaze shot to the road before landing back on Honey's naked body. "Oh shit. Oh shit."

They both scrambled to their feet, snatching clothes off the field before hightailing it to the truck, where they ducked down against the fender, dragging garments over their heads and up their legs. At least this way, no one could see them from the road. When the car rumbled past without stopping, they looked at each other and released the breath they'd been holding. Honey was the first to laugh, but Ben joined in almost immediately, both of them landing on their—thankfully clothed—asses in the grass.

Honey wiped the tears from her eyes. "We might have avoided a public indecency charge, but we still have my parents to contend with."

"You don't think they'll buy it if we tell them we saw a double feature?" Ben buried his face in his hands, but he was smiling. "I'm going to be shot on sight, aren't I?"

"I can't believe you of all people fell asleep." She got to her feet and buttoned her jean shorts. "You're so punctual. Never late. Never early. Always timing your lectures down to the minute."

"Noticed that, did you?" He stood as well, backing her against the side of the truck, making her tip her head back to look at him. "Maybe when I have a sweet little blonde who smells like cinnamon wrapped around me, I stop giving a shit about what time it is."

She narrowed her eyes at him. "Is that so?"

"Yeah. I can't wait to have that smell in my bed. All over my sheets." He tilted his head to the side, considering. "Is there any chance your father might demand I marry you to protect your honor?"

Her heart tried to leap from her chest. If it succeeded, she had no doubt it would cling to Ben, because that's what she wanted to do. Wanted to climb his body, dig her face into his neck, and never let go. Wanted to see his face in the morning, just like this, every single day. Sanity took hold, though, at the very last second. What if he was only joking and she came across crazy? He had to be joking, right? He looked serious—very serious—but she couldn't be sure.

She gave a halfhearted push against his chest. "How many nineteen-year-olds do you know that are ma—" She broke off in the middle of her own sentence, the day's date dawning on her. "Wait a minute. I'm twenty today." A laugh tumbled out. "It's my birthday."

He pushed a hand through his hair, looking slightly ill. "No, don't tell me that. I don't have a gift."

Her mouth spread into a smile. "The day is young."

A flicker of relief in his eye quickly disappeared. "Something tells me there aren't a lot of shopping options in Bloomfield."

An idea took root in her mind. "I know what I want from you." Hoping she wasn't pushing or overstepping, she twined her arms around his neck. "Write me something."

His throat worked, gaze darting to the side. "What?"

She shrugged one shoulder, chuckling when his eyes dropped to her breasts. "You've read dozens of my assignments, but besides the notes you leave me, I've never read anything of yours. I'll even let you choose the topic." When he still looked dubious, she went up on her toes and kissed his neck once, twice. "Just think about it."

Without waiting for an answer, she dropped her arms from around his neck and climbed into the truck. The keys were on the seat, where she'd apparently thrown them last night when Ben had pulled her from the truck. Had that only been last night? It seemed like ages had passed since then, so much having been resolved. She understood him now. Understood why he'd pushed her away back in New York. As of last night, she'd let the hurt go. Put it behind her. How could she continue to be upset, when he'd actually changed jobs for her? She still hadn't quite wrapped her mind around that.

A smile flirting with the corners of her mouth, Honey turned the key in the ignition. Nothing happened.

Ben slid onto the seat beside her, frowning. "Problem?"

She turned the key again and got silence in return. "The truck is dead."

He pushed up his glasses, understanding dawning on his face. "We left the headlights on."

"It drained the battery." Honey smacked her forehead, then let her hand drop into her lap. "Guess we're walking."

Just because she liked watching him walk and wanted his hands on her again, Honey stayed in the driver's seat until Ben came around to let her out. His expression told her he knew what she was about, too, and felt the same way. He hooked an arm around her waist and dragged her out of the truck, letting her dangle in the air against his hard body, their mouths hovering inches apart.

"I advise against tempting a man with morning wood, Honey. It can be vicious when not seen to properly."

She rubbed their mouths together. "I'll cure you of it later. Even if I'm reduced to sneaking into my brother's room tonight to get it on with my boyfriend."

"*Boyfriend*," he growled, stooping down to wrap an arm around her legs. Before Honey could get her bearings, he'd thrown her over his shoulder, kicked the truck door shut, and started off down the road.

When Honey stopped laughing, she smacked him on the butt. "The farm is the other way."

He turned without missing a beat, heading back in the right direction. "So, if I'm officially your boyfriend, does that mean you're dropping my class until I switch jobs?" He laid a kiss on her thigh. "I want to be with you in the open now, please. No waiting."

Thank God he couldn't see the dopey grin on her face. "Yes, Ben. I want that, too."

They walked like that for a while, Honey more than content to be carried like a sack of potatoes. It gave her one hell of a view. Two cars passed in a row, honking at Ben, who simply waved back, as if walking down the road with a girl over his shoulder was the most natural thing in the world. She finally convinced him to let her down and they walked side by side, holding hands the rest of the way.

This. Right there at that moment stood everything she'd hoped for, all in one place. Ben. The town she'd been missing so much. It couldn't last, she knew that. Ben didn't go with this place, they were just her two favorite ships passing in the night. But she could savor it while it lasted. She would return to New York in a few days and have the memories of Bloomfield to content her while she and Ben made their own. Maybe someday soon, they could even come back. Together.

When the farm came into view, their steps slowed simultaneously. *How odd.* Two extra cars were parked outside the house, one of them Elmer's truck, the other a taxicab. Why would either be there so early in the morning? Or at all, for that matter. Honey felt a tiny pinch of foreboding in her midsection, but she immediately shook it off. Worst-case scenario, her father had overreacted and called in a search party to go find them.

"Uh-oh." Ben put an arm around her shoulders. "What's going on?"

"I don't know," she murmured. "Let's go find out."

The first thing Honey saw when they started up the driveway

was her mother. She was sitting on the porch. Crying. It caused Honey's stomach to plummet right down to her knees. Her mother cried about as often as she did, which was never. It meant something bad. Very bad. Her father was leaning up against the side of the truck with Elmer, their arms crossed over their chests as they watched her and Ben close the distance to the house. Silence. So much silence.

Ben's grip on her hand tightened, and he angled his body in front of hers. She didn't need or want him to fight her battles for her. After all, she was a grown woman who lived on her own in a major city. If she wanted to spend a night with her boyfriend, same as her parents had done at her age, she damn well had the right. But it felt cruel to let Elmer see her like this. Very obviously coming home from a night out, engaging in all manner of naughty with her new boyfriend. So she let Ben take the lead for now. "Sir, I'm sorry we worried you. I can explain. We—"

"Which part are you going to explain first?" her father interrupted, pushing himself off Elmer's truck. "The fact that you're my daughter's teacher? Or the fact that you got her kicked out of school?"

Ben froze, as did Honey. Her gaze shot to her mother's questioningly, but her mother only swiped away more tears. Every inch of Honey's skin started to prickle, all the way to her scalp. What the hell was going on here?

"Kicked out of school?" Ben's voice cracked like a whip. "What are you talking about?"

Honey's mother stood and came toward the four of them. "He wrote a letter to the dean at Columbia. Said you'd been harassing him. Pursuing him relentlessly with no encouragement." She gave their joined hands a sharp look. "Forgive me if I find that hard to believe."

"Your financial aid has been rescinded," her father added, a hint of shame showing in his face. He'd always hated not being able to pay her entire way.

She might have voiced a denial, because in *what* fucking world did something like this happen? How could it happen? It got stuck in her throat, however, when Ben dropped her hand and fell back a step. His fingers threaded into his hair slowly and stayed there as he shook his head. Dammit, his eyes were closed, so she couldn't read him. "No, this isn't real. This isn't happening. In my lesson plan. I left it in my lesson plan . . . Peter must have . . ."

"Ben?" She took a deep breath when she heard her voice waver. "Did you write a letter to Dean Mahoney?"

He didn't answer. Just looked at her as though the earth was crumbling underneath her feet but his hands were tied behind his back, preventing him from reaching out to help her. Or maybe the earth really was crumbling beneath her feet. That was what it felt like. It matched the horrible crumbling taking place inside her. No, please. Why wouldn't he answer her?

"Yes or no, Ben?" she whispered.

When he nodded a single time, a rushing sound started in her ears, as if she'd been pulled under a tidal wave. It wasn't just the knowledge that Ben had written a letter to the dean about her, had written down those terrible lies on paper. That alone would have been enough to kick her in the teeth. It was more, though. Her parents had worked so hard to send her to New York, to pay what they could while she pursued her dreams. She'd let them down. Oh God, she could face almost anything except that.

Vaguely, she registered Elmer coming to stand behind her. Ben bared his teeth at her oldest friend. All hell broke loose then. Elmer laid a comforting hand on her shoulder that she immediately wanted to fling off. She didn't want comfort. She wanted the pain to kill her on the spot so she wouldn't have to deal with it.

"If you don't take your fucking hands off her," Ben grated, "I will rip them off."

"You're not in a position to be issuing demands, bro," Elmer returned. "I'll be here to pick up the pieces when you leave. In fact, we already called you a cab."

Words still hanging in the air, Ben moved. It happened so fast that Honey was snapped out of her stupor. One minute Elmer was standing beside her, the next he was lying on the ground, clutching his jaw. The boy who'd never hurt her a day in her life felled by the man who'd just shattered her heart? Unacceptable. Honey held up a hand to stay her approaching father and rounded on Ben, who looked as if he was considering going for round two with Elmer. When she blocked Ben's view of Elmer, he looked up at her, his eyes clouding over.

"Get in that cab. Get on an airplane. And get the hell out of Kentucky." She wouldn't cry. She wouldn't. Not in front of him. Or anyone. "God, I hope I never see you again."

He took a step toward her, shaking his head. "I'm going to make this right. You don't understand—"

"Looks like you wrote me something after all for my birthday." She skirted past him and opened the cab door. "Wasn't really what I had in mind, but that'll teach me to be careful what I wish for."

His hand clutched at his stomach a moment before he straightened. "Once I fix this, you'll have to listen to me. It's not what you think."

When a tiny part of her hoped that was true, Honey knew she had to end this once and for all. No more hope. No more maybes. Since meeting Ben, she'd had enough of those to last her a lifetime. She got right in his face. "There is nothing you can say, nothing you can fix, to make this better. You've embarrassed me in front of my family. You've hurt me, Ben. So bad that it's not repairable. Every time I think of you, I'll think of the words you wrote. I'll never see anything else. Give up."

He looked hollow, but she didn't have it in her to care. Not when she was hollow, too. He swept a glance over her before falling heavily into the backseat of the cab, wincing when Honey slammed the door. His eyes were solemn as they watched her through the glass, like he wanted to communicate something to her, but she turned away and allowed her father to toss Ben's carry-on sized suitcase unceremoniously into the trunk. As the cab reversed down her driveway, she refused to look back.

Chapter 19

*B*en hated the fact that it was sunny when he landed in New York. He wanted thunder, hail, and darkness. Fuck light and warmth, he wanted ice on the sidewalks. Gloom. Weather that signaled the Apocalypse. Wasn't that what *this* was? Too much. He'd been feeling far too much to sit in the tiny airplane seat for three hours. Rage, self-disgust, loss . . . so much loss. It didn't seem possible that he was leaving Honey one place and going to another. The girl he'd slept beside last night, feeling each of her breaths, smelling her hair . . . she should be with him always. She wasn't, though. She was so far from being *with* him that last night seemed like a dream. A perfect, golden-edged dream that one stupid action had burned to a cinder.

The second his flight landed, people around him began chatting excitedly into their cell phones. Making plans. He had no plans beyond getting to the school. After that, he had nothing. There was nothing beyond the meeting he had with Dean Mahoney one hour from now. Needing the situation handled immediately, he'd called the man from the airport to schedule it. And he just needed to get there and repair what he'd done so he could breathe. Until he knew he hadn't ruined her future with his past insecurities, he would just move on autopilot. Otherwise he might bum-rush the nearest ticket counter and buy a return ticket to Kentucky.

Leaving her standing there with tears in her eyes had been the shittiest thing he'd ever experienced, followed closely by the betrayal on her face when he'd walked into the Longshoreman with another woman. Jesus, how many times had he hurt her? Enough. Enough times that he knew she'd meant what she'd said before slamming the door of the cab. Honey was done. Wanted him out of her life. Fuck, he didn't blame her. Maybe he didn't know how to be with someone without inflicting pain on them. *You certainly are your father's son. A chip off the old block. The apple doesn't fall far from the tree.* On and on the clichés went in his head, until he wanted to slam it against the tray table attached to the seat in front of him.

The passengers around him started to deplane and he followed suit, taking his carry-on out of the overhead compartment and moving down the slim aisle with a serious effort. Self-disgust billowed off to the side and let rage take its turn. That fucker. She was crying to that fucker about something he did, and it was unbearable. It was goddamn unbearable knowing that. Only *that* guy wasn't the fucker. Same with Johnny Jerk Off who'd taken her to the poetry reading. It had been *him* all along.

When one of the flight attendants gave him a concerned look, he reined in the thoughts that were obviously showing on his face. He needed to focus. Just focus on getting to the dean's office and making sure his screw-up didn't have a lifelong consequence for

Honey. Then he would go home. And that was all he had. Did something exist beyond today if he didn't have *her* to look forward to? No more of her thoughts. No more of those golden eyes to devastate him, or burying himself in her body. What did it matter what he did or where he went if he couldn't have those things? If he couldn't have Honey.

Ben walked through the airport, feeling as though some cosmic Fast Forward button had been hit, affecting everyone but him. He was in slow motion while people zipped past and announcements came from overhead that were impossible to focus on. A low buzz had started in the back of his head, growing louder as he reached the exit. He saw Russell waiting at the curb, leaning against his company truck, complete with the Hart Brothers Construction logo, but Ben couldn't lift his hand in greeting or even acknowledge him. Russell didn't make his usual joke, thankfully, simply giving Ben a nod and returning to the driver's side. Ben stowed his carry-on in the backseat and got into the car, painfully aware that leaving the airport meant he was going even further from Honey. Severing one more connection.

"Where we headed?" Russell asked, starting up the truck.

Ben hadn't told Russell the full story of what happened with Honey. He wasn't ready to say the words out loud yet. Maybe ever. Anyway, he suspected the news had already reached Russell through the super group pipeline. Thankfully, his friend left it alone, simply taking the directions Ben gave him to the administration building at Columbia. As they got closer, something inside him started to coil tight. His skin felt stretched, his muscles strained. The buzzing in the back of his head moved to the front, and no amount of ordering himself to relax helped.

"We need to make a stop first," he said to Russell. At his direction, Russell drove past the administration building and pulled up outside the English department building. "Wait here."

"You sure you don't want some company?" Russell scratched the back of his neck. "Don't take this the wrong way, but you look like the poster for every revenge movie ever released."

Ben gripped the door handle. "That's not completely inaccurate, but I'm going alone."

"They *always* say that in revenge movies." Russell sighed when Ben responded by pushing open the truck door. "I'll wait here. Like the fifth-billed lackey in the film."

Before he shut the door, Ben paused. "Why aren't you giving me a hard time? You know what happened. How much of a shit swamp I've landed her in. Otherwise, you'd have asked me."

Russell looked away. "You're giving yourself a hard enough time for the both of us." He cleared his throat, fingers drumming on the steering wheel. "And anyway, fuck you for thinking I'd leave you hanging because of what happened with a girl. Louis wanted to be here, too, but the community center he was fighting to keep open had to close."

Ben absorbed that information, feeling a flash of sympathy for Louis and the kids that would have nowhere to go. But he didn't have the strength to carry anything else just then. "She's not just a girl."

"I get that." Russell looked thoughtful a moment. "Shit, I wish I didn't get that."

"Are you talking about Abby?" When Russell didn't answer, Ben didn't press. Not after the solid Russell had done him by keeping quiet about Honey. Just the thought of her name propelled him from the car toward the English building. He knew where Peter would be at this time of day because he'd just finished covering one of Ben's lectures. Normally, Ben would be horrified by the idea of walking into this building without wearing his work clothes and jacket, but today he didn't give a single fuck. His hair was wild on top of his head, his jeans were creased and dusty. His T-shirt smelled like cinnamon and sugar, so he inhaled deeply as students he recognized as his own stopped to gape at him.

The door of the faculty lounge came into view, and Ben's pace picked up. He'd managed to lower the dimmer switch on his anger until now, but just knowing he was about to see the son of a bitch's face sent it into full wattage. Without breaking his stride, Ben yanked the door open and strode inside. Peter stood on the opposite side of the room, sipping coffee and reading through a lesson plan. *Ben's* lesson plan.

Peter turned at Ben's entrance and lifted an eyebrow. "Hey, Ben. You're back? What's up with the outfit—"

"Go fuck yourself."

The other three professors in the room stood and left. Ben briefly wondered if they'd thought he'd meant *they* should go fuck themselves, but he flicked the thought aside. He had more important things to worry about, namely Peter, who was staring at him as if he'd just sprouted horns. "What's going on with you, Ben? You take off unexpectedly. Now you show up looking like you just woke up after a bender."

Funny, that was exactly how he felt. Like he'd woken up from the best damn dream of his life and had no way of falling back to sleep to finish it. "Why did you do it?"

"Do what?"

Ben ground his molars together. "You sent my letter to Dean Mahoney. About Hon—Ms. Perribow." He pointed to the notebook lying on the counter, way too close to the coffeemaker. "You're the only one who had access to it. I want to know *why*."

"I thought you wanted me to." Peter threw up his hands, cursing when he splashed coffee on his jacket sleeve. "I saw the letter and thought maybe you hadn't quite worked up the nerve to do it yourself. So I sent it in. I did you a *favor*."

Ben had rounded a lunch table and advanced on Peter before he realized his feet were moving. His blood roared in his ears. No way. No way had he lost Honey over some stupid misunderstanding. Fate couldn't be that cruel. But no. He'd written the letter either way, hadn't he? He was just as much to blame here as Peter. It didn't lessen the driving need to fix this for her, though. "You didn't do me a favor, Peter," Ben grated, barely holding on to the urge to punch the other man. "You did me the opposite of a favor, multiplied by one fucking thousand. Okay? In the process, your taking the matter into your own hands might have cost a brilliant student her education. What the hell is wrong with you?"

It finally seemed to dawn on Peter that his actions might have had dire consequences. "So, you're not grateful I sent in the letter?" Or maybe not.

"*No.* I'm not grateful." Ben scrubbed his hands down his face, briefly upsetting his glasses. His chest hurt. Everything hurt.

Nothing felt right, and he just wanted to be back, lying in that baseball field, dammit. He swallowed the massive knot in his throat. "I have a meeting with the dean in fifteen minutes. You're coming with me."

ONCE, DURING HIS parents' messy divorce, Ben had acted out in school. A fellow third-grader had made a comment during recess about his father—his father who'd spent the week being crucified by the media—and Ben had slugged him. He could feel the crunch of nose cartilage under his fist. Could still remember how damn good it had felt to release frustration. Inflict pain on someone or something besides himself or his mother. Even sitting in the principal's office afterward had been worth it. His bruised knuckles had felt like a badge of honor.

This? This was nothing like that. Ben and Peter sat across from Dean Mahoney in silence as he read the letter—the fucking letter Ben wanted to burn and stomp on—what appeared to be several times, while not-so-inconspicuously checking out his refelctive head in his computer screen. Time stretched, and Peter began to crack his knuckles, sending Ben a little closer to the edge. How close could he get before he went over?

Finally, the dean set down the letter and leaned back in his chair. "Professor Dawson, you're telling me this letter was turned in by mistake, and I understand that." He nodded at Peter. "Signing a colleague's name is not a wise practice, either, whether or not you believe you're helping the situation." His sharp gaze swung back toward Ben. "But you clearly wrote it, Professor Dawson. Did you not? These accusations are yours."

"I did write it." An image of Honey's stricken face forced him to pause. "But it was a mistake. Ms. Perribow has done nothing wrong." *Nothing about our time together was wrong. None of it. Except the fact that it's over.* "If Peter thinks the student pursued me inappropriately, he was wrong, too." Ben might have paid lip service to pushing Honey away, but he'd encouraged her in ways that counted. This belonged to both of them.

"Is that possible, Peter?"

Ben ground his teeth together when Peter shrugged. "I don't know. Maybe?"

Dean Mahoney sighed, picked up the letter again. "I like you, Professor Dawson. Your end-of-semester evaluations were the highest in the department. You have the fewest number of drops. I think you take the job seriously, as you should, and we need the new blood around here." He shook his head, nearly blinding Ben as the fluorescent light glinted off its shiny surface. "But I can't ignore this. Especially in the wake of Ms. Perribow missing classes over the last week. Where there's smoke, there's fire. It speaks of a young girl trying to get your attention, as the letter you wrote implies. I appreciate you not wanting to cost a student her education, but I can't ignore evidence when it's right in my hand. That would be remiss."

"I'm resigning." The words fell from his lips so easily. He'd only planned to transfer to NYU because of Honey, but now that it had come to this, he realized he would have done it anyway to protect her. To make things right, he would do *anything.* "If this is how Columbia treats their students, putting them on trial when they haven't even had a chance to defend themselves, this isn't the right place for me. Especially when they're lucky to have the student in question within their walls." He leveled the dean with a look. "Consider this my notice. I'll be leaving at the end of the semester."

"You can't be serious," Dean Mahoney said. "You're not being penalized here."

I should be. It should be me. Could he say what came next? It could backfire. It might not even work, but without the dean's agreement to reinstate Honey as a student and restore her financial aid, a noose was tightening around his neck. "I am serious." Ben leaned forward in his chair. "I'll miss a lot of things about this university. The traditions, the people. The *library*." And here Ben was, subtly insinuating that he had material with which to blackmail the dean of a major university. *No going back from here.* "Have you noticed how . . . polished . . . the floors are in the library, Dean Mahoney? I swear someone must stay after hours and *shine* them every single night." He dropped his gaze to the dean's gold wedding ring. "Miss Woodmere, perhaps?"

Dean Mahoney went so still that the only sign of movement was red creeping over his bald head. If a pin dropped, it would have sounded like a bomb going off in the office. Instead, Peter cracked his knuckles, making Dean Mahoney jump in his seat and upset a cup of Bic pens.

The older man's fingers moved over the keyboard of his computer. "I'll just take one more look at Ms. Perribow's file before I make a final decision."

Tension seeped from Ben's body, nearly causing him to fall off the damn chair, but right on its heels, the grief of losing Honey rushed back in where it belonged. He cleared his rusted throat. "Thank you. That's all I ask."

HONEY SAT ON the floor of her childhood bedroom, staring at the Dixie Chicks poster hanging over her desk. She could remember putting it up the morning after she returned from the concert with her mother. Placing the tape carefully along the edges and corners, positioning it perfectly before smoothing it down. Stepping back and admiring it, allowing herself to giggle, since no one was in the room with her.

There were memories overflowing in every room of this house. Comforting memories that she desperately needed right now, when she felt as if she'd crack down the middle if she moved. It didn't help that two days later, her lips were still swollen from kissing Ben in her baseball field. Every time she washed herself in the shower, the lingering twinge between her legs brought images to her mind that had no place around her broken heart. She didn't want to think about his breath rasping against her ear as he moved inside her. Or the way he tasted. The way he'd held her so tightly afterward.

No. She wanted to keep on hating him. Hating him gave her one more excuse to stay here indefinitely. Rolling around in her pile of fond memories and reliving the past. Every inch of this house, this town, her family was written on her soul. New York had only just started to creep in. She missed her roommates like hell and knew they were waiting to welcome her back. She'd gone there mostly for school, and now school wasn't an option. Ben had said he would fix what he'd done, but there was no guarantee it was possible. Even if he did work some kind of magic, did she *want* to go back?

Honey flopped onto her back. Adventure. The other reason she'd gone to New York. Wanting to live and have experiences no one else in her family could boast of. Look where it had landed her. Right back where she'd started. Only now it felt like she had a knife permanently stuck in her gut, courtesy of one gorgeous, complicated professor who'd finally overcome his writer's block in the form of a letter that slandered her character. God. *God*, it hurt to think about.

She'd tried out the big city, hadn't she? No one could accuse her of laziness or wasting her potential. There were colleges within driving distance of home where she could get the same quality education. Right?

Coward. You're running.

A knock on her door interrupted her pity party. "Honey?"

"Yeah, Mom?"

"Get on some pants if you need to. I'm coming in."

Honey sat up and pushed her hair out of her face. Her family had mostly left her alone since the scene with Ben. After her mother had patched up Elmer, he'd hung around on the porch for a while before taking the hint and leaving, too. She'd felt genuinely bad about that, since she was the reason he had a broken nose, but her own grief outweighed the politeness that had been instilled in her.

She put on what she hoped was a brave smile for her mother, who took a seat at the end of the bed. "How long are you planning on staying here?"

"Probably until dinnertime. Why? You need help peeling spuds?"

"No, I've got your brother doing it. His legs are broken, but his hands most certainly are not." Her mother leaned back on the bed. "And I wasn't talking about this room. I meant Bloomfield. How long are you planning on staying here?"

Honey dropped her gaze to the faded blue carpet. "Are you saying I've worn out my welcome?" She'd meant it as a joke, but when her mother stayed silent, her head came up. "Mom?"

"The dean called this morning. They've reinstated you as a student and restored your financial aid."

Every cell moving in her body screeched to a halt, leaving her light-headed. "H-how? Are you . . . sure?"

"I wouldn't tell you if I wasn't sure." Her mother watched her closely. "As for *how,* I think you know Ben had something to do with it."

"I don't want to talk about him," Honey wheezed. Just hearing his name spoken out loud felt like a sledgehammer being taken to her ribs. How long would it be like this? If she went back to New York, she'd hear his name all the time from her friends, Louis, Russell. Just another reason to stay put. He'd made everything right, just like he'd promised he would, but it didn't change anything. Didn't change the horrible, run-down way she was feeling.

"Well?" her mother prompted. "Why aren't you throwing clothes into your suitcase?"

Honey didn't have an answer for that, so she just stayed perfectly still. Same as she'd been doing all morning. If she rattled any of the checked emotions inside her, they would all bleed together and erupt out of her.

"All right, if you don't want to talk, you can just listen." Her mother tucked a stray hair back into her bun. "I never told you this, Honey, but I had my chance to get out of Bloomfield. Nothing so important as school, just a couple of my friends heading to Florida for the summer in a rusted orange VW van." She smiled, as if she could see it right in front of her. "I'll admit it. I was scared. Scared to miss something back home. Scared of the unknown. Everything you probably felt moving to New York City. The difference is, you did it."

"I'm here now, though, aren't I?" Honey forced past numb lips. "I didn't last."

"This ain't the same thing," her mother said. "You actually . . . went out and found a place to live, tried new restaurants, made friends. Things I could only dream about." A flush moved up her neck. "I waited too long to see the world. Made excuses to stay where I didn't have to try. And now I'm scared to visit my own daughter where she lives. Can you imagine that?"

Honey was shocked. "Scared? I don't understand."

"You shouldn't understand. This burden is mine to carry." Her mother looked up at the ceiling, and Honey suspected she was trying to keep tears from falling. "I don't regret a single second I spent here, raising you two kids, loving your father. But I should have gone to Florida in that stupid van for the summer. I should have seen something."

"You still can." Honey swiped at the moisture in her own eyes. "It's never too late."

"Well." Her mother humored her with a smile and fussed with the hem of her shirt. "Have you ever read that sealed letter I sent you off to college with?"

"No." Honey glanced at her backpack, propped in the corner. "I was saving it for a rainy day."

"This is as rainy as it gets, baby girl." Honey's mother stood to leave, but she stopped at the door with her hand on the knob. "I should hate Ben for making my daughter cry. Yes, I should. But I just can't, and I hope that doesn't make me a bad mother." She shook her head. "I just remember the way he looked at you, and I can't bring myself to hate someone who sees exactly what's there. Like he wouldn't change a single thing about you if he could."

It took Honey a moment to move after her mother closed the door behind her. The ache in her chest was too great, so overwhelming. Eventually, she gathered the willpower to crawl across the room and unzip her backpack, pulling out the sealed letter from her mother. She took a deep breath, turning it over in her palm, tapping it against her knee. Finally, she tore open the sealed edge. What she pulled out wasn't at all what she'd been expecting. She'd always thought she'd find a school-lunch-type note, something encouraging. Instead, she found postcards. From Florida. Dozens and dozens of them, sent from familiar names, friends her mother had had all her life.

Wish you were here. We went jet skiing today. . .

We can see the beach from our deck. It goes on forever. You should have come!

Honey couldn't keep the dam from breaking any longer. As tears blurred her vision, she recognized what her mother's intentions had been. In her own way, she was telling Honey not to give up. To go live her own life so she wouldn't have the same regrets later. It was damn effective, she'd give her mother that. She started to nestle down into the carpet, postcards spread out around her, but she caught sight of a framed picture on her wall and sat up again. Two men with grudging smiles flanking a much younger version of her at the diner as she sipped a chocolate milk shake. The day she'd negotiated the town's little league merger had always been so fresh in her mind, but it had been blurred by all the new. New days and nights and sounds and people. *Good,* new experiences. But she'd let the old slip away. Let herself forget that she wasn't the type of girl who laid curled up on her bedroom floor and forgot to get the hell up. Honey Perribow took what life offered and made it work for *her.* Nothing—especially not a man—was going to beat her or steal the new away. She'd been raised to fight for it.

Honey rose to her feet and turned in a circle, taking a long look at her bedroom, committing it to memory so she could draw from the strength she felt there if she ever needed it again. Then she pulled the diner photo off the wall and placed it carefully in her suitcase.

Time to go home.

Chapter 20

*H*oney had dropped his class.

Ben dropped into a wobbly chair at the Longshoreman, shaking his head when Russell started to pour him a beer from the frosty pitcher. "Water," he murmured instead. It wasn't what he wanted. He wanted to drown himself in every available liquor so he wouldn't have to remember what it felt like to stand in front of his class and not see her. But he needed to feel every ounce of agony, or he'd lose another connection to her. Being miserable because of Honey was better than not feeling anything, and that was exactly what excessive drinking would achieve.

They'd agreed back in Kentucky, before a fucking tornado had landed down in the middle of their happiness, that she would drop the class. That they would continue on as they had been, keeping a low profile around campus for the remaining months until he officially started at NYU. He wasn't deluded enough to think that was why she'd followed through. It had been three days since he'd left Kentucky and she still hadn't come back, even though they'd undone her expulsion and restored her scholarship. His efforts had come too late and hadn't been enough.

Louis walked into the bar still wearing his work suit and collapsed into the chair beside Russell, shoving his fingers through his hair. "Hey. I'm shitty company today. Pretend I'm not here."

Russell poured beer into a plastic cup and slid it in front of Louis. "Once again it appears I'm the glue holding this crew together." He threw them both a disgusted look. "Allow me to point out when all this bad shit started happening in your lives. When the girls showed up."

"Wrong." Louis held up a finger as he chugged the frothy drink. "Roxy has nothing to do with this. She's the best thing that ever happened anywhere in the world, and she's going to bear my children. Right after I convince her to move in with me." He gave Russell a pointed look. "This is work related."

"Don't spare any details," Ben said. "I need a distraction."

Louis heaved a sigh. "I'm trying to help those community center kids relocate elsewhere, but the city is reluctant to give them another lease, and private commercial spaces are too expensive." He tapped his empty cup against the table. "They're meeting at an outdoor park, but I can see the group starting to thin. They need more space. Resources. And there's nothing I can do."

"Sorry, man," Russell said. "Sometimes you can't fix something, no matter how hard you try."

"A sincere comment from Russell." Louis held his cup up to the light. "What is in this beer?"

"You know, there is such a thing as being *too* clever, Louis."

Ben needed them to keep this up. To keep talking so he could try and focus on the words. As soon as he walked out of here, he'd be back where he started, but for now the banter was dulling the rougher edges. For the last few weeks, he'd been a shitty friend, and they hadn't given up on him. So he would make an attempt to put his own motherfucker of a situation aside and return the favor. "You have something on your mind, Russell?"

A dark blond eyebrow went up. "What?"

Yeah, okay. That question had been pretty out of character for any of them. They tended to needle each other and drop personal information only when enough beer had been consumed to make talking about their feelings acceptable. They'd just gotten to the Longshoreman five minutes ago.

Ben pushed up his glasses and immediately thought of Honey saying she found that sexy. Jesus, he missed her. *Distract. Distract.* "Don't take this the wrong way," he said to Russell, "but you've been acting kind of . . . sensitive lately."

Russell split an incredulous look between them. "How am I not supposed to take that the wrong way?"

"He's right," Louis jumped in. "You've already got the shaved head, now you're channeling Gandhi in two ways. What gives, man?"

"It wouldn't have anything to do with Abby, would it?" Ben asked into his just-delivered water.

"Hey, just because you've both got your balls in a vise doesn't mean I do." When neither of them took the bait, Russell's big shoulders dipped, head falling forward. "It might, maybe, possibly have something to do with Abby. That's all you're getting from me, though."

"Oh, come on—"

"Fine. Twist my arm." Russell signaled the waitress for another pitcher of beer before delivering them both a stern look. "Nothing we say here leaves this table." Ben and Louis waved him on. Russell started to talk, but stopped. Then started again. "She's out of my league."

Louis's mouth dropped open. "Did you just admit that out loud?"

Ben shook his head. "Who are you anymore?"

"See, I knew you would react this way." Russell sprawled back in his chair. "I shouldn't have said anything."

Ben picked up a wadded-up napkin and threw it at him. "Keep going. Your pathetic condition is the only thing distracting me from mine."

"Oh, how comforting." Russell tugged at his collar. "Look, here's the bottom line. Abby is . . . she's . . ." He blew out a breath. "She's fucking *Abby*. Do you know how smart she is? Her mind is like one of those fancy calculators, but she doesn't want anyone to know because she thinks it makes them uncomfortable." His throat worked. "She's so smart and yet she thinks I want to be her friend. *Just* her friend. And you know what? I'm not going to shatter that illusion for her. I don't want to smash those rose-colored glasses. She's perfect and I'd only fuck that up, anyway. So I'm her friend. *Just* her friend."

In what world did Ben think this would distract him? His sympathy for his friend was in danger of being eclipsed by Honey. No, it was done. There she was, stunning him speechless with a smile, arms stretched out above her head in the grass. "You're right." His voice sounded dull to his own ears. "If I could go back and even have Honey as a student—*only*—I would do it. It would be painful, but I'd do it. So I could at least be near her, the way you can do with Abby." He cleared his throat. "It's like she doesn't exist for me anymore. It's worse. So much worse. You're doing the right thing."

"*What*? What the—" Louis sputtered. "No. *No.* You are both fired. I wasn't supposed to tell you this, Ben, because there's this little thing called boyfriend-girlfriend privilege, which is apparently just as binding as attorney-client privilege—"

"The point," Ben muttered. "Get to it."

"Honey is in New York." Louis paused to let that sink in, but it didn't. Not right away, at least. It poked holes in him, head to toe, and let him bleed out onto the floor before rocketing straight to his gut. "She landed this afternoon," Louis continued. "Rox doesn't know if she's staying permanently or just collecting her things, but—"

"She needs to stay," Ben shouted, loud enough to make both of his friends jump.

Russell gestured at him with his beer. "Why, Ben? Why does Honey need to stay?"

For me. She needs to stay for me. Even if I don't see her, at least there will be a chance I might see her. At least I'll know she's there. Selfish, selfish thoughts. He couldn't be selfish anymore when it came to her. He'd done enough. "School, for one. She . . . she can't just start over somewhere else."

"Actually, she can." Louis lifted a dark eyebrow. "It's called a transfer."

"That's something a professor should probably know," Russell observed with a smirk.

Ben gave him a cursory middle finger. "What about her friends?"

"They'll miss her. A lot. But she can make more," Louis said, leaning forward. "Give her a fucking reason, Ben. She's five blocks from here, man. Go get her."

"You think it's that easy?" Ben's fist clenched with the need to hit the table. "This isn't like you and Roxy. I didn't just fuck up *once*. I had three strikes, and I used them all. One when I accused her of coming on to me for a better grade. Two when I showed up here with someone else. The letter makes three—" He shook his head. "I don't have any strikes left. The game's over."

"Far be it from me to knock a baseball reference, but—"

"Wait." Ben's hand came up to quiet Russell. An idea had just winged through the fog surrounding his brain. Dots were connecting, stars aligning. A weight pressed down on his chest as tiny squares sewed themselves together into a patchwork quilt. It could work. This idea. *This. Idea.* Not to get them back together. He wouldn't give himself a moment's hope she would ever let him hold her again. Touch her, kiss her. But he wouldn't be part of the reason she gave up and went home. No way. Never.

There might be a way, however, to keep her here. He thought back to her essays, the ones he'd read so many times the last three days that his vision had blurred. Above everything in this world, Honey valued being part of a team. Surrounding herself with people she could help. She loved her hometown so much because it was a community. *Her* community. Could he create that for her in New York City?

It was selfish to desire any kind of proximity to her, so that couldn't be why he pulled this idea together. It had to be for her. It *would* be for her. An apology. A solution. An expression of how he felt about her, if nothing else.

He looked between Louis and Russell. "I need your help."

"You've got it," they said at the same time.

Chapter 21

Where did you say we're going?"

Honey pulled her legs up onto the hard, plastic subway seat, unconcerned about taking up too much space, since she, Roxy, and Abby were the only souls left on the 7 train headed to Queens. Her roommates were behaving . . . strangely. To say the least.

"There's a new Mexican place we want to try," Roxy said without skipping a beat. "Abby had a craving for an enchilada."

Abby gave her a serious look. "And guacamole."

Honey played with the zipper of her leather boot. "We can't get that in Manhattan?"

"Where's your sense of spontaneity?" Abby asked her. "We had to learn to fend for ourselves when you left. Procure our own meals. There was a few minutes there where I didn't think I was going to make it."

"You've turned us into major food snobs. Look at us. One week without your cooking and we're riding an hour on the train to get decent Mexican food." Roxy made a sound of disgust. "I used to eat all my meals from food trucks."

"*Maybe*," Honey drew out the word, "if you hadn't hidden my cooking utensils, I could have made us enchiladas from scratch."

"No idea what you're talking about," Roxy said.

Abby, avoiding all eye contact, started to whistle.

Honey gave them both the stink eye. She'd been back in New York for three days, and slowly but surely, her possessions had started to disappear. One morning, she'd woken up and reached for her phone on the nightstand to find it gone. A search of the apartment had yielded no results. Then her favorite pair of Converse had vanished from her closet without a trace. When she'd asked Abby if she'd seen them, the leggy brunette had shoved a Saltine cracker into her mouth and given a helpless shrug.

At first, Honey thought maybe she'd been imagining their twitchy behavior whenever she walked into the room, but this afternoon had confirmed her suspicions. When she'd returned home from a meeting with her counselor at Columbia, they'd been lying in wait for her in the living room. Roxy had thrown her worn-in jean jacket at her and hustled her out the door, each of them sending what they thought were discreet text messages at their sides. Honey had an apprehensive feeling about this little adventure, but she was going along with it because she felt guilty.

Despite her assurances, they expected her to fly back to Kentucky at any second. If she'd been able to maintain an upbeat attitude, she might have convinced them to the contrary, but Ben was still there, blocking the positivity trying to push its way through. Returning to New York, going back to school, had clobbered her in memories, but she was working her way through it.

Abby and Roxy seemed to sense that, so they hadn't pressured her to talk, choosing instead to hoard her possessions so she couldn't leave. She kind of loved them for that. She owed them the truth, too, but when she started talking, Ben would appear, and that sealed bottle of emotions would shatter at her feet. He was already there every time she blinked or managed to fall asleep, and maintaining her sanity meant keeping the memory of him in check during daylight hours. Not that she was even remotely pulling it off.

The subway doors rolled open, and still neither Abby nor Roxy made a move to get off.

"Okay, are we going to Queens or Mexico for this Mexican food?"

Abby's whistle turned into a giggle. "One more stop. Right, Roxy?"

Roxy eyeballed her phone. "I think so . . ."

"Okay, you two." Honey couldn't take the mysterious behavior anymore. When she thought of what could potentially lay on the other side of this subway ride, she started to panic. "I'm just going to come right out and ask. Does this little trip have something to do with Ben? Is he . . . going to be there?" She swallowed hard. "Because—"

"Honey." Abby looked affronted. "Do you really think we'd blindside you like that? He won't be there."

"Good." Oh, the sweeping disappointment she felt was so obnoxious and unwanted. "I just had to check. You guys have been acting weird since I got back."

"We wouldn't let that jerk near you." Roxy's expression was blank. "Not after what he did."

"Yeah," Abby said, once again refusing to meet Honey's gaze. "I hope we never have to see him again."

Indignation had the back of Honey's neck turning red. It was all well and good for her to mentally refer to Ben as a jerk, but quite another for her friends to say it out loud. *Keep your mouth shut. Don't say anything.* "Well, I wouldn't go that far, Abby." Honey's knee started to bounce. "You'll have to see him some-time. He's part of the super group."

"Nope." Roxy pursed her lips. "I told Louis that Ben was no longer welcome."

"*What?*" Honey shot forward on the seat. "He—that's—not exactly fair. I mean . . . he only wrote the letter because he was scared. You don't know everything that happened with his father. He had his reasons. For everything."

Abby inspected her nails. "Not good enough. There's no excuse for him hurting you."

"I hurt him, too," Honey whispered, but it got lost in the hum of the train, so she said it louder. "I hurt him, too." The way he'd looked at her as she'd ordered him into the cab—completely devastated—came crashing down on her, and suddenly the subway car felt too close, stifling. It became difficult to inhale, as though someone had laid a metal plate down on top of her lungs. This was why she'd sealed everything up, because now the contents whooshed out and surrounded her on all sides. Honey looked up at her roommates. They were both staring back at her sympathetically. Holy shit, she'd walked right into an interven-tion. A *Ben*tervention.

"Well played," she murmured shakily, just in time for the subway doors to slide open. Roxy and Abby each grabbed one of her hands and tugged her off the train. She stayed lost in her own thoughts as they descended the stairs of the elevated train station and headed down a busy avenue.

Was she in the wrong here? Staying away from Ben had seemed like the best way to mend her heart, but every moment she spent away from him ruptured it a little more. Was he going through the same thing? Suddenly, she resented the fact that she'd been brought all the way to Queens. Not that she would go to Ben if she were in Manhattan, but at least she'd know he was close by.

"Guys, I think I'm going to head back." As soon as she said it, she felt better. With every stop on the way back to Manhattan, she'd be closer to him. Too bad her friends shook their heads adamantly and continued to pull her down the avenue, turning into a side street after a few blocks. The sound of the rumbling train overhead and honking cars faded, and she could see the East River in the distance. Warehouses lined the block, but she could see a park up ahead. Or a field of some kind. Where were they taking her?

When they reached the field, Honey felt a small flutter in her throat. Not just any field. A baseball field. Roxy and Abby remained closemouthed as they pushed through a rusted metal gate and urged her inside. They got as far as the pitcher's mound when Louis walked out of the dugout, carrying a mesh bag full of bats and baseball helmets. Honey could only watch in confusion as several kids, a variety of ages, followed him onto the field. Russell brought up the rear, tossing a baseball up in the air and catching it with his mitt, two smaller boys hanging off each of his shoulders.

"They need a place to play ball, Honey," Louis called as he set the bag down near home plate. "What do you think? Can they play here?"

She shook her head slowly, at a complete loss as to what was happening. "Why are you asking *me*?"

Abby slipped an envelope into her hand. "Because it's your field."

"What?" She croaked the word, her pulse speeding to a frantic pace. This had to be a crazy dream. Yet she could feel the slope of the mound beneath her feet, the cool wind off the river. When Roxy nudged the envelope, Honey willed her fingers to open it. She tugged out a long yellow piece of paper. A deed? It had her name on it, though. That couldn't be right. "I don't understand."

"There's a letter in there, too," Abby said. "Read it."

Jogging off to join the guys, her friends left her standing dumbfounded on the pitcher's mound. Honey reached back into the envelope and found a folded piece of notebook paper, the edges torn neatly off. Her fingers felt numb as she unfolded it and started to read.

What I Should Have Written by Ben Dawson

Dean Mahoney,

There is this girl in my class. This brave, intelligent, golden-eyed girl who glows so brightly that once I saw her, I never had a chance. I'm being paid to teach her, when it should be the opposite. I've learned through her that we're not the past that made us but the choices we make. I've learned what it means to forgive and be forgiven. I've learned what it's like to live in the sun. Unfortunately, I hurt her in the process of learning those things, and now she's gone. Once you've lived in the sun, anything else feels desolate. My hope is that she can live in it now for the both of us.

I fell in love with this girl in my class. I could have met her anywhere and I would have loved her. On a ship, passing her on Fifth Avenue, across a busy restaurant. She would have been loved by me in all those places. Any place I'm in for the rest of my life, wherever I'm standing, I will be standing there loving her. Because while I don't deserve her love, she deserves mine, and she has every ounce of it.

I bought this girl a baseball field. She let me live in the sun for a while, and this is my attempt to return the favor, though it doesn't compare. It took me some time to figure out what she missed back home that New York couldn't offer. This girl needs to be needed. She cooks for the friends she loves, she farms for her family. She studies to become a doctor to mend their pain. Perhaps it took me so long to figure it out because I was busy needing her, too. Now these lucky kids get to live in the sun with her.

This girl is Honey Perribow, and she's extraordinary.

Sincerely,
Professor Ben Dawson

Ben watched Honey through the chain-link fence, his fingers curled around the metal. Oh God, she looked gorgeous, but more fragile than usual. Eyes tired, skin pale. He wanted to press his lips to all of her, warm her, but he wouldn't. Couldn't. He'd told himself he would come and make sure she received his gift, but that was all he would allow. If he went in there now, she might feel obligated to give him another chance, and that was not what this was about. This was atonement. It was giving her a reason to stay where she was loved. Knowing this city for the good in it, not the bad. Not what he'd done.

His mother had been shocked when he'd called to let her know he'd be withdrawing his portion of the money from the bank. It would have sat there forever if he hadn't thought of the one use for it he could tolerate. It was kind of a relief, not having it there, actually. He hadn't even realized how the very idea of such an excessive amount of money had been hanging over his head, taunting him. He'd always viewed the funds as tainted, but with the purchase of the ball field, he'd converted it. Made it new, he hoped.

Honey's blond hair was whipping around her in the wind, obscuring the side of her face from his view on the sidewalk. Knowing she was reading his words made him ache everywhere, head to toe. Maybe it had been selfish of him to tell her he loved her, but there had been no help for it. The words had poured out onto the page, as if they'd been clamoring to get out. So now she knew. There was something freeing about having it out in the open, even if it made being without her somehow worse.

She swayed a little on the pitcher's mound, and he shot forward on instinct, rattling the gate by accident. Honey's head whipped around, and they locked eyes. His heart sped up . . . then dropped to his stomach. She looked . . . *miserable*. Jesus, had he been all wrong about this? Maybe he'd been presumptuous. Why would she want a single damn thing from the fucker who'd hurt her in the first place? Maybe she'd mentally moved on and he was dragging her back.

Ben backed away from the gate. This is why he shouldn't have come. Should have left her with the gift and stayed away. Taking one last memorizing look at her, he turned and walked briskly toward the subway. He'd almost made it to the end of the block when he heard her.

"*Ben.*"

Damn. It felt painfully good to hear her say his name. It meant he was still in her consciousness, if nowhere else. He knew he should keep walking, let her off the hook from having to thank him, or, worse, making an attempt at friendship. They would never be friends. Not now, when he knew what it felt like to have it all. But he couldn't leave her there on the sidewalk, calling after him. His entire being rebelled against it, so he turned around.

She was running, blond hair flying out behind her. So god-damn beautiful he cursed under his breath. For a split second, he let himself imagine Honey throwing herself into his arms, but when she skidded to a stop a few yards away, the fantasy popped like a balloon over his head.

A sound of anguish fell from her mouth. "Where are you going?"

It took him a moment to speak. He hadn't expected to have her this close ever again. "Home."

"*Home.*" Her lips trembled. "I don't even know where you live. I hate that."

Something akin to hope flared to life in his stomach, but he doused it. "I hate it, too."

Her eyes were bright with tears. "You bought me a baseball field."

"Yeah."

"I don't want it." Ben fell back a step on the sidewalk, positive no one could survive that kind of pain, but she followed him. And she kept coming. "Not without you, Ben. I don't want it without you." She wrapped her arms around him, followed by her legs, and then he had her full weight against his body and it was so fucking intoxicating it took all his willpower to stay standing. Her curves found his muscle and they reacquainted themselves, interlocking like they'd never been apart. He could feel her fingers in his hair, her lips kissing his cheek, his neck, and he could only stand there, stunned and grateful. "I'm sorry. I'm so sorry," she sobbed. "I shouldn't have made you leave. I should have understood."

"No," he breathed into her hair, finally allowing his arms to wrap around her. Oh, God. It felt like everything good in the world was concentrated right where they were pressed together. "You're not sorry. I can't handle you being sorry."

"No?" She pulled back to swipe at her eyes. "Can you handle me loving you? Because I do. I love you so much, Ben." When his head dropped forward into her neck, a watery laugh bubbled from her lips. "Not because you bought me a baseball field, even if it's the best—*the best*—gift I'll ever get for the rest of my life. *Thank you*." She slid her fingers into his hair. "I love you for knowing what I needed even when I didn't. For stealing my alarm clock. Learning how to work the damn tractor. So many reasons. If you still need me, too, you have me. You never stopped having me."

Ben was pretty sure he would never breathe again, but he forced oxygen into his lungs. "*If* I need you?" He gave her a hard kiss. "Honey, I don't need anything else."

She opened her mouth for his kiss, tongues sliding together, drawing groans from both of them. "Later, you're going to take me home and show me where you live. Where you sleep." Her lips edged into a smile. "But first, we've got a baseball game to win."

As he carried her down the sidewalk toward the field, they were greeted by loud, noisy cheers from their friends. Ben could barely hear it over the pounding of his heart.

Don't miss the other books in the
Broke and Beautiful series . . .

Chase Me and Make Me

The full series is available now wherever books are sold.

And keep an eye out for the next book from
#1 *New York Times* bestselling author Tessa Bailey . . .

Wreck the Halls

Coming October 2023
Read on for a sneak peek at this fun,
spicy holiday rom-com!

Prologue

2009

*T*he second Beat Dawkins entered the television studio, it stopped raining outside.

Sunshine tumbled in through the open door, wreathing him in a halo of glory, pedestrians retracting their umbrellas and tipping their hats in gratitude.

Across the room, Melody witnessed Beat's arrival the way an astronomer might observe a once-in-a-millennium asteroid streaking across the sky. Her hormones activated, testing the forgiveness of her powder-fresh-scented Lady Speed Stick. She'd only gotten braces two days earlier. Now those metal wires felt like train tracks in her mouth. Especially while watching Beat breeze with such effortless grace into the downtown studio where they would be shooting interviews for the documentary.

At age sixteen, Melody was in the middle of an awkward phase—to put it mildly. Sweat was an uncontrollable entity. She didn't know how to smile anymore without looking like a constipated gargoyle. Her milk chocolate mane had been carefully styled for this afternoon, but her hair couldn't be tricked into forgetting about the humidity currently plaguing New York, and now it was frizzing to really *accentuate* the rubber bands connecting her incisors.

Then there was Beat.

Utterly, effortlessly gorgeous.

His chestnut-colored hair was damp from the rain, his light blue eyes sparkling with mirth. Someone handed him a towel as soon as he crossed the threshold and he took it without looking, rubbing it over his locks and leaving them wild, standing on end, amusing everyone in the room. A woman in a headset ran a lint brush down the arm of his indigo suit and he gave her a grateful, winning smile, visibly flustering her.

How could she herself and this boy possibly be the same age?

Not only that, but they'd also been named by their mothers as perfect complements to each other. Beat and Melody. They were the offspring of America's most legendary female rock duo, Steel Birds. Since the band had already broken up by the time Beat and Melody were born, their names were bestowed quite by accident, without the members consulting each other. Decidedly *not* the happiest of coincidences. Not to mention, children of legends with significant names were supposed to be interesting. Remarkable.

Obviously, Beat was the only one who was meeting expectations.

Unless you counted the fact that she'd chosen teal rubber bands.

Which had seemed a lot more daring in the sterility of the orthodontist's office.

"Melody," someone called to her right. The simple act of having her name shouted across the busy room caused Mel to be *bathed in fire*, but okay. Now the backs of her knees were sweating—and oh God, *Beat was looking at her.*

Time froze.

They'd never actually met before.

Every article about their mothers and the highly publicized band breakup in 1993 mentioned Beat and Melody in the same breath, but they were locking eyes for the very first time IRL. She needed to think of something interesting to say.

I was going to go with clear rubber bands, but teal felt more punk rock.

Sure. Maybe she could cap that statement off with some finger guns and really drive home the fact that he'd gotten all the cool rock royalty genes. Oh God, her feet were sweating now. Her sandals were going to squeak when she walked.

"Melody!" called the voice again.

She tore her attention off the godlike vision that was Beat Dawkins to find the producer waving her into one of the cordoned-off interview suites. Just inside the door was a camera, a giant boom mic, a director's chair. The interview about her mother's career hadn't even started yet and she already knew the questions she would be answering. Maybe she could just pop in very quickly, recite her usual responses, and save everyone some time?

No, I can't sing like my mother.

We don't talk about the band breakup.

Yes, my mother is currently a nudist and yes, I've seen her naked a startling number of times.

Of course, it would be amazing for fans if Steel Birds reunited.

No, it will never happen. Not in a million, trillion years. Sorry.

"We're ready for you," sang the producer, tapping her wrist.

Melody nodded, flushing hotter at the suggestion she was holding things up. "Coming."

She snuck one final glance at Beat and walked in the direction of her interview room. That was it, she guessed. She'd probably never see him in person again—

"Wait!"

One word from Beat and the humming studio quieted, ground to a halt.

The prince had spoken.

Melody stopped with one foot poised in the air, turning her head slowly. *Please let him be talking to me*, otherwise the fact that she'd stopped at his command would be a pitiful mistake. Also, *please let him be talking to someone else.* The train tracks in her mouth were approximately four hundred pounds per inch, the teal dress she'd worn—oh God—to match her rubber bands, didn't fit right in the boob region. Other girls her age managed to look normal. *Good*, even.

What was it *TMZ* had said about her?

Melody Gallard: always a before picture, never an after.

Beat *was* talking to her, however.

Not only that, but he was also jogging over in this athletic, effortless way, the way a celebrity might approach the mound at a baseball game to throw out the ceremonial first pitch, the crowd cheering him on. His hair had arranged itself back to a perfect coif, no evidence of the rain she could see, his mouth in a bemused half smile.

Beat slowed to a stop in front of her, rubbing at the back of his neck and glancing around at their rapt audience, as if he'd acted without thinking and was now bashful about it. And the fact that he could be shy or self-conscious with charisma pouring out of his eyeballs was astounding. Who *was* this creature? How could they possibly share a connection?

"Hey," he breathed, coming in closer than Melody expected, that one move making them coconspirators. He wasn't overly tall, maybe five eleven, but her eyes were level with his chin. His sculpted, clean-shaven chin. Wow, he smelled so good. Like a freshly laundered blanket with some fireplace smoke clinging to it. Maybe she should switch from powder fresh Speed Stick to something a little more mature. Like ocean surf. "Hey, Mel. Can I call you that?"

No one had ever shortened her name before. Not her mother, classmates, or any of the nannies she'd had over the years. A nickname was something that should be attained over time, after a long acquaintance with someone, but Beat calling her Mel somehow seemed totally normal. Their names were counterparts, after all. They'd been named as a pair, whether it had been intentional or not.

"Sure," she whispered, trying not to stare at his throat. Or inhale him. "You can call me Mel."

Was this her first crush? Was it supposed to happen this fast? She usually found members of a different sex sort of . . .

uninspiring. They didn't make her pulse race, the way this one did. *Say something else before you bore him to death.*

"You stopped the rain," she blurted.

His eyebrows shot up. "What?"

I'm dissolving. I'm being absorbed by the floor. "When you walked in, the rain just . . . stopped." She snapped her fingers. "Like you'd turned it off with a switch."

When Melody was positive that he would cringe and make an excuse to walk away, Beat smiled instead. That lopsided one that made her feel funny *everywhere.* "I should have thought of switching it off before walking two blocks in a downpour." He laughed and exhaled at the same time, studying her face. "It's . . . crazy, right? Finally meeting?"

"Yeah." The word burst out of Melody and quite unexpectedly, her chest started to swell. "It's definitely crazy."

He nodded slowly, never taking his eyes off her face.

She'd heard of people like him.

People who could make you feel like you were the only one in the room. The world. She'd believed in the existence of such unicorns, she just never in her wildest dreams expected to be given the undivided attention of one. It was like bathing in the brightest of sunlight.

"If things had been different with our mothers, we probably would have grown up together," he said, blue eyes twinkling. "We might even be best friends."

"Oh," she said with a knowing look. "I don't think so."

His amusement only spread. "No?"

"I don't mean that to be offensive," Melody rushed to say. "I just . . . I tend to keep to myself, and you seem more . . ."

"Extroverted." He shrugged a single shoulder. "Yeah. I am." He waved a hand to indicate the room, the crew who were still captivated by the first—maybe only—meeting of Beat Dawkins and Melody Gallard. "You might think I'd be into this. Talking, being on camera." He lowered his voice to a whisper. "But it's always the same questions. Can you sing, too? Does your mother ever talk about the breakup?"

"Will there ever be a reunion?" Melody chimed in.

"Nope," they said at the same exact time—and laughed.

Beat eventually turned serious. "Look, I hope this isn't out of line, but I notice the way the tabloids treat you. Online and off. It's . . . different from how they treat me." Fire scaled the sides of her neck and gripped her ears. Of course he'd seen the cringe-inducing critiques of Melody. They were usually included in articles that profiled him, as well. The most recent one had whittled her entire existence down to the line, *In the case of Trina Gallard's daughter, the apple didn't just fall far from the tree, it's more of a lemon.* "I always wonder if it bothers you. Or if you're able to blow that bullshit off."

"Oh, I mean . . ." She laughed, too loudly, waved a hand on a floppy fist. "It's fine. People expect those gossip sites to be snarky. They're just doing their job."

He said nothing. Just watched her with a little wrinkle between his brows.

"I'm lying," she whisper-blurted. "It bothers me."

His perfect head tilted ever so slightly to one side. "Okay." He nodded, as if he'd made an important decision about something. "Okay."

"Okay what?"

"Nothing." His gaze ran a lap around her face. "You're not a lemon, by the way. Not even close." He squinted, but not enough to fully hide the twinkle. "More of a peach."

She swallowed the dreamy sigh that tried to escape. "Maybe so. Peaches do have pretty thin skin."

"Yeah, but they have a tough center."

Something grew and grew inside of Melody. Something she'd never felt before. A kinship, a bond, a connection. She couldn't come up with a word for it. Only knew that it seemed almost cosmic or preordained. And in that moment, for the first time in her life, she was angry with her mother for her part in breaking up the band. She could have known this boy sooner? Felt . . . *understood* sooner?

Someone in a headset approached Beat and tapped his shoulder. "We'd like to get the interview started, if you're ready?"

Unbelievably, he was still looking at Melody. "Yeah, sure."

Did he sound disappointed?

"I better go, too," Melody said, holding out her hand for a shake.

Beat studied her hand for several seconds, then gave her a narrow-eyed look—as if to say, *don't be silly*—and pulled her into the hug of a lifetime. The hug. Of a lifetime. In a millisecond, she was warm in the most pleasant, sweat-free way. All the way down to the soles of her feet. Light-headedness swept in. She'd not only been granted the honor of smelling this boy's perfect neck, he was encouraging her with a palm to the back of her head. He squeezed her close, before brushing his hand down the back of her hair. Just once. But it was the most beautiful sign of affection she'd ever been offered, and it wrote itself messily all over her heart.

"Hey." He pulled back with a serious expression, taking Melody by the shoulders. "Listen to me, Mel. You live here in New York, I live in LA. I don't know when I'll see you again, but . . . I guess it just feels important, like I need to tell you . . ." He frowned over his own discomposure, which she assumed was rarer than a solar eclipse. "What happened between our mothers has nothing to do with us. Okay? Nothing. If you ever need anything, or maybe you've been asked the same question forty million times and can't take it anymore, just remember that I understand." He shook his head. "We've got this big thing in common, you and me. We have a . . ."

"Bond?" she said breathlessly.

"*Yeah.*"

She could have wept all over him.

"We *do*," he continued, kissing her on the forehead hard and pulling Melody back into the second hug of a lifetime. "I'll find a way to get you my number, Peach. If you ever need anything, call me, okay?"

"Okay," she whispered, heart and hormones in a frenzy. He'd given her a *nickname*. She wrapped her arms around him and held tight, giving herself a full five seconds, before forcing herself to release Beat and step back. "Same for you." She struggled to keep her breathing at a normal pace. "Call me if you ever need someone who understands." The next part wouldn't stay tucked inside of her. "We can pretend we've been best friends all along."

To her relief, that lopsided smile was back. "It wouldn't be so hard, Mel."

A bell rang somewhere on the set, breaking the spell. Everyone flurried into motion around them. Beat was swept in one direction, Melody in the other. But her pulse didn't stop pounding for hours after their encounter.

True to his word, Beat found a way to provide her with his number, through an assistant at the end of her interview. She could never find the courage to use it, though. Not even on her most difficult days. And he never called her, either.

That was the beginning and the end of her fairy-tale association with Beat Dawkins.

Or so she thought.

Chapter 1

December 1
Present Day

*B*eat stood shivering on the sidewalk outside of his thirtieth birthday party.

At least, he assumed a party was waiting for him inside the restaurant. His friends had been acting mysterious for weeks. If he could only move his legs, he would walk inside and act surprised. He'd hug each of them in turn, like they deserved. Make them explain every step of the planning process and praise them for being so crafty. He'd be the ultimate friend.

And the ultimate fraud.

When the phone started vibrating again in his hand, his stomach gave an unholy churn, so intense he had to concentrate hard on breathing through it. A couple passed him on the sidewalk, shooting him some curious side-eye. He smiled at them in reassurance, but it felt weak, and they only walked faster. He looked down at his phone, already knowing an unknown caller would be displayed on the screen. Same as last time. And the time before.

Over a year and a half had passed since the last time his blackmailer had contacted him. He'd given the man the largest sum of money yet to go away and assumed the harassment was over. Beat was just beginning to feel normal again. Until the message he'd received tonight on the way to his own birthday party.

I'm feeling talkative, Beat. Like I need to get some things off my chest.

It was the same pattern as last time. The blackmailer contacted him out of the blue, no warning, and then immediately became persistent. His demands came on like a blitz, a symphony beginning in the middle of its crescendo. They left no room for negotiation, either. Or reasoning. It was a matter of giving this man what he wanted or having a secret exposed that could rock the very foundation of his family's world.

No big deal.

He took a deep breath, paced a short distance in the opposite direction of the restaurant. Then he hit call and lifted the phone to his ear.

His blackmailer answered on the first ring.

"Hello again, Beat."

A red-hot iron dropped in Beat's stomach.

Did the man's voice sound more on edge than previous years? Almost agitated?

"We agreed this was over," Beat said, his grip tight around the phone. "I was never supposed to hear from you again."

A raspy sigh filled the line. "The thing about the truth is, it never really goes away."

With those ominous words echoing in his ear, a sort of surreal calmness settled over Beat. It was one of those moments where he looked around and wondered what in the hell had led him to this time and place. Was he even standing here at all? Or was he trapped in an endless dream? Suddenly the familiar sights of Greenwich Street, only a few blocks from his office, looked like a movie set. Christmas lights in the shapes of bells and Santa heads and holly leaves hung from streetlights, and an early December cold snap that turned his breath to frostbitten mist in front of his face.

He was in Tribeca, close enough to the Financial District to see coworkers sharing sneaky cigarettes on the sidewalk after too much to drink, still dressed in their office attire at eight P.M. A rogue elf traipsed down the street yelling into his phone. A cab drove by slowly, wheels traveling over wet sludge from the brief afternoon snowfall, "Have a Holly Jolly Christmas" drifting out through the window.

"Beat." The voice in his ear brought him back to reality. "I'm going to need double the amount as last time."

Nausea lifted all the way to his throat, making his head feel light. "I can't do that. I don't personally have that kind of liquid cash and I will not touch the foundation money. This needs to be *over.*"

"Like I said—"

"The truth never goes away. I heard you."

Silence was heavy on the line. "I'm not sure I appreciate the way you're speaking to me, Beat. I have a story to tell. If you're not going to pay me to keep it to myself, I'll get what I need from *20/20* or *People* magazine. They'd love every salacious word."

And his parents would be ruined.

The truth would devastate his father.

His mother's sterling reputation would be blown to smithereens.

The public perception of Octavia Dawkins would nose-dive, and thirty years of the charitable work she'd done would mean nothing. There would only be the story.

There would only be the damning truth.

"Don't do that." Beat massaged the throbbing sensation between his eyes. "My parents don't deserve it."

"Oh, yeah? Well, I didn't deserve to be thrown out of the band, either." The man snorted. "Don't talk about shit you don't know, kid. You weren't there. Are you going to help me out or should I start making calls? You know, I've had this reality show producer contact me twice. Maybe she would be a good place to start."

The night air turned sharper in his lungs. "What producer? What's her name?"

Was it the same woman who'd been emailing and calling Beat for the last six months? Offering him an obscene sum of money to participate in a reality show about reuniting Steel Birds? He hadn't bothered returning any of the correspondence because he'd gotten so many similar offers over the years. The public demand for a reunion hadn't waned one iota since the nineties and now, thanks to one of the band's hits going viral decades after its release, the demand was suddenly more relevant than ever.

"Danielle something," said his blackmailer. "It doesn't matter. She's only one of my options."

"Right."

How much had she offered Beat? He didn't remember the exact amount. Only that she'd dangled a lot of money. Possibly seven figures.

"How do we make this stop once and for all?" Beat asked, feeling and sounding like a broken record. "How can I guarantee this is the last time?"

"You'll have to take my word for it."

Beat was already shaking his head. "I need something in writing."

"Not happening. It's my word or nothing. How long do you need to pull the money together?"

Goddammit. This was real. This was happening. *Again.*

The last year and a half had been nothing but a reprieve. Deep down, he'd known that, right? "I need some time. Until February, at least."

"You have until Christmas."

The jagged edge of panic slid into his chest. "That's less than a month away."

A humorless laugh crackled down the line. "If you can make your selfish cow of a mother look like a saint to the public, you can get me eight hundred thousand by the twenty-fifth."

"No, I can't," Beat said through his teeth. "It's impossible—"

"Do it or I talk."

The line went dead.

Beat stared down at the silent device for several seconds, trying to pull himself together. Text messages from his friends were piling up on the screen, asking him where he was. Why he was late for dinner. He should have been used to pretending everything was normal by now. He'd been doing it for five years, since the first time the blackmailer made contact. Smile. Listen intently. Be grateful. Be grateful at all times for what he had.

How much longer could he pull this off?

A couple of minutes later, he walked into a pitch-black party room.

The lights came on and a sea of smiling faces appeared, shouting, "*Surprise!*"

And even though his skin was as cold as ice beneath his suit, he staggered back with a dazed grin, laughing the way everyone would expect. Accepting hugs, backslaps, handshakes, and kisses on the cheeks.

Nothing is wrong.

I have it all under control.

Beat struggled through the inundation of stress and attempted to appreciate the good around him. The room full of people who had gathered in his honor. He owed them that after all the effort they'd clearly put in. One of the benefits of being born in December was Christmas-themed birthdays, and his friends had laid it on thick. White twinkling lights were wrapped around fresh garland and hanging from the rafters of the restaurant's banquet room. Poinsettias sprung from glowing vases. The scent of cinnamon and pine was heavy in the air and a fireplace roared in the far corner of the space. His friends, colleagues, and a smattering of cousins wore Santa hats.

As far as themes went, Christmas was the clear winner, and he couldn't complain. As far back as he could remember, it had been his favorite holiday. The time of year when he could sit still and wear pajamas all day and let his head clear. His family always kept it about the three of them, no outsiders, so he didn't have to be *on*. He could just be.

One of Beat's college buddies from NYU wrestled him into a playful headlock and he endured it, knowing the guy meant well. God, they all did. His friends weren't aware of the kind of strain he was under. If they did, they would probably try to help. But he couldn't allow that. Couldn't allow a single person to know the delicate reason why he was being blackmailed.

Or who was behind it.

Beat noticed everyone around him was laughing and he joined in, pretending he'd heard the joke, but his brain was working through furious rounds of math. Presenting and discarding solutions. Eight hundred thousand dollars. Double what he'd paid this man last time. Where would he come up with it? And what about next time? Would they venture into the millions?

"You didn't think we'd let your thirtieth pass without an obnoxious celebration, did you?" Vance said, elbowing him in the ribs. "You know us better than that."

"You're damn right I do." A glass of champagne appeared in Beat's hand. "What time is the clown arriving to make balloon animals?"

The group erupted into a disbelieving roar. "How the hell—"

"You ruined the surprise!"

"Like you said"—Beat saluted them, smiling until they all dropped the indignation and grinned back—"I know you."

They don't know you, though. Do they?

His smile faltered slightly, but he covered it up with a gulp of champagne, setting the empty glass down on the closest table, noting the peppermints strewn among the confetti. The paper pieces were in the shape of little B's. Pictures of Beat dotted the refreshment table in plastic holders. One of him jumping off a cliff in Costa Rica. Another one of him graduating in a cap and gown from business school. Yet another photo depicted him on-stage introducing his mother, world-famous Octavia Dawkins at a charity dinner he'd organized recently for her foundation. He was smiling in every single picture.

It was like looking at a stranger. He didn't even know that guy.

When he jumped off that cliff in Central America, he'd been in the middle of procuring funds to pay off the blackmailer the first time. Back when he could manage the sum. Fifty thousand here or there. Sure, it meant a little shuffling of his assets, but nothing he couldn't handle in the name of keeping his parents' names from being dragged through the mud.

He couldn't manage this much of a payoff alone. The foundation had more than enough money in its coffers, but it would be a cold day in hell before he stole from the charity he'd built with his mother. Not happening. That cash went to worthy causes. Well-deserved scholarships for performing arts students who couldn't afford the costs associated with training, education, and living expenses. That money did not go to blackmail.

So where would he get the funds?

Maybe a quick call to his accountant would calm his nerves. He'd invested in a few start-ups last year. Maybe he could pull those investments now? There had to be something.

There isn't, whispered a voice in the back of his head.

Feeling even more chilled than before, Beat forced a casual expression onto his face. "Excuse me for a few minutes, I just need to make a phone call."

"To whom?" Vance asked. "Everyone you know is in this room."

That was not true.

His parents weren't here.

But that's not who his mind immediately landed on—and it was ridiculous that he should still be thinking about Melody Gallard fourteen years after meeting her *one time*. He could still recall that afternoon so vividly, though. Her smile, the way she whisper-talked, as if she wasn't all that used to talking at all. The way she couldn't seem to look him in the eye, then all of a sudden she couldn't seem to look anywhere else. Neither had he.

And he'd hugged thousands of people in his life, but she was the only one he could still feel in his arms. They were meant to be friends. Unfortunately, he'd never called. She'd never used his number, either. Now it was too late. Still, when Vance said, *Everyone you know is in this room*, Beat thought of her right away.

It *felt* like he knew Melody—and she wasn't here.

She might know him the best out of everyone if he'd kept in touch.

"Maybe he needs to call a woman," someone sang from the other side of the group. "We know how Beat likes to keep his relationships private."

"When I find a woman who can survive my friends, I'll bring her around."

"Oh, come on."

"We'd be on our best behavior."

Beat raised a skeptical brow. "You don't have a best behavior."

Someone picked up a handful of B confetti and threw it at him. He flicked a piece off his shoulder without missing a beat, satisfied that he'd once again diverted their interest in his love life. He kept that private for good reason. "One phone call and I'll be back. Don't start the balloon animals without me. I'm going to see if the artist can create me a sense of privacy." He gave them all a grin to let them know he was joking. "It means a lot that you organized this party for me. Thank you. It's . . . everything a guy could hope for."

That sappy moment earned him a chorus of boos and several more tosses of confetti until he had to duck and cover his way out of the room. But as soon as he was outside, his smile slid away. Back on the sidewalk like before, he stood for a full minute looking down at the phone in his hand. He could call his accountant. It would be a waste, though. After five years of having the blackmailer on his back like a parasite, he'd wrung himself dry. There simply wasn't eight hundred thousand dollars to spare.

You know, I've had this reality show producer contact me twice.

Maybe she would be a good place to start.

His blackmailer's words came back to him. Danielle something. She'd contacted Beat, too. Had a popular network behind her, if Beat recalled correctly. His assistant usually dealt with inquiries pertaining to Steel Birds, but he'd forwarded this particular request to Beat because of the size of the offer and the producer's clout.

Instead of calling his accountant, he searched his inbox for the name Danielle—and he found the email after a little scrolling.

Dear Mr. Dawkins,

Allow me to introduce myself. I'm your ticket to becoming a household name.

Since Steel Birds broke up in ninety-three, the public has been desperate for a reunion of the women who not only cowrote some of the world's most beloved ballads, but inspired a movement. Empowered little girls to get out there, find a microphone, and express their discontent, no matter who it pissed off. I was one of those little girls.

You're a busy man, so let me be brief. I want to give the public the reunion we've been dreaming about since ninety-three. There are no better catalysts than the children of these legendary women to make this happen. It is my profound wish for you, Mr. Dawkins, and Melody Gallard to join forces to bring your parents back together.

The Applause Network is prepared to offer each of you a million dollars.

Sincerely,
Danielle Doolin

Beat dropped the phone to his thigh. Had he seriously only skimmed an email that passionate? He hadn't even made it to the middle the first time he'd seen the correspondence. That much was obvious, because he would have remembered the part about Melody. Every time someone mentioned her, he got a firm sock to the gut.

He was getting one now.

Beat had zero desire to be a household name. Never had, never would. He liked working behind the scenes at his mother's foundation. Giving the occasional speech or social media interview was necessary. Ever since "Rattle the Cage" had gone viral, the requests had been coming in by the mother lode, but remaining out of the limelight was preferable to him.

However.

A million dollars would solve his problem.

He needed to solve it. *Fast.*

And if—and it was a *huge* if—Beat agreed to the reality show, he'd need to talk to Melody first. They might have grown up in the same weird celebrity offspring limelight, but they'd gotten vastly different treatment from the press. He'd been praised as some kind of golden boy, while every single one of Melody's physical attributes had been dissected through paparazzi lenses—all when she was still a *minor*. He'd watched it from afar, horrified.

So much so that the first and only time they'd met, he'd been rocked by protectiveness so deep, he still felt it to this very day.

Was there any way to avoid bringing her back into the spotlight if he attempted to reunite Steel Birds? Or would she be dragged into the story, simply because of her connection to the band?

God, he didn't know. But there was no way in hell Beat would agree to anything unless Melody was okay with him stirring up this hornet's nest. He'd have to meet with her. In person. See her face and be positive she didn't have reservations.

Beat's pulse kicked into a gallop.

Fourteen years had passed and he'd thought of her . . . a weird amount. Wondering what she was doing, if she'd seen whatever latest television special was playing about their mothers, if she was happy. That last one plagued him the most. Was Melody happy? Was he?

Would everything be different if he'd just called her?

Beat pulled up the contact number for his accountant, but never hit call. Instead, he reopened the email from Danielle Doolin and tapped the cell number in her email signature, with no idea the kind of magic he was setting into motion.

Chapter 2

December 8

Melody stood at the top of the bocce ball court, the red wooden ball in hand.

This throw would determine whether her team won or lost.

How? How had the onus of demise or victory landed on her birdlike shoulders? Who'd overseen the lineup tonight? She was their weakest player. They usually buried her somewhere in the middle. Her heartbeat boomed so loudly, she could barely hear the *Elf* soundtrack pumping through the bar speakers, Zooey Deschanel's usually angelic voice hitting her ears more like a witch's cackle.

Her team stood at the sides of the lane, hands clasped together like it was the final point at Wimbledon or something, instead of the bocce bar league. This was low stakes, right? Her boss and best friend, Savelina, had *assured* her this was low stakes. Otherwise, Melody wouldn't have joined the team and put their success at high risk. She'd be at home watching some holiday baking championship on the Food Network in an adult onesie where she belonged.

"You can do it, Mel," Savelina shouted, followed by several cheers and whistles from her coworkers at the bookstore. She hadn't known them well in the beginning of the season, considering she worked in the basement restoring young adult books and almost never looked up from her task. But thanks to this semi-torturous bocce league, she'd gotten to know them a lot better. She *liked* them.

Oh, please God, grant me enough skill not to let them down.

Ha. If she didn't screw this up, it would be a miracle.

"Do you need a time-out?" asked her boss.

"What made you think that?" Melody shouted. "The fact that I'm frozen in fear?"

The sprinkle of laughter boosted her confidence a little, but not by much. And then she made the mistake of glancing backward over her shoulder and finding the entire Park Slope bar watching the final throw with bated breath. It was the equivalent of looking down at the ground while walking on a tightrope. Not that she'd ever experienced such a thing. The craziest risk she'd taken lately was hoop earrings. *Hoops!*

Now she was breathing so hard, her glasses were fogging up.

Was everyone looking at her butt?

They had to be. She looked at everyone's butts, even when she tried not to. What would make this crowd any different? Did they think her floor-length pleated skirt was a weird choice for bocce? Because it totally was.

"Mel!" Savelina gestured to the bocce lane with her pint of

beer. "We're going to run out of time. Just get the ball as close to the jack as possible. Slice of cake."

Easy for Savelina to say. She owned a bookstore and dressed like a stoned bohemian artist. She could pull off gladiator sandals and had a favorite brand of oolong tea. Of course she thought bocce was simple.

The crowd started cheering behind Melody in encouragement, which was honestly very nice. Brooklynites got a bad rap, but they were actually quite friendly as long as they were being offered drink specials and strangers regularly complimented their dogs.

"Okay! Okay, I'm going to do it."

Melody took a deep breath and rolled the red wooden ball across the hard-packed sand. It came to a stop at the farthest position possible from the jack. It wasn't even remotely close.

Their opponents cheered and clinked pint glasses, the home team bar heaving a collective sigh of disappointment. They probably thought an underdog-to-hero story was unfolding right in front of their eyes, but no. Not with Melody in the starring role.

Savelina approached with a sympathetic expression on her face, squeezing Mel's shoulder with an elegant hand. "We'll win the next one."

"We haven't won a game all season."

"Victory isn't always the point," her boss suggested. "It's trying in the first place."

"Thanks, Mom."

Savelina's tight, brown curls shook with laughter. "Two weeks from now, we have the final game of the season and I have a good feeling about it. We're going to head into Christmas fresh from a win and you're going to be a part of it."

Mel didn't hide her skepticism.

"Let me clarify," Savelina said. "You *must* be a part of it. We only have enough players if you show up. You're not taking off early to visit family or anything, are you?"

As a rare book restoration expert, Mel's work schedule was loose. She could take a project home with her, if needed, and her presence in the store largely depended on whether or not there was even a book that currently required tender loving care. "Uh, no." Mel forced a smile onto her face, even though a little dent formed in her heart. "No, I don't have any plans. My mother is . . . you know. She's doing her thing. I'm doing mine. But I'll see her in February on my birthday," she rushed to add.

"That's right. She always comes to New York for your birthday."

"Right."

Mel did the tight smile/nodding thing she always did when the conversation turned to her mother. Even the most well-intentioned people couldn't help but be openly curious about Trina Gallard. She was an international icon, after all. Savelina was more con-scientious than most when it came to giving Mel privacy, but the thirst for knowledge about the rock star inevitably bled through. Mel understood. She did.

She just didn't know enough about her mother to give anyone what they wanted.

That was the sad truth. Trina love-bombed her daughter once a year and once a year only. Like a one-night sold-out show at the

Garden that left her with a hangover and really expensive merch she never wore again.

Melody could see Savelina was losing the battle with the need to ask deeper questions about Trina, probably because it was the end of the night and she'd had six beers. So Mel grabbed her kelly green peacoat from where it hung on the closest stool, tugged it on around her shoulders, and looked for a way to excuse herself. "I'm going to settle my tab at the bar." She leaned in and planted a quick kiss on Savelina's expertly highlighted brown cheek. "I'll see you during the week?"

"Yeah!" Savelina said too quickly, hiding her obvious disappointment. "See you soon."

Briefly, Mel battled the urge to give her friend something, anything. Even Trina's favorite brand of cereal—Lucky Charms—but the information faltered on her tongue. It always did. Speaking with any kind of authority on her mother felt false when most days, it felt as though she barely knew the woman.

"Okay." Mel nodded, turned, and wove through some Friday night revelers toward the bar, apologizing to a few customers who'd witnessed her anticlimactic underdog story. Before she could reach the bar, she made sure Savelina wasn't watching, then veered toward the exit instead—because she didn't really have a bar tab to settle. Customers who recognized her as Trina Gallard's daughter had been sending her drinks all night. She'd had so many Shirley Temples she was going to be peeing grenadine for a week.

Cold winter air chilled her cheeks as soon as she stepped out onto the sidewalk.

The cheerful holiday music and energetic conversations grew muffled behind her as soon as the door snicked shut. Why did it always feel so good to leave somewhere?

Guilt poked holes in her gut. Didn't she *want* to have friends? Who didn't?

And why did she feel alone whether she was with people or not?

She turned around and looked back through the frosty glass, surveying the bargoers, the merry revelers, the quiet ones huddled in darkened nooks. So many kinds of people and they all seemed to have one thing in common. They enjoyed company. None of them appeared to be holding their breath until they could leave. They didn't seem to be pretending to be comfortable when in reality, they were stressing about every word out of their mouth and how they looked, whether or not people *liked* them. And if they did, was it because they were a celebrity's daughter, rather than because of their actual personality? Because of who Melody was?

Melody turned from the lively scene with a lump in her throat and started to walk up the incline of Union Street toward her apartment. Before she made it two steps, however, a woman shifted into the light several feet ahead of her. Melody stopped in her tracks. The stranger was so striking, her smile so confident, it was impossible to move forward without acknowledging her. She had dark blond hair that fell in perfect waves onto the shoulders of a very expensive looking overcoat. One that had tiny gold chains in weird places that served no function, just for the sake of fashion. Simply put, she was radiant and she didn't belong outside of a casual neighborhood bar.

"Miss Gallard?"

The woman knew her name? Had she been lying in wait for her? Not totally surprising, but it had been a long while since she'd encountered this kind of brazenness from a reporter.

"Excuse me," Melody said, hustling past her. "I'm not answering any questions about my mother—"

"I'm Danielle Doolin. You might recall some emails I sent you earlier this year? I'm a producer with the Applause Network."

Melody kept walking. "I get a lot of emails."

"Yes, I'm sure you do," said Danielle, falling into step beside her. Keeping pace, even though she was wearing three-inch heels, her footwear a stark contrast to Melody's flat ankle boots. "The public has a vested interest in you and your family."

"You realize I was never really given a choice about that."

"I do. During my brief phone call with Beat Dawkins, he expressed the same."

Melody's feet basically stopped working. The air inside of her lungs evaporated and she had no choice but to slow to a stop in the middle of the sidewalk. Beat Dawkins. She heard that name in her sleep, which was utterly ridiculous. The fact that she should still be fascinated by the man when they hadn't been in the same room in fourteen years made her cringe . . . but that was the *only* thing about Beat that made her cringe. The rest of her reactions to him could best be described as breathless, dreamlike, whimsical, and . . . sexual.

In her entire thirty-year existence, she'd never experienced attraction like she had to Beat Dawkins at age sixteen when she spent a mere five minutes in his presence. Since then her hormones could only be defined as lazy. Floating on a pool raft with a mai tai, rather than competing in a triathlon. She had the yoga pants of hormones. They were fine, they definitely *counted* as hormones, but they weren't worthy of a runway strut. Her lack of romantic aspirations was yet another reason she felt unmotivated to go out and make human connections. To be in big, social crowds where someone might show interest in her.

It was going to take something special to make her set down the mai tai and get off this raft—and so far, no one had been especially . . . rousing. A fourteen-year-old memory, though? Oh mama. It had the power to make her temperature peak. At one time it had, anyway. The recollection of her one and only encounter with Beat was growing grainy around the edges. Fading, much to her distress.

"Well." Danielle regarded Melody with open interest. "His name certainly got your attention, didn't it?"

Melody tried not to stumble over her words and failed, thanks to her tongue turning as useless as her feet. "I'm sorry, y-you'll have to refresh my memory. The emails you sent me were about . . . ?"

"Reuniting Steel Birds."

A laugh tumbled out of Melody, stirring the air with white vapor. "Wait. Beat took a phone call about *this*?" Baffled, she shook her head. "As far as I know, both of us have always maintained that a reunion is impossible. Like, on par with an Elvis comeback tour."

Danielle lifted an elegant shoulder and let it drop. "Stranger things have happened. Even Pink Floyd set aside their differences for Live 8 in 2005 and no one believed it was doable. A lot of time has passed since Steel Birds broke up. Hearts soften. Age gives a different perspective. Maybe Beat believes a reunion wouldn't be such an impossible feat after all."

It was humiliating how hard her heart was pounding in her chest. "Did . . . did he say that?"

Danielle blew air into one cheek. "He didn't *not* say it. But the fact that he contacted me about the reunion speaks for itself, right?"

Odd that Melody should feel a tad betrayed that he'd changed his position without consulting her. Why would he do that? He didn't owe her anything. Not a phone call. Nothing. "Wow." Melody cleared her throat. "You've caught me off guard."

"I apologize for that. You're very difficult to get in contact with. I had to dig quite a bit to find out where you worked. Then I saw a picture of your bocce team on the bookstore's Instagram. Thank goodness for location tags." Danielle gestured with a brisk, gloved hand to the general area. "I assure you, I wouldn't have ventured into Brooklyn in twenty-degree weather unless I had a potentially viable project on the table. One that, if done correctly, could be a cultural phenomenon. And it *would* be done correctly, because I would be overseeing production personally."

What was it like to be so confident? "I'm afraid to ask what this project entails."

"That's why I'm not going to tell you until we're in my nice, warm office with espresso and a selection of beignets in front of us."

Melody's stomach growled reluctantly. "Beignets, huh?"

"They piqued Beat's interest, as well."

"They did?" Melody's breathless tone hit her ears, cluing her in

Beat Dawkins was eons and galaxies out of her league. Not only was he blindingly gorgeous, but he had *presence*. He commanded rooms full of people to give speeches for his mother's foundation. She'd seen the pictures, the occasional Instagram reel. His grid was brimming with nonstop adventures. Equally glamorous friends were pouring out of his ears. He was loved and lusted after and . . . perfect.

Beat Dawkins was perfectly perfect.

And he'd taken her into consideration.

He'd thought of her.

This whole Steel Birds reunion idea would never fly—the feelings of betrayal between their mothers ran deeper than the Atlantic Ocean—but the fact that Beat had said her name out loud to this woman basically ensured another fourteen years of infatuation. *Sad, sad girl.*

"You mentioned money," Melody said offhandedly, mostly so it wouldn't seem her entire interest was Beat-related. "How much? Just out of curiosity."

"I'll tell you at the meeting." She smiled slyly. "It's a lot, Melody. Perhaps even by the standards of a famous rock star's daughter."

A lot of money. Even to her.

Despite her trepidation, Melody couldn't help but wonder . . . was it enough cash to make her financially independent? She'd been born into comfort. A nice town house, wonderful nannies, any material item she wanted, which had mainly turned out to be books and acne medication. Her mother's love and attention remained out of reach, however. Always had—and it was beginning to feel as though it always would.

Melody's brownstone apartment was paid in full. She had an annual allowance. Lately, though, accepting her mother's generosity didn't feel right. Or good. Not when they lacked the healthy mother-daughter relationship she would gladly take instead.

Could this be her chance to stand on her own two feet?

No. Facilitating a reunion? There had to be an easier way.

"At least take the meeting," Danielle said, smiling like the cat who'd caught the canary.

The woman had her and she knew it.

To be in the same room with Beat Dawkins again . . .

She wasn't strong enough to pass up the chance.

Melody shifted in her boots and tried not to sound too eager. "What time?"

About the Author

#1 *New York Times* bestselling author TESSA BAILEY can solve all problems except for her own, so she focuses those efforts on stubborn, fictional blue-collar men and loyal, lovable heroines. She lives on Long Island, avoiding the sun and social interactions, then wonders why no one has called. Dubbed the "Michelangelo of dirty talk" by *Entertainment Weekly*, Tessa writes with spice, spirit, swoon, and a guaranteed happily ever after. Catch her on TikTok @authortessabailey or check out tessabailey.com for a complete list of her books.

Normally, he was the type to stop and suffer through their silly questions with a golden grin. But this time, he didn't. He halted abruptly on the sidewalk and, to this day, she could still remember what came out of his mouth, word for word.

I'm done talking. You won't get another word out of me. Not until you—and all the similar outlets—stop exploiting girls for clicks. Especially my friend Melody Gallard. You praise me for nothing and disparage her no matter how hard she tries. You can fuck right off. Like I said, I'm done talking.

That day, Melody hadn't come out of the bathroom until third period, she'd been so frozen in shock and gratitude. Just to be seen. Just to have someone speak up on her behalf. That clip had been shared all over social media. For weeks. It had started a conversation about how teenage girls were being portrayed by celebrity news outlets.

Of course, their treatment of her didn't change overnight. But it slowly shifted. It lightened in degrees. Bad headlines started getting called out. Shamed.

And shockingly, her experience with the press got better.

Melody was so lost in the memory, it took her a moment to notice the smile flirting with the corners of Danielle's glossy mouth. "He's coming to my office on Monday morning for a meeting. I've come all the way here to invite you, as well." She paused, seemed to consider her next words carefully. "Beat won't agree to the reunion project unless *you* are comfortable with it moving forward. He made your approval a condition."

Melody hated the way her soul left her body at Danielle's words. It was pathetic in so many ways.

to what was happening. The tactic that was being employed. "You keep bringing him up on purpose."

Danielle studied her face closely. "He seems to be my biggest selling point. Even more than the money the network is willing to pay, I'm guessing," she murmured. "If I hadn't mentioned his name, you never would have stopped walking. Surprising, since the two of you haven't maintained any sort of contact. According to him."

"No, I know," Melody rushed to blurt, heat clinging to her face and the sides of her neck. "We don't even know each other."

And that was the God's honest truth.

Fourteen years had passed.

However. Beat was a good person. He'd proven that to her—and he couldn't have changed so drastically. The kind of character it took to do what he'd done . . .

About a month after they'd met in that humid television studio, she'd passed through the gates of her Manhattan private school, expecting to walk to class alone, as usual. But she'd been surrounded by buzzing girls that morning. Had she seen Beat Dawkins on *TMZ*?

Considering she avoided that program like the plague, she'd shaken her head. They'd cagily informed her that Beat had mentioned her during a paparazzi ambush and she might want to watch the footage. Getting through first period without exploding was nearly impossible, but she'd made it. Then she'd rushed to the bathroom and pulled up the clip on her phone. There was Beat, holding a grocery bag, a Dodgers ball cap pulled down low on his forehead, being pursued by a cameraman.

ALSO BY
Tom McCarthy

REMAINDER

A man is severely injured in a mysterious accident, receives an outrageous sum in legal compensation, and has no idea what to do with it. Then, one night, an ordinary sight sets off a series of bizarre visions he can't quite place. How he goes about bringing his visions to life—and what happens afterward—makes for one of the most riveting, complex, and unusual novels in recent memory. *Remainder* is about the secret world each of us harbors within, and what might happen if we were granted the power to make it real.

Fiction

ALSO AVAILABLE

C
Men in Space
Transmission and the Individual Remix
Satin Island